Nigel McCrery worked as a policeman, until he left the force to become an undergraduate at Cambridge University. He is the author of *Silent Witness*, *Strange Screams of Death*, *Spider's Web* and *All the King's Men* – which has also been made into a television drama starring David Jason. He is now Director of Drama at Ardent Productions, Prince Edward's production company. Married with children, he lives in Nottingham.

Also by Nigel McCrery

Silent Witness
Strange Screams of Death
Spider's Web
All the King's Men

Faceless Strangers

Nigel McCrery

POCKET
B O O K S

LONDON · SYDNEY · NEW YORK · TOKYO · SINGAPORE · TORONTO

First published in Great Britain by Simon & Schuster, 2001
This edition first published by Pocket Books, 2001
An imprint of Simon & Schuster UK Ltd
A Viacom Company

13 5 7 9 10 8 6 4 2

Simon & Schuster UK Ltd
Africa House
64–78 Kingsway
London WC2B 6AH

Simon & Schuster Australia
Sydney

A CIP catalogue record for this book is available from the British Library

ISBN 0-671-03325-5

Typeset by SX Composing DTP, Rayleigh, Essex
Printed and bound in Great Britain by
Omnia Books Limited, Glasgow

For my children
Luke, Emily and Rebecca
who brighten my life

Introduction

She would have to die, and he would have to kill her. That fact above all others was the most apparent. He'd known for weeks. It had only really taken him a few days of serious contemplation to come to that conclusion. He was still surprised how quickly and easily he had arrived at his decision. Of course he'd mulled the problem over for a few days, considering different remedies, various solutions, but he knew he was only playing with options and theories. In the end it came down to the same obvious answer, murder. Now it was just a case of where, how and when.

He'd thought about hiring a hit man, but after doing some careful research he'd realized it was impossible. Firstly, he wouldn't know where to find one and secondly, it brought another person into the equation, and that might prove difficult later. He wanted no complications; the murder itself would be complicated enough. He would have to do it himself. With all other options eliminated, he set about planning the 'perfect crime', an intellectual obstacle course in itself. He was good at planning, he'd done it all his life. Now he was about to see how well that training had prepared him for the unexpected. In a bizarre way, he was actually looking forward to it. It would at least stretch his mind beyond the ordinary and benign. Despite the macabre nature of the deed before him, he was quick to realize that the principles and practices were the same as for any other career move. Once he'd made his plans, as long as he stuck to them everything would be fine. In his experience only when a plan wasn't strictly adhered to did problems emerge. He was quite aware that if he was to avoid getting caught, and he had no intention of allowing that to happen, then everything would have to be carried out with military precision. Pulling a notebook from his desk drawer, he began to make notes.

After all these months Claire knew it didn't really matter where they met, but this was a very unusual place and a little more remote then she'd imagined. A narrow and deeply rutted dirt track led approximately a quarter of a mile from the main Cambridge road, disappearing into a large deciduous wood before cutting through several fields of sugar beet. After about two hundred yards, the track re-emerged by the side of a high and heavily over-grown railway embankment. Following the edge of this embankment for four or five hundred yards, it finally ended in front of a low Victorian railway arch, which linked two sections of track together.

She had hitched her way to Cambridge before walking the three miles across country to the location. It had only taken her half a day and the journey had been trouble-free. The lorry driver who had taken her most of the way had been both kind and friendly and had kept his hands to himself, which made a pleasant change. Claire was used to hitching and people in general were both affable and pleasant, so as long as you stayed on your toes you were normally OK. Occasionally she found herself in a tricky situation and had once, a few years before, been raped, but that was only because she'd been careless. It had put her off hitching for a while but realizing she still needed to move around cheaply, she'd eventually returned to it, only now she took more care. The odd thing was that the guy who had raped her had seemed perfectly respectable. So, she thought, you never could tell. She often wondered afterwards whether he had just been driving around on the off-chance of finding some girl to assault, or whether he was just an ordinary man who took advantage of that particular situation. She eventually came down on the side of the latter, but it was a frightening realization and a cautionary lesson.

Examining the tired and ageing bridge closely, she wondered how it ever coped with the weight and speed of the trains as they rattled over it. 'There's a disaster waiting to happen here,' she thought.

Picking up a stick, she scratched away at the crumbling masonry from between the brickwork. It fell away easily, too easily for her liking. As she waited a long freight train rattled over the bridge and the entire structure shook. She gazed about her surroundings. Like all remote but convenient places, this one had been used as a dumping ground for years. The interior of the bridge was littered with every kind of rubbish imaginable. As well as bags full of rotting, smelly household waste, large metal drums lay both upright and on their side, a distinctly unpleasant brown liquid oozing from their leaking lids. Ripped and stained mattresses lay around the floor or were propped up against the side of the walls, drooping over like water-starved flowers in a vase. Worn-out and damaged tyres were strewn everywhere, giving the place a sort of ugly permanence. She wondered why people acted so badly and seemed to have no consideration for the environment in which they lived, or for the long-term care and protection of the planet. It was the main concept she hung on to, to justify her chosen lifestyle. People might not like her, or the way she lived, but at least she cared about her surroundings. Then there were the rats, she'd already seen two and they were big, almost the size of a small dog or cat. Ugh! She shuddered.

Looking down at her watch she noticed the hour: it was quarter past two, he was late. Spade had given her the watch the previous month for her twenty-fifth birthday. She was sure he'd nicked it. Despite the fact that he and

his mates were making a fortune doing illegal booze and
cigarette runs to the Continent, he still nicked everything.
It was an expensive looking gold Rolex, she'd seen them
in the shop and they cost thousands, where would he get
that sort of money? No, he'd definitely nicked it. He'd
filed something off the back of the watch as well. Spade
knew what he was doing and had done a good job, but
then she'd have expected nothing less, he'd had enough
practice over the years. She slipped the watch back inside
her pants. She never wore it, just in case it got stolen, and
as much as she loved her friends, they weren't the most
honest in the world. She had to hand it to Spade, at least
he didn't steal crap. Even though the watch was pinched,
it was still a bloody nice one, and it was good of him to
have given it to her.

Sitting down on the embankment she began to wonder
if he was going to turn up at all. She had expected him to
be there when she arrived and was a little irked when he
wasn't. Cupping her hand across the top of her eyes to
protect them from the powerful sun that blazed down
from the scorching July sun, she examined the horizon.
For a moment there was nothing, then she noticed the
small hazy cloud of swirling dust in the distance. As
she watched the cloud got closer and the shape of a
car began to emerge through the twisting dust. He'd
finally arrived.

He was late and he knew it. Like all the best-laid plans,
there was always something to help change your
direction. In this case it was an ageing rust-bucket of a car.
The bloody thing wouldn't start and it had taken him a
quarter of an hour to get the ignition working. He had
wanted to be there before she arrived so he could get it
over with quickly. He'd had to wait in the woods for a
short time, while the two-fifteen train passed through. He
had hoped it would all be over before the train arrived,
but that was one of the penalties of a badly executed plan.
Now he would have to be a little more flexible to allow for
changes, and that could be dangerous. He had spent days

at the site checking the times the trains went through. Luck, or the lack of it, wasn't going to be a factor as far as he was concerned. All he needed was a sharp-eyed train driver to see something and he was lost. There were to be no witnesses, accidental or otherwise. After the train had passed through he started the car and made for the bridge, finally stopping about twenty-five yards in front of it. He looked around carefully; she wasn't there.

Claire watched intensely as the car drew closer. She tried to get a look at the occupant but the car was too far away, and the dust thrown up from the dried-out track was too thick to see through. For a moment, as the car swerved from side to side along the track, she thought the driver was either drunk or ill, then she realized that he was only trying to avoid the potholes and ruts. As the car got closer she was suddenly frightened. In any other situation she would have run – all her instincts were on edge, telling her she was in danger. Normally she would have listened to them, they rarely let her down, but this time she didn't, putting her unease down to her natural nervousness at the meeting. All the same, until she was sure, she decided to hide. Jumping quickly behind the drums she waited to see who would eventually emerge from the car.

The man inside the car hesitated for a moment, searching the area with his eyes, before stepping out and walking slowly across the track towards the bridge. Although she knew it must be him, he wasn't at all what she'd expected. He was scruffy, dressed in stained blue overalls, with a pair of old and worn-out black working men's boots forced uncomfortably over his feet. He was also wearing thick-rimmed glasses, which she didn't know he needed. His hair was longer than she remembered, and black. She seemed to remember it as brown. Still, she considered, she could be wrong: memories play tricks. The thing that amazed her most, however, was the beard. He must have grown it quickly. In all the photographs she'd seen of him, he'd never had a beard. It was a funny shape too. Whoever told him it suited him wanted shooting. His car was the other odd thing. It was old and speckled all over with spots of rust as if someone had thrown handfuls of gravel at it. It was in such a poor condition that Spade wouldn't even have lowered himself to steal it. However odd his appearance, though, she still knew it was him, and despite her instincts she stood up and looked across at him. She had practised what she was going to say for weeks and now as the curtain was finally drawn back she repeated her well-rehearsed line.

'Hello, I'm Claire.'

Her sudden appearance from behind a group of large waste cans under the bridge startled him for a moment, but he quickly collected his thoughts and composed himself. He smiled back, trying to bring as much warmth to the smile as he could. She was far more attractive than he had expected, long and slim with a crop of dark black hair, which was tied tightly back into a ponytail. Her face was oval and beautifully proportioned, with full lips and small pert nose. But it was her eyes that were by far her most striking feature. They were emerald-green, he could not remember seeing eyes quite so striking before. To destroy something quite so beautiful was a crime in itself, but it had to be done, as tragic as it was. As he began to walk across to greet her he glanced at his watch. The next train was due in ten minutes. He would have to be quick.

'Are you on your own?'

Claire nodded and smiled broadly. 'As requested.'

He smiled and nodded his approval. 'Good, well done.'

As he reached her he put his left arm around her waist, pulling her tightly into his body before pressing his lips hard against hers in a passionate kiss. Looking into Claire's eyes he could see the shock brought on by his amorous approach. This look however quickly changed to one of pain and horror, as with his free hand, he pulled a lock knife from his pocket and plunged it hard into her stomach, twisting it as he pushed it deeply inside her. She tried to pull free but he had her tightly and the shock had already weakened her. He could feel her screaming against his mouth but he kept his lips pressed down hard on to hers, muffling any sound she might try to make. Again and again he plunged the knife deeply into her, twisting and ripping at her body as he did, each time finding a new fresh spot to cut into. He knew he had to keep the blows low, driving the blade upwards towards her heart and lungs whilst avoiding leaving any telltale signs on her ribcage, but as she struggled with the pain and attempted to free he found it increasingly difficult to be accurate. Finally, and to his relief, she stopped struggling and became limp in his arms. He knew she was dead. He looked into her half-open eyes. They were dull, the life and twinkle that had been there only moments before had disappeared for ever.

It had been easier than he'd thought. Quicker too. With the exception of the slight delay at the beginning of the operation, everything was going perfectly to plan and he was pleased with himself. 'Planning,' he murmured, 'it's everything.' After searching Claire's body for anything that might help identify her, he dragged it to a far wall. This proved to be harder going then he imagined, for such a small girl she was quite a weight – 'dead weight'. He smiled at his own macabre joke. Once she was in position he dropped two or three syringes, some silver foil, a lighter and a drug-smoking pipe around her remains. If she was ever found, the drugs paraphernalia should throw the police off the trail for a while, if not for ever.

Once he was satisfied with the scene he covered her body with several old mattresses and bags of refuse, holding it all in place with a few tyres. As he threw the last of the tyres he noticed several rats scurrying about the place, and he smiled to himself. They were certain to help the cause, even if she was discovered there wasn't going to be much of her left. As a particularly big rat ran across one of the mattresses before disappearing into a black plastic bag of rubbish, he wondered how much bigger they were all going to get over the next few weeks. He also realized that in the July heat the stink of the place would help disguise the smell of the decomposition that was bound to follow, and give the rats time to do their work. Every eventuality had been considered and acted upon. He really had done a good job, he silently congratulated himself.

He took one last look around to make sure nothing had been left behind before jumping back into his car and driving away. He looked at his watch. It was another three minutes before the next train was due and by then he would be long gone. No farmer in his field, no one walking any stupid dogs, not even a kid on a bike, no witnesses; it was all going like clockwork.

A few miles further along down the Cambridge road he turned off on to yet another track, this one leading up to a thick evergreen wood. Passing his own car, which he had parked carefully a few hours before in a small clearing, he drove on for a further hundred yards before stopping and climbing out. Going to the boot he pulled out a black plastic bin liner, which was full of his neatly folded clean clothes. Stripping off all his clothes, wig and beard, he threw them into the car together with Claire's belongings. Then he ripped off both the front and back number plates and dropped them into a large plastic bag. Later he would remove all the numbers from the plates and drop the lot into the Cam. Content with what he had done he changed quickly into a smart shirt, jacket, trousers and tie. Then, after emptying a drum of petrol over the car, he set it alight before walking back to his own vehicle. Still unobserved he pulled out on to the Cambridge road and accelerated away from the scene. Before the black smoke from the burning car was visible above the tree line, he was well away from the scene listening to Radio 2 and singing along to Robbie Williams' 'Angels.' It had all gone perfectly.

CHAPTER ONE

Detective Sergeant Stanley Sharman took one final and deeply satisfying draw from his cigarette before flicking it aimlessly through the car's open window and into the street beyond. Lying isolated in the dirty rundown alley, its glowing embers burnt brightly for a few moments more then faded into the menacing darkness. Blowing the last of the cigarette smoke through his nose, he began to search through the deep shadows that stretched across the alley filling it with a dark melancholy. Finally he discovered what he had been searching for. The smart Mercedes coupé was parked just beyond the only fluorescent light left unshattered along the passage. From its gentle rocking movement Sharman knew that he had the right vehicle, and it would only be a matter of time before the woman he had been searching for emerged.

After a further five minutes, during which time Sharman rolled and sparked up another cigarette, Kate finally leapt from the car. Pulling her clothes back into place she turned angrily and looked back inside the car. Sharman could tell from her demeanour that all was not well. He was right.

'You bastard. You agreed the price, now pay up!'

The figure inside the car was clearly screaming back. Sharman was too far away to make out what the punter was saying, but he guessed it wasn't complimentary. Whatever it was, it seemed to enrage Kate still further.

Stepping back, she kicked out at the car, smashing her foot hard against the front wing and denting it. This final explosion of temper was clearly too much for the unseen man inside the car. In an instant he'd swung open the driver's door, jumped out into the alley and was moving purposefully towards Kate. As he got closer she stepped back and began to cower, putting her hands out in front of her face to protect herself. She began to plead with her attacker, 'All right, mate, all right, you've made your point, leave it out now. Keep your bloody money.'

Sharman started to become agitated and he felt in his pocket for the wrapped roll of fifty pence pieces he always kept there for just such an occasion. He pressed them firmly into the palm of his hand, clenching his fist tightly around them. It was an old trick but an effective one. With the coins pressed hard inside your palm it stopped your fist collapsing, making the punch twice as hard, and twice as effective. Keeping a close eye on the punter he began to open the car door. As he did he noticed the man calm and then hesitate as Kate continued to plead with him. It was a fatal mistake. As he let his guard slip, Kate dropped her hands, stepped back smartly, and brought her right foot up hard into the man's groin, sending him crashing to his knees screaming abuse and gasping for breath. The sight made even Sharman wince. With her punter sprawled out on the ground clutching his groin and screaming in pain Kate moved in again, clearly unsatisfied with the results of her initial attack. Kicking out again she caught him hard under his chin, sending him rolling across the alley, blood pouring from an injury inside his mouth. Finally, content with the outcome, she marched towards Sharman's car and clambered in. Sharman looked across at her.

'Difficult customer?'

She glared across at him. 'Nothing I couldn't handle. Where the fuck were you, anyway?'

'On my way.'

'Just like the bloody cavalry. But as I remember they were always too late.'

Sharman suddenly reached out and grabbed Kate's face. As he did, just for a instant, he saw genuine fear in Kate's eyes. It wasn't what he wanted or intended. Fear was a useful tool in his trade, but not when dealing with someone you loved. Sometimes he forgot his own strength. He released his grip. 'How much does he owe you?'

She shrugged. 'Does it matter?'

Sharman nodded. 'Yes, it does. How much?'

'Twenty quid. It was only a quick one, no specials.'

Sharman nodded and stepping out of his car walked across to the punter Kate had left lying in the alley. He had recovered a little and just about managed to pull himself off his knees and onto the bonnet of his car, still clutching his groin. Sharman leaned over him. 'I think you owe my friend twenty quid?'

He looked up. 'Well, you can tell your friend to fuck off. Pimp!'

'That's Detective Sergeant Pimp to you, friend.'

That, as far as Sharman was concerned, was introduction enough. Pulling the wrapped roll of coins from his pocket and clenching them tightly in his fist, he hit the man hard just above his kidneys, sending him crumpling to the floor holding his back and screaming as loudly as before. As he went down Sharman slipped his hand inside his jacket pocket and retrieved his wallet. He opened it and removed two ten-pound notes plus the man's driving licence and a family photograph. He pushed the money inside his trouser pocket, before throwing the wallet on to the floor next to the prostrate figure. The man looked up.

'I'll have you for this, you bastard.'

Sharman smiled and glanced at the driving licence. 'Mr Robert Green, 74 London Road, Histon, is it.' He turned to the photograph. 'Nice family, good-looking kids and wife. Now, Mr Green, whatever would your wife say if she knew you went with ladies of the night? Although with a wife as good-looking as this I'm surprised you do. I would think she would be more than a little pissed off. Upset your kids as well, I expect?'

The man's head went down. 'Now my advice to you, Mr
Green, is to forget about tonight. Write it off to experience.
And next time you take a girl out, pay her what you owe,
it'll save you so much grief in the long run.' He waved the
photograph and licence in his face. 'I'll hang on to these
for a while, sort of insurance for your continued co-
operation shall we say? Any further problems from you
and I'll be forced to give them to Kate over there, who I'm
sure will find a way to get them to your wife and children.
Am I making myself clear?'

The man nodded his understanding of the situation.
Satisfied with his response Sharman slapped his face
gently.

'Good, then we'll say no more about it, shall we?'

The man raised his hand in submission and Sharman
walked away. On reaching his car, he handed over the two
notes to Kate. She snatched them from his hand and
stuffed them quickly into her bag. 'Hope you're not
expecting a freebie for this?'

'Freebie? I've seen the way you deal with freeloaders, I
think I'd rather pay.'

Kate almost smiled as Sharman pushed the car into
reverse and backed quickly out of the alley.

Sam strolled out into her garden. She enjoyed the summer.
Although spring was her favourite season, she loved the
early mornings and late evenings that the summer
brought with it. Picking up Shaw, who was rubbing
around her legs waiting to be fed, she walked up the path,
stopping every now and then to examine the stocks and
old English shrub roses and to take deep breaths over
them to take in their sweet perfume. Even at seven in the
morning the garden was full of life, colour and aromas. Of
all her senses it was still her sense of smell that mattered
most to her. Whether that was because she had almost lost
it, or she got the most pleasure from it, she wasn't sure,
probably both. As she reached the far end of the garden
and was looking at a particularly attractive hydrangea the

phone rang in the kitchen. For a moment she hesitated, considering whether to answer it or not. She knew that phone calls at odd hours of the day only meant one thing – work. The unexpected spell of hot weather had taken its toll and people, especially the old and unfit, were dropping like flies. She had already completed seventy hours overtime and the month wasn't over yet, they just kept coming. She longed for some cool refreshing weather in the hope it would at least slow the current mortality rate.

Sam liked to work fast, especially with everyday stuff. Someone had once described her as the Hurricane Higgins of pathology, but even she was having trouble keeping up with the current workload. It didn't help that Fred had cleared off on holiday the very week the hot spell had begun, so she was obliged to work with one of the other assistants. She hated doing that. She thought that she and Fred were a partnership, and a good one. Despite their different backgrounds and education, they understood each other perfectly. At times it was almost uncanny, as Fred seemed to foresee and be prepared for her every need. Compared to Fred every other assistant and technician she had worked with was found seriously wanting. Fortunately there hadn't been a major incident for some time. With half the department on holiday, away on courses, or just sick, she wasn't sure how she would have coped with it if there had been.

Listening to the continual and determined ringing from the phone, Sam had an inkling her luck had just run out. She looked down at Shaw, who was scowling hungrily at her. 'For whom the bell tolls, eh? What do you think, old friend, shall I answer it or let Trevor do something for once?'

She knew she was being unfair. Trevor Stuart had been on call for the past two weeks and had just been lucky that nothing had happened. He'd also come down to the mortuary for a few days to give her a hand with some of the outstanding PMs, which she'd appreciated.

Nigel McCrery

'Just because I'm management now, it doesn't mean I mind sullying my hands from time to time, Sam. Mustn't forget my roots.'

Sam smiled appreciatively at him every time he said it, which was more often than she could stand. Despite his patronizing tone Sam could see no point in upsetting him and risk losing a much-needed pair of hands. So she remained silent and bit her tongue. As if in answer to her question, but more likely because he was desperate to be fed, Shaw jumped down on to the path and scurried into the kitchen. Sam sighed. 'Even the cat's against me.'

Having made up her mind to answer the call, she hurried down the path as quickly as her loose-fitting slippers would allow. Reaching the kitchen she pulled the receiver from the top of the phone and pressed it to her ear.

'Dr Ryan.'

'Morning, Dr Ryan. DI Meadows here.'

Sam didn't need to be told who it was, she recognized his voice. She didn't like Meadows. Despite having known him for years, her view of him had never changed. She'd always found him weak and inefficient and could never understand how he'd ever made inspector. Belonging to secret societies that adopted funny hand-shakes or made you roll up one trouser leg had probably got more to do with it than being good at your job. Still, the medical profession wasn't free of that little game either. Her concentration returned to Meadows.

'What can I do for you, inspector?'

'We've found the body of a woman in Grantchester, and would be obliged if you would attend.'

Sam grabbed the pen from the notepad she kept by the side of all her phones. 'Give me the address.'

'The Gables, Oak Tree Avenue, Grantchester. Do you know how to get here or shall I send a car?'

Sam was infamous for her sense of direction, and was known to have got lost on more than one occasion en route to a murder scene. Despite knowing her own limitations

Sam was indignant at having them pointed out. Especially by someone like Meadows. 'I'm more than capable of finding Grantchester, thank you, Inspector.'

Sam had also had a road navigation unit fitted to her car recently, which increased her confidence.

'How long will you be?'

That was the other question Sam hated. It always seemed to imply she was a bit slow or idle.

'I'll be there as soon as I can.'

Meadows persisted, 'And how long might that be, Doctor?'

'Work it out for yourself, you're a policeman.' There was an annoyed silence from the other end of the phone before Sam added, 'Are the press there yet?'

There was a short pause before Meadows reluctantly replied, 'Not yet, but we think they're on their way. It's a high-profile job, by the way.'

Sam was intrigued. 'Why, who is it?'

'Sophie Clarke.'

'Wife of John Clarke, the MP?'

'That's her.'

'Christ.'

She felt a sense of shock, which for her was unusual.

'Thought that might make you sit up.'

'Give me half an hour.'

She put the phone down and looked across at Shaw, who was sitting by his food dish waiting impatiently. 'Better get this one right, Shaw, the entire country's going to be watching.'

Sam had met Sophie Clarke a few times over the past year. She was very young, Sam guessed in her mid- to late twenties, very beautiful with long fair hair and deep blue eyes. She was also a lot of fun. What she was doing with a man like John Clarke Sam really couldn't understand. He'd already had three wives, none of them over thirty, and God knows how many mistresses. They do say power is an aphrodisiac, and as he wasn't the most attractive man Sam had ever been introduced to she could only think it had to be the power. He had just been given his first cabinet post too, as Secretary of State for the Environment, so his profile was as high as it had ever been. Sam had always found him rather full of himself and, dare she think it, a bit of a snob. He'd asked her out once during a fund-raising party at the Park. She'd had great pleasure in turning him down. The next time she saw him he had completely ignored her, which suited her just fine. Still, she had nothing against Sophie, for her she was sad. Even now, after all these years in pathology, she still felt an extra sense of sadness when someone young and so full of life died.

Turning her mind back to the present Sam contemplated what she should wear to the scene. With so much press attention she had better look good, or at least professional. The Armani suit she had picked up in London during her last trip should do it. Smart, attractive and professional, just the image she was trying to portray. With Shaw munching happily away at his food Sam swept upstairs to change.

Sharman woke with a start as the phone by the side of the bed suddenly burst into life. He opened his eyes and tried to orientate himself. He knew he was in his own room and for that matter his own bed. He also knew, because his arm was wrapped around her waist, that Kate was lying next to him, but for the life of him he couldn't remember what day, or even what time it was. He switched on the sidelight and glanced at his alarm clock. 7.10 a.m. Who in God's name was calling him at seven in the morning when he'd been out on night crime all evening? He glanced at Kate. Well, most of it anyway. He picked up the receiver; this had to be bad news. He decided to be brisk.

'Sharman.'

'Stan? It's Dick Meadows.'

Sharman's reply was sarcastic. 'Really, I never would have guessed.'

Meadows had been his partner for over five years,

during which time he was convinced he'd developed a stoop from carrying the bastard. Then, as if to rub it in, Meadows had got promoted to inspector and he hadn't. After that he had decided to do things on his own. Less complicated that way. He'd resisted the need for a partner ever since, despite numerous offers including one from Meadows who was looking for a bag man. The bloody cheek of it, he thought. Sharman continued with his sarcastic tone, 'Do you know what fucking time it is? I'm on night crime in case you'd forgotten.'

'Sorry, Stan, know it's your day off . . .' Was it? Sharman hadn't even realized. 'But I need you down here, we've got a cold one.'

This was Meadows' usual description of a body, normally a murdered one. Sharman leaned across the bedside table and picked up a pen.

'Where?'

'Oak Tree Avenue, Grantchester. It's just off the main road, opposite side to the river.'

'Yeah, I know where it is, thanks, Dick. I'll just follow the flashing lights when I get there, shall I?'

Sharman knew the area well. One of the most sought-after addresses in Cambridge. Only the great and the good lived there. Well, the great anyway. 'Anyone we know?'

'Sophie Clarke.'

'Not the wife of our most esteemed MP John, surely?'

'The very same. Can you get across quickly?'

'Wouldn't miss it for the world. Chance to get myself on TV.'

Meadows laughed. 'Everybody wants to be somebody. Even that bitch of a pathologist wanted to know about the cameras. Anyway, they've just arrived, so make sure you've got your best bib and tucker on.'

Sharman grunted. 'I haven't got one.'

He heard Meadows laugh down the phone. 'See you here in a bit, then. Oh, and give my regards to Kate.'

Sharman slammed the phone down without replying. How the fuck did Meadows know about Kate? Fucking two-faced bastards on Vice, he expected. Meadows just had to let him know he knew. Bastard. Rolling over on to his back and pushing his hands behind his head, he looked up at the ceiling for a few moments, pondering what he had just heard. Sophie Clarke, all the big boys would be out for that one. Lots of arse-licking would get done over the next few weeks. He smiled to himself knowingly: Dick Meadows was going to be the chief arse-licker. After all, it's what he did best. He might as well pop down and be his usual disrespectful self. See how many senior ranks he could upset before he left. He looked across at Kate, who was lying motionless on her back. Sharman lifted the sheet covering her body and looked at her nakedness. Long and lean, with firm high breasts and legs that went on for ever. She could have been so much more than a prostitute. She was certainly fit enough to be a model or something like that. What a waste. If she had been any of those things, however, would she have ever looked twice at him? He didn't think so.

Kate suddenly woke. 'It'll cost you extra.'

Sharman scowled. 'For what, looking?'

She looked across at him suspiciously. 'As long as that's as far as it goes.'

As Sharman threw the sheet back across her body and began to crawl out of bed, Kate grabbed his arm and let the sheet drop away from her body again. 'Go on, you can have a freebie. After last night I think you deserve it.'

Sharman looked at her. 'What about the extras?'

She hesitated for a moment. 'No, you'll still have to pay for those.'

He laughed. 'Sorry, Kate, I've got to go, there's been a killing.'

Annoyed by his rejection, Kate pulled the sheet across her body again and turned away from him. 'Can I stay here for a while. Sleep it off a bit?'

'Cost you extra.'

'Piss off, mark it off to the free extras you got last night.'

Sharman smiled and began to make his way across the bedroom, stopping by the bathroom door. 'Are you free tonight?'

'I'm never free. In fact I'm quite expensive.'

He scowled, 'I didn't mean that. Available, then. Are you available for dinner?'

Kate knew what he meant but enjoyed playing games. 'Might be. Who's asking?'

Sharman knew what she was doing and was tiring of it. 'The *Globe*, eight o'clock, then.'

Kate didn't turn, just put her thumb up before throwing the sheet over her head and drifting back to sleep. Sharman took one last lingering look at the shape of her body under the thin cover and contemplated the evening's entertainment with a smile. Finally, his fantasy completed, he sparked up a cigarette and staggered into the bathroom for a long pee.

By the time Sam arrived in Grantchester the TV cameras were already there, together with what appeared to be an army of journalist and photographers. How they'd found out about the murder before she did was anyone's guess. Probably had a pet police officer or two in their pay, or there was a lot of back-scratching going on in Westminster. It had to be something like that. Sam recognized one of the journalists, Edward Case. He was the crime reporter for the *Cambridge Evening Star*, and had been for a good few years. Decent enough reporter, he'd been with the *Star* a few years now. Came out of Fleet Street, where he had been the Chief Crime Reporter with the *Telegraph* for over a decade. Out to grass now, or was it drink? So many reporters, like policemen, seemed to throw away their careers and often their lives over drink, and Case had a formidable reputation with a bottle. All he had left was to see out his time with a small provincial paper and hope his liver held out long enough for him to draw his pension at the end. Eventually, even the *Star* would tire of him and force him to go freelance and Sam couldn't help but notice that from the look of him it wouldn't be very much longer. Even in his current state, however, Sam knew she couldn't underestimate him. Years on Fleet Street hadn't been entirely wasted on him. He was still tenacious when it came to a good story and up to every trick in the book.

Sam had arrived in Grantchester in plenty of time for once. The navigational system she had deployed inside her car really had worked and got her there without a hitch. As she approached the scene she was hit by a curtain of white flashing camera lights that blinded her for a moment and forced her to brake sharply. As her eyes recovered, reporters began to bang on the side of her car, calling her through the closed windows, 'Dr Ryan, Dr Ryan, any comment?' 'What time did you get the call?' 'What are you expecting to find?' 'Can we expect a statement later?'

Sam ignored them and drove on. She could never really understand why they did it. They must realize that she wasn't going to make a comment that was likely to prejudice any further proceedings. Perhaps they just felt it was part of their job and they had to be seen to be doing something. One of these days there was going to be a serious accident because of those bastards, she just hoped she wasn't involved.

Stopping by the booking officer, a fresh-faced youth of about twenty, Sam introduced herself and was directed along the drive to the front of the house. As she drove away the booking officer carefully noted the time she had arrived at the house on his notepad. That completed, he then noted down the make and number of Sam's car before throwing the clipboard back inside his Panda to await the next VIP investigator. As Sam reached the end of the drive Colin Flannery was there to direct her into her parking place. She smiled and waved at him. She was always glad to see Colin. With him there she knew the job was going to get done properly. Some people considered him fussy, but Sam just considered him professional and wished there were more like him. The house itself was a large and impressive Mock Tudor manor house. The grounds, or what she could see of them through the police lamps, were impressive too. Large and green with hundreds of trees, plants and bushes. She wondered how many people Clarke employed to keep the garden in shape. Under happier circumstances she would have loved to look around, and stolen the odd cutting. As she stepped out of her car Flannery approached her, holding up a pair of white protective overalls.

'See the circus out there, did you? One wonders how the hell they find out about these things almost before we do.'

Sam smiled at him and slipped into her overalls. 'I think we both have a good idea how they find out, don't we, Colin?'

Flannery shrugged and nodded. 'Well, precisely. It's ridiculous.'

Sam looked down at her feet. 'Got my shoe covers?'

Flannery handed her a pair and she slipped them over her feet.

'Superintendent Adams here yet?'

Flannery shook his head. 'No, not yet, had trouble finding him. It's probably that new young wife of his, she—'

Flannery checked himself and could have bitten his tongue off. 'Sorry, thoughtless. I'm sure he'll be here shortly.'

Sam knew Flannery wasn't malicious so she paid the comment no heed, just made for the front door. 'What have we got?'

'Young woman upstairs on her bed, believed to be Sophie Clarke, wife of the local MP, John. Looks like she's been strangled—' He checked himself again, knowing he'd perhaps gone too far, it was becoming an uncomfortable habit. 'But of course that's for you to determine, Dr Ryan, I'm just making a general observation.'

Sam smiled at his awkwardness. Colin was so proper

and kind. 'I'm sure you're right, Colin. We'll take a look, though, shall we? What about her husband?'

'They're getting a message to him now. There was some Commons party he had to go to. So you can imagine what the alibi list is going to read like.'

'Sophie didn't go?'

'MPs only apparently'.

Sam wondered if the police had a list of his mistresses' names and addresses. They'd probably need them. 'Who found her?'

'Housekeeper, a Mrs Waddam, been with the family for years, apparently, comes from Histon. She used to be Clarke's bedder when he was at John's.'

'Bit of a drive from Histon?'

'Husband drops her off every morning, picks her up at night. Discovered the body just before six this morning and called the local plods.'

'Six, Christ, she starts early. Don't they mind the noise?'

'She does a bit of cooking as well. Gets here in time to make breakfast for herself and the rest of the staff before they start work.'

'How many staff are there?'

'Four including Mrs Waddam. There's a driver-handyman, whatever that means.'

His disapproving and judgemental tone amused Sam. 'He lives in the cottage at the back of the house. There's also a gardener who lives somewhere in the village, but he only works part time, and a cleaner who comes in about nine.'

Flannery directed Sam through the giant hall and up the winding stairs towards the main bedroom. The interior of the house was as impressive as the exterior. Original works of art, both modern and ancient, covered the walls, while expensive-looking antiques littered the floors, tables and sideboards. It wasn't Sam's style but it was stylish. Money and style, she would never have thought it from a man like Clarke. Perhaps there was more to him than met the eye after all. On the other hand he probably had someone else do his interior design for him. Although Sam always thought well of people she liked, she hated thinking good of anyone she disliked. It was a failing, but one she was happy to live with.

It took Sharman half an hour to drive from his one-bedroom council flat in Arboury to leafy middle-class Grantchester. It would normally take him twice that time but it was early and the roads were quiet. Cambridge, like everywhere else, suffered from too many people in too many cars and having a few empty roads to cruise down made a pleasant change. He arrived to the normal chaos that surrounds the early part of any murder inquiry. People, cars, and vans everywhere. Detectives and uniform trying to look as if they mattered when most of them didn't. White-suited Socos with plastic bags full of God knows what running to and fro, while endless rolls of blue and white location tape were spread across everything. The press were also there in force, but after glancing into his car and realizing he wasn't important they ignored him, which suited him fine. As he approached the main gate a young constable stepped out in front of his car and stopped him. Sharman opened the window and the young man leaned in.

'Can I help you, sir?'

Sharman didn't like uniform, he hadn't liked uniform even when he was one, especially ones that didn't know him. He considered himself a bit of a legend amongst the Cambridge Constabulary. He had more arrests, had recovered more property, had more commendations then the rest of the idle bastards put together, and it irritated him when a 'still wet behind the ears' kid didn't know who he was. Waste of space as far as he was concerned, all of them. He looked up at the young enthusiastic face. Christ, he thought, they're giving us children now. 'Does your mother know you're out, son?'

He could see at once that the comment had got through and irritated the little sod. He found himself enjoying the experience and decided to press home his advantage. For now, however, he decided to play along.

'I'm afraid I'll have to ask you to turn your car around and follow the diversion signs away from this scene, sir. They're clearly marked. Perhaps if you wore your glasses you wouldn't have missed them in the first place, sir?'

Now it was Sharman, turn to be irritated, although he had to admire the lad's spunk. He loved sarcasm – it was his favourite form of wit. However, it was never a good idea to piss off a detective sergeant, especially one that was as bitter and twisted as he was. He'd wait until he could pay the little bastard back. What goes around comes around, he considered.

He pulled his warrant card from the inside pocket of his jacket and flashed it in the young constable's face. 'Detective Sergeant Sharman. Want me to follow the diversion signs now, do you, son?'

The young constable looked surprised and a little nervous. 'Sorry, I didn't recognize you, sir.'

The word 'sir' irritated Sharman further. 'It's not "sir", it's sergeant. Don't they teach you anything at that posh police college any more? Or aren't you old enough to read yet?'

'No, sir, Sergeant, I mean, yes. Sorry, Sergeant.'

Sharman slipped his warrant card back in his pocket and pushed his car into gear. Before pulling off, however, he took one last shot at his victim. 'There's not enough cones out. I want lots more cones. It's a murder scene, for Christ's sake, cones are everything.' He could see that he had the cheeky young sod on the run.

'I'll arrange it at once, sir, Sergeant.'

Sharman shook his head sarcastically. 'No, son, don't *arrange* it, do it. I want you to do it. Now get on with the bloody job.'

He nodded. 'Yes, Sergeant.'

'Good. I'll want a lot more cones out by the time I've finished. I'll have me glasses on by then so I'll be able to see, savvy?'

The young constable nodded nervously again as Sharman pulled on to the long drive that led up to the house. As he did he looked up into his rear-view mirror and could have sworn he saw the little sod put two fingers up at him. Sharman laughed. He'd have done just the same.

As he approached the house Sharman spotted a parking place just off the drive and close to the front door. He pulled into it. Stepping out of the car, he was approached by yet another baby-faced flat-foot.

'Sorry, Sergeant' – at least this time he had been recognized – 'but that spot's reserved for Superintendent Adams.'

The only thing Sharman hated more than being told what to do by a fresh-faced flat-foot was Superintendent bloody Adams. As far as Sharman was concerned Adams had got to his current rank off the back of two women. Harriet Farmer, who he had to admit, despite being a woman, was a bloody good cop, and the pathologist Samantha Ryan. Mark you, he, like most of the force, wanted to get inside her knickers, so he couldn't hold that one against him. Although she had the reputation of being a bit of an ice maiden, Adams certainly seemed to have thawed her out. Didn't marry her, though. Married that other looker from Fire Investigation. Odd that, Sharman thought, he'd have gone for the pathologist. Cold she might be, but there was something about her that was – well, he wasn't quite sure, but there was definitely something. He glared at the uniform standing in front of him. 'So clamp me.'

With that he strode into the house leaving a bemused and confused constable wondering what to do next.

Entering the large hall he was met by Tinker Graham who smiled up at him.

'Better late than never, Stanley.'

Detective Constable John (Tinker) Smith had been

Sharman's partner shortly after he joined CID and they had a long history. Sharman had always found Tinker a bit on the idle side and become a little sick of carrying him. Not that changing his partner to Meadows made that much difference. But when Tinker found out he was on the take, he engineered a divorce. He'd never told the police complaints department about his friend's private income; he knew enough about the code of silence not to break that particular rule. And although he'd never taken bribes himself he had bent the rules enough to get a conviction, and Tinker was well aware of it. If he put Tinker in the frame then he was bound to return the favour and then they'd all go down together. That was the way it was, after all they were friends.

'Up your giggy with a wire brush, Tinker. What's going on?'

'Shit, that's what's up. Whole world's gone mad. Local MP's missus is upstairs, dead as a doornail. Adams is running around like a headless chicken and passing all the grief down the line to us. So I'd make yourself scarce if I were you, Stan. No good can come of your presence here.'

Sharman shook his head. 'Meadows invited me.'

Tinker laughed. 'Then you're already in the shit. You know the Chief Constable's on his way down with half his staff?'

Sharman shrugged. 'Chief Constables might bother you, they don't bother me.'

Tinker laughed again. 'Accepted, mate, but you're sure going to bother him. Ever thought of shaving or running a comb through your hair before you turn up for duty?'

Sharman felt his chin and ran a hand through his hair. 'It's my day off. Didn't expect to be here.'

Tinker stroked a hand across Sharman's jacket. 'If I'm not wrong, that's Gypsy Smith's blood, and we nicked him two months ago.'

Sharman gave him a sarcastic smile. 'Like to keep a few mementoes. Which room's the body in?'

'Just follow your nose.'

Sharman glared at him.

'OK, keep your hair on. Up the stairs, turn right, third door on your left. Can't miss it, full of men in white suits. With luck one of them will take you away.'

As Tinker began to walk away, Sharman called after him. 'Tinker!'

Tinker turned to face his former partner. 'What?'

'Go fuck yourself.'

Tinker laughed. 'That's it, Stan, you keep the moral high ground.'

Sharman ignored him and continued to climb the stairs.

Turning right at the top he followed the bright lights and white-suited Socos into the room. Before he had a chance to enter, however, he was met by an angry-looking Colin Flannery.

'Why aren't you suited up?'

For once Sharman didn't have a clever reply. He might be a bit rough around the edges, but he took his work seriously and knew he was wrong.

'Sorry, never thought. Haven't got one handy, have you?'

Flannery, still annoyed, stuck a suit and overshoes in his hand. 'Don't let it happen again, Stan.'

Sharman wasn't sure if he liked Flannery but he did respect him and that was enough as far as he was concerned. He suited up quickly.

'Heavy night.'

Flannery shook his head. 'When aren't they, Stan? It's going to kill you in the end.'

Flannery stood guarding the door until Sharman was fully prepared then stood aside. 'You can go in now, Detective Sergeant.'

Sharman nodded and entered. The room was awash with light from various lamps that had been established around the room, and white-suited Socos were every-where. It was funny how things had changed over the years. Not so long ago he'd never heard of Scene of Crime Officers. Now they were an entire department. When he'd first joined the job you had your pathologist, normally a middle-aged man in a tweed jacket, more often than not smoking a cigarette or munching on a sandwich over the body, and a few detectives thrown in at the last minute to help collect evidence, and that was your lot. Now everything was delegated to a specialist department and was all very skilful and professional. Still, it was no bad thing and Flannery's team did seem to get results. He surveyed the scene. Dick Meadows was already there, looking as austere as he could. Two Socos were taking photographs at Dr Ryan's request, while a third videoed the entire scene. Meadows stepped across to Sharman and whispered in his ear. Everybody, with the possible exception of the pathologist, seemed to whisper, and despite the organized chaos that surrounded a murder scene there was always an odd hush about the place. Sharman was never quite sure why, but it just seemed like the proper thing to do. A sign of respect, really.

'Bloody hell, Stan, you look like you've been pulled through a hedge backwards. Ever thought of shaving? Take years off you. The Chief will be here in a minute, I want you out the back door when he does. One look at you and he'll lose faith in all of us.'

Sharman ignored him, his eyes drawn instinctively to the bed. Lying naked and spreadeagled across it, her hands and feet tied firmly to the bed's four corner posts, was a young and once beautiful woman. Her fair hair lay partially across her face and partially across the sheets. She had a fine athletic body with a flat stomach and firm, high breasts. She had clearly been beautiful in life but now her face was black and bloated almost beyond recognition. Around her neck was a sort of noose, which dug so deeply into her flesh that the skin folded over it making the cord difficult to distinguish. Sharman looked across at Sam, who was already in the middle of her commentary. She really was a beautiful woman. Why Adams had thrown her over for Webber was a mystery to him and most of the force. Rebecca Webber might have been younger, but there really was much more of a depth about Dr Ryan.

He waited for her to finish. He knew it wouldn't take long. She never hung about at the scene, left that for others. Just made general notes and then she was away. The real work was done in the mortuary. Watching Ryan conduct a PM was like watching a fine artist at work. Skilful, never missing a stroke, and knowing how to lift the ordinary to the extraordinary. As she completed her commentary Sharman stepped forward and glanced across at her.

'May I take a closer look, Dr Ryan?'

Sam looked up at him.

'Stan Sharman! Haven't seen you for a while. Thought you'd been retired quietly, like most troublemakers.'

Sharman gave her a half-smile. 'Force would fall apart without me.'

Sam liked Sharman but she wasn't quite sure why. He was probably one of the scruffiest men she'd ever met and certainly the crudest. His private life didn't bear much scrutiny either, apparently. There was an honesty about the way he dealt with his work, however, that appealed to her. He was also one of the best thief-takers in the force. Even Adams, who made his dislike of Sharman very clear, had to admit that. She indicated the body. 'Help yourself, I've just about finished anyway.'

Sharman accepted her invitation and stepped closer to the bed. He didn't touch the cord, he knew better than that, just crouched down and took a closer look. It was a garrotte, he'd seen them before, far too often for his liking. Although it was twisted tightly around her throat, he could see the knot and the small bar that had been threaded through it to give her attacker control over her life and ultimately her death. The slightest turn of the bar this way or that either tightened or loosened the cord, making the difference between a person being able to breathe and being choked to death. In this way an attacker could play with his victim for hours before making the

final twist and finishing them off. Like a cat playing with
a mouse until it got bored and gave it one final and fatal
swipe. It was a painful and unpleasant way to die. The
cord looked cheap, like washing line. He looked at the
cord around her wrists: it was the same. She'd struggled,
all right, not that there was any chance of her escaping.
The knots had been tied tightly and well, someone knew
what they were doing, no granny knots here.

Sam noticed Sharman's interest in the knots.

'Round turn and two half-hitches. Used by the boating
fraternity, I think?'

She looked at Flannery, who nodded in agreement. Both
wrists were cut where the cord had bitten deeply into the
flesh. He examined her feet; they had been tied in a similar
fashion. Sharman stood back examining the scene and
became thoughtful. She hadn't been gagged, but then
whoever was going to hear her screaming out here?
Perhaps hearing her scream, beg for her life, was all part
of it. But then, where were the servants? He couldn't
believe a place like this ran itself, and Mrs Clarke didn't
look the type to push a trolley around Tesco's. There were
marks on her breasts and nipples too. He leaned across her
body. Burn marks. Someone had used her like an ashtray
and stubbed their cigarettes out on her. He'd seen similar
injuries a dozen times before, especially after domestic
disputes and too often on children. He looked around the
room. There was no sign of the rest of the cord or of a
packet of cigarettes. He glanced across at Flannery, who'd
re-entered the room. 'Your boys find any cigarette stubs
lying around the room?'

Flannery looked across at two white-suited Socos
who were standing at the far side of the room waiting for
Sam to finish her initial examination so they could tape
and wrap the body. They held up a clear plastic exhibit
bag.

'Two.'

Sharman stepped across the room and took the exhibit
bag. 'Do we know the make?'

'Not yet. Forensics will tell us later.'

Sharman looked at them closely through the bag. There was something odd about them, but he wasn't sure what. Whatever it was, forensics would pick it up later. While he was still examining the cigarettes Sam was suddenly by his side, peering into the bag with him.

'Why do you think the filter tips have been torn off?'

Sharman looked at the cigarettes again. Dr Ryan was right, they had been torn off. He shook his head. 'I've no idea. Perhaps he liked his tobacco raw.'

Sam wasn't convinced. 'Then why buy filter tips?'

Sharman found himself agreeing with her. He turned to Meadows. 'Did she smoke?'

Meadows shrugged. 'No idea. But we'll soon find out, I'm sure.'

Sharman turned his attention to Colin Flannery. 'Any sign of a break?'

Flannery shook his head. 'Nothing so far. My boys haven't finished looking around yet, though.'

'What about the rest of the cord?'

Again Flannery shook his head. 'Nothing so far. But like I said, they're still looking.'

Sharman traced his eyes around the room carefully, looking for anything ordinary or extraordinary that might give him a clue to the identity of her attacker. But there was nothing obvious. He'd have to leave that one to Flannery and his team.

Adams' angry and irritated voice broke Sharman's train of thought. 'Is that your pile of junk in my parking place, Sharman?'

Sharman turned. He first glanced at Meadows, who was standing next to the Superintendent, shuffling his feet, looking both embarrassed and concerned, and then at Adams. 'If you mean the 1969 Ford Cortina, it's not a pile of junk, it's a classic car.'

Adams glared at him. 'Call it what you like, Stan, it's still in my place. Now shift it or I'll have it towed away.'

Sharman didn't answer, just gave Adams a sarcastic half-smile and began to walk out.

As he passed the Superintendent, Adams hissed in his ear, 'And for crying out loud smarten your bloody self up, will you? You smell.'

Sharman looked at him. 'It's my suit.'

Adams shook his head. 'Then bloody well burn it and buy another. That style went out ten years ago.'

Sharman looked him straight in the eye. 'About ready to come back into fashion, then, isn't it? You know how these things are, sir.' With that he stepped out of the room and started to make his way to the front door.

After Sharman had disappeared, Adams turned his attention to Sam, who was smiling, having enjoyed the little argument between Sharman and her former boy-friend. She still hadn't forgiven Adams for leaving her for another woman, especially for a younger one.

'Thought you were never going to get here. Rebecca keeping you up, is she?'

It was unfair and unprofessional and Sam regretted it at once, but by then it had been said. Adams looked both annoyed and embarrassed by the comment. Despite her reservations about what she had just said, Sam enjoyed his discomfort. Since they'd parted she had been avoiding him, and had, up to now at least, been fortunate. He'd phoned, written and on at least two occasions visited the cottage. She'd been in the second time he'd called but had refused to answer the door. She'd been hurt and wasn't really interested in any more of his lame excuses.

'Is there anything you can tell us, Dr Ryan?'

Very formal, Sam thought. Well, she could be formal, too.

'She's dead, almost certainly strangled, and it looks like she was tortured beforehand. From the swelling and bruising around the vagina, and from the position of the body, I think it's fair to assume she was probably raped as well. I've taken swabs from the vagina, nipples, mouth and anus so we'll know soon enough.'

'When do you propose to do the PM?'

Sam began to leave the room, wanting to spend as little time as possible in the same room as him. 'Depends.'

Adams sounded exasperated. 'On what?'

'How long it takes you to get the body to the mortuary.'

As Sam left the room Adams' attention returned to his team. It was then that he noticed that every eye in the place seemed to be on him. Lovers', or former lovers', tiffs weren't normal in the middle of a murder inquiry and they were lapping it up. His confrontation with Sam would be around the force in hours. Things really couldn't go on like this, he considered, something serious would have to be done.

Bringing himself back to reality, he called Dick Meadows across to him. 'Dick, a word if you don't mind.'

As Stan Sharman reached his car, still parked in Adams' spot, Meadows called after him, 'Hang on, Stan, need a word.'

Sharman waited for his former partner as he crossed the drive. Meadows smiled at him. When Meadows smiled he had the look of a cobra about to strike. Some people in the force actually called him the Snake, and it wasn't a bad description. Sharman had seen that smile before and knew instinctively that whatever Meadows wanted to say it wasn't going to be good.

'Fancy a fag?'

Sharman nodded. 'If you like.'

He didn't really want one and he certainly didn't want one with Meadows, but then, what choice did he have? Besides, it was one way of getting Meadows to say what he'd been sent to say.

As the two men walked to a quiet spot at the back of the house they passed Sam, who was being helped out of her white protection suit by Colin Flannery. She looked up when she saw the two men.

'Will I be seeing you later at the PM, Stan?'

Sharman shrugged. 'Doubt it.'

He nodded to Meadows, who looked at Sam sheepishly. Sam shook her head. Sharman was a great cop but he was his own worst enemy. Goading Adams was never a good idea.

On reaching the back of the house Sharman and Meadows sat on two deckchairs by the side of the over-large swimming pool. Meadows offered him a cigarette, which he took. Meadows then lit them both up.

'Sorry, mate, but you're off the case.'

Sharman kept staring across the pool. 'Now there's a surprise. Didn't know I was even on it. It's my day off, remember?'

Sharman was seriously disturbed that he was being thrown off the case before he'd even had a chance to start on it, but he wasn't going to give Meadows or Adams the satisfaction of letting them know that.

Meadows continued, 'It's not me, Stan, you know that. I'd keep you on, you're a good copper – a copper's copper. It's Adams. Why do you have to rub him up the wrong way all the time?'

Sharman gave a sarcastic laugh. 'Because he's a pratt. Bastard couldn't detect a cold.'

Meadows looked across at his former partner. 'He's perhaps not in the same league as you, Stan, but his record's not that bad.'

Sharman realized that, but he was determined not to give credit where credit was due.

'Anyway, he's not happy with your attitude and wants you back at section.'

Sharman shrugged. 'Fine by me.'

Meadows shook his head. 'Liar. Look, if you keep winding the boss up like that, you're likely to find yourself in a funny hat pounding the beat in the sodding rain. Do you really want that?'

Sharman shrugged again, like a spoilt child determined to defy logic to get his own way.

'Times are changing, Stan, you've just got to change with them or you'll get left behind. Look, if anything else comes up I'll put you on it. Just keep out of Adams' way for a bit, that's all. Out of sight out of mind. Know what I mean?'

Sharman looked at his friend. He still couldn't stand the sight of him but knew he was only trying to help.

'Yeah, all right Dick, I'll keep out of the way.'

Meadows nodded. 'It's just for a while. He knows you're a good detective, that's why you're still on the job. He'd have got rid of a lesser bloke ages ago.'

Sharman didn't reply, just took a prolonged drag on his cigarette.

'Spot anything in there, did you?'

Sharman had but wasn't in the mood to pass on the information. 'Nothing. I'm sure the Socos will sort it out. Besides they've got Sherlock Adams on the case now. I'm sure Super Sleuth will make an early arrest.'

Meadows knew he was lying. Sharman was the best copper he'd ever known. It was almost uncanny, as if he had second sight or something. Yet Stan Sharman was about as mystical as a truck. He also knew that until he'd had time to calm down and change his current belligerent mood, he wasn't likely to get any information out of him. He realized he'd have to box clever for a while and wait until Stan was ready to cooperate. Vice had been in to talk to him about Stanley's nocturnal habits as well. It was Kate Armstrong as usual, Stan never used any other girl. Why he'd taken up with a prostitute was beyond Meadows' understanding. It wasn't as if Sharman was unattractive, he'd had plenty of regular girlfriends, even a couple of long-term ones, but he'd never settled down with any of them. Perhaps Kate presented him with no pressures or commitments, just easy sex. It had to be something like that, surely. He'd got Vice off Stan's back for now, but wasn't sure how much longer he could cover for him. As soon as he'd got what he needed he'd have to have a serious talk to him about Kate. Try to persuade him to get her to visit him, at least – that way his car wouldn't be seen roaming around the back streets of Ditton Fields any more.

'Anyway you'd better get your car shifted, Stan. I can't cope with any more stress, especially from Adams.'

Meadows finished his cigarette and flicked it carelessly into the swimming pool.

Sharman watched him, bemused by his stupidity. Kneeling down by the side of the clear water he picked the nub end out before dropping it, along with his own cigarette, into his pocket. Meadows looked at him.

'Sorry, Stan, bit stupid. Wasn't thinking.'

You never bloody think, Sharman thought, but he kept silent. He needed to keep Meadows on his side for now, so there was no point upsetting him further. He felt he'd crossed enough senior officers for one day.

As Sam began her drive home, she decided to get changed and have some breakfast before going into the hospital to perform the PM. She began to feel guilty about the way she'd treated Adams. Perhaps it was time to forgive and forget. She could never stay angry for long anyway, took after her dad in that way.

If she was honest with herself it wasn't really Adams' fault. She'd had plenty of opportunities to marry him. She knew, even now, that it had been her he really wanted and not Rebecca bloody Webber, as young as she was. She'd certainly got her claws into Tom a bit quick, though. Didn't give her time to think, or consider, now it was all too late. What a fool she'd been. Did her independence really mean that much to her? She'd achieved as much as she was likely to in her career, was marriage and a bit of happiness really going to get in the way of her life or just add to it? As she pulled into her drive, her mobile phone burst into life. She looked down to see who was calling her but the monitor indicated 'anonymous'. She turned it on. It was Adams.

'Sam, don't hang up, we need to talk.'

Sam hesitated for a moment, contemplating whether to press the off switch or not. She decided against it.

'I wasn't going to,' she lied. 'What can I do for you, Superintendent?'

There was a pause. 'How much longer are we going to go on like this, Sam?'

'You tell me. You're the one that walked out and found a younger woman.'

'You know that's not what I wanted, I wanted you but you wouldn't have me. What was I suppose to do, wait for ever? Grow old while you made up your mind? I needed someone in my life, Sam, I wanted you, but you wouldn't come. What was I suppose to do?'

She knew that everything he was saying was true, but somehow it didn't help. 'Perhaps I just need time, Tom.'

'Well, that's a result, at least you're calling me Tom again.'

Tears began to roll down Sam's face, streaking it with mascara.

'But not in public, eh?' There was a short silence. 'You can call me Tom whenever and wherever you want. It doesn't bother me.'

Adams' gentle attitude was more than Sam could bear. 'Look, Tom, I've got to go. Sorry, really, look, it's dangerous driving like this. I'll talk to you later. Bye.'

She turned off the phone and sat perched at the wheel of her car, her eyes so full of tears she couldn't see her cottage only a few yards away.

As they began to walk back towards the front of the house Meadows suddenly grabbed Sharman's arm. 'Hang on a second, Stan.'

Sharman stared through a gap in the hedge and saw several braided officers walk across the drive and into the house. One of them was clearly Robert Shaw, the Chief Constable. Another size ten to walk all over the scene of crime, he thought. He wondered if Flannery would stand up to the Chief like he had done to him. Knowing

Flannery, he probably would. Not that Sharman had much to do with chief officers, avoided them like the plague if he could. Shaw was one of the new breed of chiefs, intellectual liberal – but then weren't they all these days? They all seemed to be vying with each other to see who could be the most liberal and impress the politicians. Pity they couldn't all vie with each other to nick villains.

'Wouldn't do for the Chief to see me now would it, Dick?'

Sharman had a way of making Meadows feel uncomfortable, he always had. In truth, as far as the modern police force was concerned, Sharman was a bloody liability. Far too unconventional to make anything of himself, he also had the ability to drag those who supported him down with him. Meadows knew he needed him, but also knew that he had to keep his distance. Just in case. As much as Meadows respected Sharman, he always made sure there was clear blue sky between the two of them. As soon as the coast was clear, Meadows bustled him back around the side of the house and on to the drive.

'Give us a call tomorrow, Stan. I'll see what I've got.'

Sharman walked across to his car. 'Yeah, sure Dick.' Before Meadows had time to reply Sharman was inside his car and heading along the drive towards the main gate. As he passed through the gate he noticed there were hundreds of police cones everywhere. The young constable he'd seen earlier was still putting out more cones, and remembering the V sign he'd made at Sharman earlier, he called the hapless young lad across.

'What the bloody hell do you think you're doing? It looks like the M6 on a bad day. Get the lot cleared up.'

The constable looked bemused. 'What, all of them? But you said . . .'

Sharman glared at him. 'Never mind what I said, get the lot cleared away now. That's a bloody order.' With that he pulled up his window and drove away chuckling to himself. That should take him all night. With luck Kate would still be in bed when he got back and then he could take serious advantage of her. It's an ill wind, he considered.

CHAPTER TWO

Andrew Walker had exercized his dogs on Poppy Fields since he was a child, and considering he was now fifty-five, that was a great many years. He had always considered Poppy Fields to be his special place, a sort of secret garden where he could be alone with his thoughts and memories. But since the developers had moved in and destroyed the fields he and hundreds like him had been forced to change their habits.

He was now forced to walk along the edge of the old railway embankment. It wasn't a bad walk, about five miles, and his two retrievers seemed to like it well enough. There were numerous fields, a couple of large woods and dozens of rabbits and squirrels for the dogs to chase, but it wasn't the same, never would be. The end of the walk was a bit unpleasant too. It ended by an old and crumbling railway bridge that had been used as a tip for many years. It wasn't too bad during the winter, but in the summer it stank to high heaven. Lots of rats, too, but then the dogs liked that, and they had already killed a good few. He'd informed both the council and Railtrack about the state of the place, but they'd both blamed each other, and as usual nothing had been done, and the rubbish continued to pile up. He tried to keep away from it, but the dogs loved it and he had trouble keeping them under control whenever they got near the place. Anything evil-smelling or something to chase and they were eager to be there rolling in it or chasing it. It was all quite disgusting. He tried to call them back but when their tails were up there really was no stopping them.

As he approached the bridge the dogs were already under the arch, bounding through the rubbish and scratching about in God only knew what. He called to them, 'Jasper, Conrad, here boys, come on now or I'll bath you both when we get back.' Despite their size and energy Andrew knew their weak point. Despite their love of water this only involved ponds, rivers and lakes, when it came to taking a bath they would cower like strays being taken for that final injection.

As if they'd understood the threat he'd just made they came bouncing back towards him. As they got closer he noticed that Jasper was carrying something in his mouth. It looked like a bit of old meat or perhaps a bone of some sort. Oh my God, thought, it's some kind of dead animal, the bugger would smell for weeks after this.

Jasper dropped whatever it was he had been holding in his mouth at Andrew's feet and waited at bay, his eyes flashing with expectation. Andrew looked at him. 'If you think I'm going to throw that for you then you've got another think coming, mate.'

He looked down at the object lying in the dirt by his right foot. For a moment he fought to control the horror that was welling up inside him. He knew he had to concentrate on the object and make sure there was no mistake and his mind wasn't playing tricks on him. It wasn't. There, lying on the ground beside him, was a human foot, or rather, what was left of one. The shape was distinct enough, but most of the flesh had disappeared, leaving the white skeletal bones exposed. What flesh remained was black and putrid. Four sharp bones stood out where the toes had once been. The remaining fifth toe hung limp and black from the bone, only a few threads of flesh securing it to the foot.

Jasper began to move forward to retrieve his prize, tired

of waiting for his master to act. Walker pushed him away. 'Get away, you daft bugger, leave it!'

He pulled the dogs' leads from his pocket and secured them to their collars, and then, with one last look at the badly decomposed foot to make sure there was no doubt about what it was, he raced back along the embankment towards his house.

Sam had composed herself quickly after Adams' call. She knew she'd have to pull herself together eventually, and now seemed as good a time as any. She stood under the shower for what seemed an age, letting the warm water run and drip over her naked body, enjoying the calming and soothing effect it had on her. The only reason she finally dragged herself out was a loud and continual banging on her front door. Wrapping a towel tightly around her body and covering her hair with a second, Sam marched down stairs to see who had had the nerve to interrupt her private time. Reaching the door she pressed her eye to the security spy hole in the centre of the door and peered through.

Edward Case was standing on the doorstep waving to her. He'd always been a cheeky sod – came with the job, she supposed – but this really was too much, this was an invasion of her privacy.

She opened the door in a rage. 'What the hell are you doing here, Ed? You know the rules, no comment and no doorstepping, especially at this stage of the inquiry.'

Case gazed at her for a moment, raised his hat and smiled. 'And what makes you think I've come to talk to you about the Clarke murder? It might just be a social call.'

Sam folded her arms defensively. 'Cut the crap, Ed, and leave, before I'm forced to ring Superintendent Adams.'

Case smiled. 'From what I understand you have to be forced to call our beloved Superintendent these days, Dr Ryan?'

The comment stunned her for a moment, leaving her

confused, her mind racing for a clever and innocuous
reply. She hadn't realized until then how much her former
relationship with Adams was a matter of public record,
and she didn't like it. Her eyes narrowed. 'I think that's
quite enough, Ed. My relationships, true or imagined,
have nothing to do with this inquiry. You really should
know better. Now please leave.'

'Listen, Dr Ryan, I'm not interested in your private life.
My readers might be, but I'm not . . .'

Sam could feel her temperature beginning to rise. 'And
what the hell has my private life got to do with your
bloody readers?'

Case shook his head. 'Nothing, but you know people.
Pathologist in major murder inquiry having a relationship
with the senior investigating officer. Is that likely to
prejudice the outcome of this inquiry?' He moved his
hand across the space in front of him as if reading a
headline before continuing. 'A matter for public concern,
and debate perhaps, what do you think? You know what
people are like, they love a bit of scandal.'

'I know what you are, Ed, I don't know about the
people. Besides, I'm not having a relationship with
Superintendent Adams. As you are well aware.'

Case's smile broadened, 'Makes matters worse, surely. I
understand there was a certain amount of tension
between the two of you while you were conducting your
initial examination. Very unprofessional, not like you at
all, Dr Ryan. I'm sure my source just misinterpreted the
situation. But once again it could be a matter for public
concern if he didn't, wouldn't you say? I mean, can the
inquiry be conducted properly with you two at each
other's throats the entire time? Something's bound to get
missed, isn't it?'

Sam stared angrily at him. 'Nothing will get missed. I
can assure you of that.'

Case smiled. 'Maybe not.' He suddenly changed his
tack. 'Look, Dr Ryan, we're both people of the world, all
I'm looking for is a bit of an edge with this story. Try and

keep one step ahead of the game. After all it is a local story, we don't want the gang from Wapping all over it, do we?'

Sam remained silent but guessed what was coming next.

'If you could give me that inside track so to speak, Dr Ryan, I'm sure none of this rather sordid story about your good self and Superintendent Adams need ever come out. If you follow what I mean?'

Sam did, only too well. It was blackmail plain and simple and she wasn't falling for it. She grabbed the side of the door ready to slam it in his face.

'Superintendent Adams and I have a close working relationship—'

'Not as close as it once was, though, eh?'

Sam continued, 'Nothing will get missed and the work will be carried out in a highly professional manner. Now print that and be damned. Good day!'

With that, Sam had the satisfaction of finally slamming the door in Edward Case's face. She was only sorry he didn't try and put his foot in the way then she might have broken it. His neck would have been better still, she pondered. After a few minutes she looked back through her spy hole to see him making his way slowly back down her drive towards his car. As he did, however, she noticed that he was met by a second man, who appeared from behind the hedges at the front of the cottage. What concerned her more however was the fact that this second man was carrying a very professional looking camera, with a very long lens attached. She pulled away from the spy hole and leaned back against the door. '*Shit!*'

The desire to chase after them both and pull the camera out of the photographer's hand was strong, but she knew it would be futile and embarrassing. Why had she answered the door in just a towel? She should have known better. Now not only did they have their story, they had a titillating photograph to go with it.

*

Sam changed quickly before grabbing a couple of slices of toast and making her way back to the Park Hospital to perform the PM on Sophie Clarke. By the time she arrived the crowd of journalists who had been parked outside John Clarke's house earlier that morning were now encamped outside the hospital, including she noticed, Edward Case. As Sam drove through them, she was met with another wall of flashing camera lights and people banging on the side of the car screaming questions at her through the tightly closed windows. There was so much noise she couldn't understand a word they were saying, and she wondered why they behaved like a bunch of alley cats after the last fishtail. She eventually made her way to the underground car park, black spots from the camera flashes still affecting her eyes. She wondered how celebrities coped with it all the time and why more hadn't gone blind.

Jean was waiting in her office when she arrived. She looked at her boss earnestly.

'Time for a coffee before you start, Dr Ryan?'

Sam smiled up at her secretary. 'Please, Jean. Not too hot, I haven't got long.'

Sam walked across to her desk and sat down. 'Just thought you ought to know the phone's been ringing off the hook. Press mostly. I've got the switchboard to monitor the calls so it shouldn't be so bad now. The police team is waiting for you in the mortuary . . .'

'Really, well they'll just have to wait a little longer, won't they,' Sam snapped.

Jean judged her mood and decided to be cautious, 'Oh, and Dr Stuart would like to see you when you've got a minute.'

Sam looked up at her. 'Then he's likely to be waiting a very long time, isn't he, Jean?'

Jean thought it prudent to keep the rest of the messages concerning Superintendent Adams' visit to herself.

Sam looked down at the pile of papers on her desk. 'What is all this, Jean? I only cleared my desk last week!'

Jean gave a nervous smile. 'I've put all the urgent stuff at the top, and tried to work down in order of priority.'

Sam shook her head despondently. 'I'll be here for ever. I'll die at this desk and I still won't have done it all.'

Jean backed out of the office slowly. 'I'll make the coffee.'

After undertaking a few urgent and essential administration tasks in order to keep her department ticking over, Sam made her way down to the mortuary, taking her mug of coffee with her in an attempt to finish it off en route and before the PM started. As she entered the mortuary she called out for her assistant, who'd only arrived back from holiday that morning.

'Fred, let's get on with it shall we?'

Fred emerged from behind the corner of the mortuary and put a finger to his lips, pointing in the direction of the small room by the side of the mortuary that was used to allow relatives and friends the privacy of identification. Sam winced and calmed, making her way uneasily to her small office to prepare. After a few moments there was a gentle rap on the door and Sam looked up. It was Trevor Stuart, looking very serious and formal.

'Mr Clarke would like a word, Dr Ryan, if that's OK?'

'Dr Ryan'; that must be the first time since she had known Trevor Stuart that he'd addressed her so formally. She wondered who was listening. She didn't have to wonder long. A few moments later John Clarke MP entered accompanied by Robert Shaw, the Chief Constable. In all her years at the Park this was the first time a chief constable had ever visited her mortuary, or for that matter, as far as she knew, the scene of the crime. Sam directed them to two seats opposite her desk while Trevor Stuart waited anxiously by the door.

Shaw began.

'Mr Clarke, er, John, would like to ask you a few questions, about proceedings, if that would be in order, Dr Ryan?'

Sam nodded and turned her attention to Clarke. He was clearly distressed, his face was red and blotchy, while his eyes were swollen and watery. He spoke nervously and in jerks.

'I know you have to do your job, Dr Ryan.' He stopped to breathe deeply and maintain his composure. Shaw put a reassuring hand on his arm. 'But if at all possible will you treat her as gently as you can. She was really very beautiful, not just to look at I mean, but as a person. She was just lovely.' Tears began to flow across his cheeks.

For the first time since Sam had known the man, she felt sorry for him. Despite his reputation, he seemed genuinely distressed and upset at what had happened to his young wife. She spoke as gently as she could. 'I'll take my time and take great care of her. I promise.'

Clarke nodded his head in understanding and thanks and, unable to say more stood up, aided by Shaw, who still had hold of his arm. The Chief Constable nodded to Sam. 'Thank you, Dr Ryan, much appreciated.'

As they left, Shaw had a few quiet words with Trevor Stuart, before Trevor returned to the office and perched himself in the seat Clarke had just vacated. 'The world's going to watch this one, Sam, you'll need to be at your very best.'

'He certainly looked upset.'

Trevor nodded. 'She was very young and very beautiful. I'm not surprised.'

'Older men and their young wives, eh, Trevor?'

He fidgeted uncomfortably on his chair but ignored the remark. 'So we're going to take extra special care over this one aren't we, Sam?'

Sam stood and began to make her way out of the office to scrub up. 'Trevor, I always take special care. It doesn't matter whether they're the wives of MPs or the wives of down and outs, they're all the same to me.'

Trevor shouted after her as she vanished from sight, 'Down and outs can't affect this department, Clarke can, remember that.'

*

By the time Sam arrived at the mortuary Sophie Clarke's body had already been removed from its plastic covering and laid on the table. Flannery as normal was directing the proceedings, so Sam knew that the job would get done properly. At every stage the body was photographed and a video record made. The bags containing the victim's head, hands and feet were carefully removed and stored within other bags to preserve any debris that might have come loose during the removal of the body. The nails were scraped and hair combed. Hair cuttings from both the head and pubic region were taken and sealed in separate bags. Both the back and front of the body were taped again for any contact traces or further loose debris.

Sam looked across at Flannery. 'Has the body been X-rayed?'

Flannery nodded. 'I had it done before you arrived, Doctor. Thought it might save us some time?'

She should have guessed, but she had to make sure. Pulling the microphone that was attached to the front of her green surgical scrubs she began her commentary.

'The remains are those of a white female approximately twenty-six years of age, with fair hair and blue eyes. She is well nourished and developed.' Sam picked up a chart from a small side table. 'She weighs eight stone three pounds and is five feet four inches tall.' Sam still worked in old weights and measures, leaving Jean to convert it to metric later. She put the chart back on to the table.

'X-rays and general photographs have already been taken. A cord has been tied tightly around both wrists and ankles to restrain the victim. A similar cord has been pulled tightly around the victim's neck.'

Sam looked at Flannery again. 'Have we got shots of the wrists and ankles?'

Flannery nodded.

'Including the knots?'

'Several close-ups, Doctor.'

'What about the neck?'

Flannery nodded again. 'Cord and knot.'

Satisfied, Sam took a pair of surgical scissors and cut away the cord first from the ankles and wrists and then, more carefully, from the neck, as the cord had been pulled so tightly that it was difficult to get the scissors under the cord without causing further injuries. Once the cords had been cut free they were dropped into exhibit bags and removed for analysis.

'The cord appears to be of a common type, similar in size and construction to a washing line. There are deep cuts and bruising around both the ankles and wrists where I have removed the cord. There are also several deep furrows around the neck where the cord seems to have been loosened and then tightened several times.' Sam turned to the photographer again. 'Can you get close-ups of the wrists, ankles and neck for me, thank you.'

As the photographer did his work Sam looked around the room. The usual crowd of suspects were there. Meadows, Adams, coroner's officer and an entire host of Socos. The only person who was visible by his absence was Sharman. She wondered what had happened to him.

'Where's DS Sharman?'

Adams didn't reply, leaving it to Meadows to do his dirty work. 'He's been reassigned to another case.'

Sam nodded. She knew that was police talk for a rebuke. To be removed from a case was usually due to a reprimand, in this case probably for parking in Adams' spot. Policemen get very territorial about their parking spaces.

Although Sam had never been keen on so many people, especially the police, being in the room when she was conducting an examination, she knew it was necessary. It was important, if only to shorten the chain of continuity, that the police collected the evidence during the PM. That way Sam should be able to spend less time in court. They were also responsible for making sure the evidence was labelled and stored properly. Occasionally, and much to Sam's amazement, they even asked the odd relevant question. That's why Sam was surprised Sharman wasn't there – he was good at that. Uncomfortably so sometimes.

When the photographers had finished Sam examined the eyes. 'Close examination of the conjunctivae has revealed bloodspots caused by haemorrhaging concurrent with asphyxia.'

Sam then began to work down the body with Fred continually moving the bright overhead light to keep any shadow from creeping across her view. She next examined and measured several small scars, which covered the body's breasts and nipples. She counted them.

'There are sixteen small burn marks across both breasts and nipples. The marks are circular in appearance, possibly caused by a lighted cigarette placed against the flesh. There is considerable damage to the right nipple. There are also similar injuries to both the vagina and anus. There are further superficial injuries to her lips, chest and neck.' Sam turned to the photographer. 'I'd like several close-up shots of these injuries, please.'

She then turned to Flannery, 'I'd like a small diagram situating the injuries on the body, please, Colin.'

Flannery took his notepad and began his work at once. Sam stood back allowing both Flannery and the photographer to work.

When they had finished she turned to Fred. 'Can you turn her on her side for me, Fred?'

Fred stepped forward and turned the body as instructed, and Sam examined it carefully. 'Although there is widespread hypostasis, the back of the body appears to be clear of any injuries or marks.' Sam nodded to Fred, who rolled the body back into position.

She next took swabs from the vagina and anus, checking for the presence of semen. She wasn't disappointed. 'There appears to be strong traces of semen inside the vagina.' She continued to take swabs from the mouth and nipples, checking for the same thing. She noted that both the perineum and anus were damaged and ripped, almost certain indicators of rape and sodomy. This girl had been through a lot before finally being murdered. Picking up a scalpel from the tray, Sam looked around the room as if she was going to make some monumental announcement, which in some way she was. 'I'm now going to cut into the body.'

Pushing the scalpel through the neck she pulled it down and along the body to the pubis making the usual detour around the navel, which was both difficult to cut and even harder to sew up afterwards. She then made a V-shaped incision across the neck so that the front of the neck could be taken out for separate examination, and the larynx removed. Sam had started her work in earnest.

After Sam had finished the PM she left Fred to finish off, and stitch up. She had, as she'd promised, been as gentle and as careful as she could. Sam always liked to think she treated all her cadavers with equal respect but sometimes it was difficult, especially, as had been the case recently, when there were so many. As she finally walked away from Sophie Clarke's body she put a hand on Fred's shoulder. 'Be careful with her, Fred, do a good job.'

Fred nodded, 'Don't worry, Dr Ryan, I'll sort her out. You won't know I've been there.'

Sam felt emotionally drained. She looked at the remains lying on the table. Even now, after all the things that had happened to her, there was still a gentleness about Sophie. Even though Sam had never really known her, she still felt an overwhelming sense of sadness and loss. She always maintained a clinical distance between her and the remains she was dealing with, made it easier that way. She didn't need, or want, to know anything about their personalities, that would just have made the job harder. As indeed it had with Sophie Clarke, and she didn't want to cope with too many more of those.

Adams and Meadows were waiting in Sam's office.

'Morning, gentlemen.'

Only Meadows replied. 'It's afternoon, actually, Dr Ryan.'

Sam looked at her watch. It was almost two. Time really

had raced away with her. Meadows commenced the questions while Adams remained silent.

'So, Dr Ryan, what can you tell us. As you know, we need to get this sorted out quickly?'

Sam leaned back in her chair. 'There was tearing and bruising to both her vagina and rectum not consistent with consensual sex, so I'm assuming she was both raped and sodomized.'

Adams cut in. 'Assume?'

Sam shrugged. 'I'm quite certain she was, but I've seen similar injuries caused through rough sex too.'

Adams cut in again. 'She was tied up, for God sake.'

Sam looked at him hard. 'The games people play. My job is to outline my findings, not come to a conclusion, that's yours.'

Adams wasn't satisfied. 'Doesn't normally stop you having an opinion.'

'If I examine the body of a person who has been shot, I will tell you what I have discovered. From that information it is up to you to decided whether he was shot by another, shot himself, or whether it was an accident. I'm an examiner, not a police officer.'

Meadows could feel the tension and cut it sharply to stop it. 'Anything else, Dr Ryan?'

'As I said she's been sodomized too, but not with a penis. Something else has been used. What ever it was, it caused quite extensive injuries. A similar instrument was probably used on her vagina too.'

Meadows continued the conversation, trying to keep Adams and Sam apart. 'What about the marks on her chest?'

'Burns. From their size and shape they look like cigarette burns. I counted sixteen in all, mostly over the breasts and nipples. However, there were also several around the vaginal walls, and at least three around and inside the anus.'

Meadows shook his head. 'We're looking for one sick bastard.'

Sam looked across at him. 'Or one sane evil one.'

Meadows gave a mock laugh as Sam continued, 'She died slowly too.'

Adams cut in sarcastically, 'I take it she was strangled, but I wouldn't want you to have an opinion about that.'

Sam remained cool and calm, enjoying the superiority she felt this gave her over her former lover. 'Garroted, actually, and it's not an opinion, Superintendent, it's a clinical fact. There are several ruts in her neck showing how the cord was twisted tightly and then released several times. Whoever it was really wanted her to suffer before he finally twisted the cord tight.'

'Time of death?'

He's nothing if not persistent, Sam thought. 'Well, as you know, it's not an exact science but if I was to hazard a professional guess I would say between one and four this morning. But as I said, that's just a guess.'

Meadows shrugged. 'It'll do for now. Something to work on, anyway. Anything else?'

Sam shook her head. 'Not at the moment. Have to wait for the test results to come through before I can tell you any more.'

Meadows nodded his understanding, 'Well, thank you, Dr Ryan. When the results are through you know where we are. An early call would be appreciated.'

Sam nodded. As the two detectives left the room, Adams hesitated for a moment and looked back at Sam as if he was going to say something. Then, thinking better of it, turned back and followed Meadows out of the mortuary.

Stan Sharman wondered why Meadows had sent him out to this Godforsaken hole to deal with the death of some damn druggy. He'd managed to get himself lost twice and it finally needed a plod in a marked panda to show him the way in. As he drove past the wood, and then on through the fields of sugar beet, he couldn't help wondering why anyone would travel quite so far to die. There had to be better places, closer. At least, he thought, it should be straightforward enough and wouldn't take long. He cursed himself for the thought, knowing he was asking for trouble for just thinking it. He was looking forward to seeing Kate and nothing, especially a dead druggy, was going to stop him. He was going to spoil her tonight, in the hope that she would be in the mood to spoil him later. He liked Kate, OK she was a prostitute and he had to be careful, but he really did like her. He'd been with more than his fair share of girls, and knew himself well, but there was something about Kate that had always appealed to him. Her independence, perhaps. She didn't have a pimp and that was unusual. But then she had him. He looked after her, protected her and it didn't cost her a penny.

He finally stopped his car behind the Panda about forty yards from the edge of the railway bridge where the body had been discovered. He couldn't help comparing the scene outside the Clarkes' house, with everyone, including the Chief Constable, running around like headless chickens, with what he was approaching now. Two uninterested-looking plods, one clapped-out Panda, and a man with two dogs, presumably the person who found the body. After making a note of his arrival time, Sharman stepped out of his car and walked towards one of the police officers standing underneath the railway arch. As Sharman approached he looked up.

'Morning, Stan. Bit low-key for the likes of you, isn't it?'

'Jim.' Stan had known Jim Bogner most of his career. He'd never had any ambition other than to work section, work shifts and stay in uniform. The police force had no problem in granting him his three wishes. At first Sharman had thought he was a bit of a waster, then it had occurred to him that if it wasn't for men like Jim the entire bloody force would collapse. 'They've decided that the rest of my career should be stress-free. Bit like yours really, Jim.'

Bogner laughed. 'Hadn't realized you were in that much trouble, mate. Adams on your case?'

'He's on everybody's case. Anyway, what we got?'

'Bloke over there with the dogs found this.' Bogner held up a piece of flat card with the remains of a skeletal foot on it.

Sharman examined it for a moment. 'Where did he find it?'

Bogner laughed again. He seemed to be finding the entire situation hilarious. 'He didn't, his dogs did. Searching for rats and dug up this instead.'

Sharman looked away from the foot and back to Bogner. 'Find anything else?'

Bogner nodded. 'Unfortunately, yes.'

Kicking away a large and broken piece of chipboard, PC Bogner revealed a brown stained human skull. At first Sharman thought the skull was somehow moving. As if what flesh that was left was being pressed and manipulated. Then he realized. The skull was covered in maggots. There were thousands of them, crawling over each other through the eyes and mouth. Every inch of the remains seemed to be covered in them. Sharman crouched down, careful where he put his feet and keeping his hands well away from the remains. He, wondered who it was, why they were there, and more importantly, how they had died.

Bogner crouched down beside him. 'We could start a fishing bait shop with this one, Stan.'

Sharman ignored him but Bogner wouldn't be put off. 'I reckon she's female.'

Sharman stood up and looked at Jim Bogner, impressed. 'How the hell do you know that?'

'Got its mouth open.' Amused by his own joke Bogner began to laugh. Although he tried to stop himself even Sharman stretched out a broad smile.

'Fucking hell, Jim, let's have some respect, shall we?'

Bogner wiped his eyes and held up a syringe. 'Found a few of these scattered around the body. Heroin, I would think, tenth this year that I know about. Little doubt what we've got here, Stan. Don't know why you bothered turning out.'

Sharman glanced across at him. 'Shouldn't that be in an exhibit bag?'

PC Bogner laughed sarcastically. 'On a case like this? Waste of bloody time.'

Sharman walked back to his car and removed several small plastic exhibit bags. Returning he pulled the syringe out of Bogner's hand and dropped it into one of the exhibit bags. He did the same with the decomposed foot. 'Let's do this one by the numbers, Jim. Just in case you're wrong. Know what I mean? Are there any more needles?'

Bogner stood up. 'A few, over there.' He pointed to the wall about five yards from the body. 'Look, Stan, don't try and make something out of nothing.'

Sharman shook his head. 'I'm not. Just trying to do the job right.'

Bogner wasn't satisfied with his explanation. 'Look, just because you've been thrown off the Clarke case, don't try to make up for it by inventing your own murder story.'

Sharman looked hard into Bogner's face. He had always been impressed how quickly gossip flew around the force, but even he was surprised at the speed the information about his departure from the Murder Squad been passed about.

'Is that what you really think?'

He nodded. 'Yes, it's what I really think. You can waste your time, Stan, but don't waste mine, I've got too much to do. I'll leave it with you, mate. Don't forget to fill out the coroner's report, will you. I'm sure he'll be fascinated.'

With that Bogner called across to his colleague. After a short discussion while Bogner justified his decision to his fresh-faced probationer, they both drove away.

Sharman watched them go, incensed by Bogner's attitude.

'You always were a pratt, Jim.'

Once Bogner and his partner were gone Sharman walked across to the man with the dogs.

'I take it you found the remains?'

Walker looked down at his dogs. 'Well, they did actually, I just sort of followed them.'

Sharman nodded and crouched down rubbing his hand over their faces. 'How old are they?'

'Jasper's two and Conrad is just over three.'

'They're beautiful dogs.' Sharman straightened. 'When did you find the body?'

'Couple of hours ago now. I rang your lot straight away.'

Sharman looked back towards the bridge. 'Touch anything?'

Walker suddenly looked nervous. 'No, nothing. Jasper found a foot and brought it to me, but I gave that to the other policeman.'

Sharman nodded his understanding. 'Come here much, then?'

'I do since they bulldozed Poppy Fields.'

Sharman shook his head in sympathy. 'Tragedy that. Used to play there when I was a lad. Loved the place. Like to check a few councillors' bank accounts after planning permission was passed for that one.'

Walker smiled. 'Me too. They had to be up to something.'

Sharman changed the subject quickly, not wanting to get involved in a conversation away from the main subject for too long. 'When was the last time you were here?'

'Yesterday. I come here every day, twice a day – to walk the dogs, you understand?'

Sharman smiled and looked at the dogs. 'Nice to know they're so well looked after. They ever reacted to anything under the bridge before?'

He shook his head. 'No, never. I don't always walk up that far. It's just that they seem to like smelly places. Once they're off their leads I have trouble getting them back sometimes.'

Sharman glanced across at the two enthusiastically

panting dogs. 'Did you give your details to the two police officers? Name, address, phone number?'

'Yes.'

'Good, well that's it for now. Probably want a statement later, though. But we'll let you know.'

The man nodded his understanding, turned and walked away, fighting to keep control of his retrievers. Sharman watch him go. It was amazing how many people with dogs found bodies, and he was right about Poppy Fields, it had been a tragedy. He turned and began to walk back towards the scene. He needed to be on his own for a while before the funeral van arrived to take the body to the mortuary. He wanted to have a good look around. He didn't know why, but the whole scene somehow felt wrong.

There was nothing much to look at. There was no view of the area from the road, no houses nearby. He'd need to talk to the farmer and find out if he or any of his lads had noticed anything. He knew it was a long shot, but right now that's all he had. He noticed that trains still travelled along the embankment and over the bridge. He'd try and have a conversation with some of the drivers. Another long shot, but again one that would have to be taken. He made a note to find out what time trains passed over the bridge and who the drivers had been over the last – he thought about it for a moment – six months. Sharman's entire career was based on his ability to make lists. With so much going on in his life he had discovered it was the only way he could survive. Besides, he wasn't getting any younger and the memory wasn't what it was. Lists helped.

Pulling a small Olympus camera from his bag he photographed the surrounding area. Then he photographed the bridge and all the rubbish underneath it. Carefully removing the rubbish, cardboard, tyres and mattresses from the top of the remains, he photographed what was left of the body. He'd watched the Socos at work long enough, so he had some idea of what photographs to take, what was important and what wasn't. Once that had been covered he collected the tattered remains of the body's clothing and dropped them into exhibit bags. Not that there was much left. Part of a green T-shirt, what looked like a faded pair of jeans, a pair of approximately size six trainers and a pair of faded white thong pants. A rat suddenly scurried across the front of the remains. Sharman liked most animals, but he found rats distasteful. He kicked out at the creature as it dashed for cover, catching it under its belly and sending it sprawling across the piles of rubbish. Despite the force of the kick, the rat seemed uninjured and continued on its way disappearing into the dark recesses of the far corner of the bridge. Tough evil bastards, Sharman thought.

As he looked down at the body he noticed something glint on the floor next to the exposed hip bone. Crouching down he picked it up and examined it closely. It was a watch. In fact it was a very expensive-looking gold Rolex. He looked at the back. Something had clearly been engraved there and someone had taken the time and trouble to file the inscription off. Sharman was pleased, it was the best clue he'd had yet. He dropped it carefully into an exhibit bag.

Under Sharman's supervision the remains were carefully wrapped in a large clear plastic cover, maggots and all, before being placed into a black body bag and dropped into a coffin. Sharman continued to supervise the removal of the remains, making sure they were all there, and that nothing was accidentally lost or dropped. Satisfied that everything that should be there was, he finally gave permission for the van to leave. Once it had disappeared through the woods, he took one last careful look around. He climbed the embankment, searching it for a quarter of a mile in each direction for anything that might be of interest. There was nothing. Then he searched behind the bridge and in the fields both sides of the embankment, but still there was nothing. He finally shook his head in despair. The body had been there for too long, any relevant clues would be long gone. Despite not really expecting to find anything he was still disappointed. It probably was just another druggy who had overdosed in a lonely place. Wouldn't be the first, or the last. Perhaps Bogner was right and he was making too much of it. Trying to make up for his disappointment for being kicked off the Clarke case. He began to question his judgement, which was unusual for him. What he was sure about, however, was the tingling in his spine that told him there was a lot more to this case than just another overdose. He'd felt it when he arrived, and the feeling hadn't left him yet.

The evening with Kate was as much fun as Sharman had expected. He didn't know whether she did it for all her clients or whether she considered him special. He hoped so. Whenever she turned up for an evening with him she always looked stunning, and he felt proud to be with her. Even the way she spoke and acted seemed to be different. She was polite, reasonably spoken, even affectionate. They met at the Garden House Hotel for a drink. Sharman liked the Garden House because of its location by the river. He liked to sit out in their garden bar and watch the world go by. Young students and tourists struggling by in punts or just walking and cycling along the towpath. After they had finished their drink they walked slowly through the crowds of tourists that thronged the streets of Cambridge. Even though most of the students had gone for the summer, the city still teemed with life as representatives of what seemed every nation on earth wandered around its narrow alleys and magnificent courts.

After twenty minutes or so, they finally reached Sharman's favourite restaurant, the Tai-Chewn on John Street. Sharman never booked; he didn't need to, he was a regular, and was always generous with his tip. As usual they gave him his favourite table by the window. He always enjoyed watching people, not that with Kate with him he would have eyes for anyone but her. She was a total distraction. He wondered if one day she would marry him. He also wondered what the force would say if she did. That should liven the Christmas party up a bit. Given the choice between the force and Kate, however, he knew he would take Kate every time. He'd already got it planned. He'd got more injuries than most, several of them caused while doing his job. The second he wanted to leave he would just play on one of them, go sick, stay sick and finally leave with his pension intact and paid early. Besides, he justified himself, they owed him at least that.

As usual, the meal was wonderful and there was plenty of it. They managed to get through two bottles of wine between them. They could both hold their drink after years of practice, so although not drunk when they left, they were certainly merry. Back at Sharman's flat formalities were forgotten and they were soon undressed and bouncing across his king-sized mattress. Kate made him feel good about himself, while the rest of the world seemed to spend most of their time reminding him who he was and where he came from, fearful perhaps that one day he would become too big for his boots.

When they had finished Sharman lit up two cigarettes and they lay back on the bed relaxing and studying the marvels of his ceiling. After a few moments he turned his head towards Kate. 'Have you ever been involved in any of that bondage stuff?'

Kate didn't move. 'It'll cost you extra. But then, at least you won't have to buy the stuff, you could always use your handcuffs. I know other coppers who have.'

Sharman was alarmed by the last comment. 'You've let coppers cuff you up?'

Kate shook her head despairingly. 'No, not me, pratt. Believe me, one daft copper's more than enough. But some of the other girls have.'

'Who?'

Kate looked at him and shook her head. 'No chance. But

what I will tell you is that some of them have got a lot more than just three stripes on their arms.'

Sharman looked back at the ceiling. 'So, do they charge by rank?'

Kate laughed. 'That's why you're so cheap.'

Sharman looked across at her feeling slightly hurt. Kate squeezed his hand, which was unlike her and surprised him. 'But you're worth it. Do you want to handcuff me?'

Sharman shook his head. 'No, I like what you do with your hands too much. I just wondered if you ever have been tied up?'

Kate took a long draw on her cigarette before replying. 'Couple of times.'

'Isn't it dangerous? Could get yourself hurt or worse?'

Kate shrugged. 'Can be a bit dodgy, few of the girls have had a rough time but I only allowed it with ones I know well.'

'Do you enjoy it?'

'There's only one bloke I enjoy sex with so it doesn't really matter whether I do or not. Punters seem to, they pay well so that's OK.'

Sharman looked at her, contemplating her last comment. Kate noticed him.

'Oh, for God's sake, Stan, give it up. Yes it is you, before you ask. Happy now?'

Sharman was, more than Kate realized. He continued with his questioning.

'Do they ever hurt you?'

'A bit, but nothing I can't handle.'

Sharman could feel himself becoming angry even at the thought of someone hurting her. 'So what happens?'

Kate stubbed out her cigarette. 'It varies. Some punters like to play rape games, acting out their fantasies. Nipple clips, vibrators, canes, nothing too heavy usually. There are specialist places for those that want that sort of thing. Some of the other girls have been cut but that's never happened to me. I tend to offer the straightforward variety of relief, it's safer.'

'Cigarette burns?'

Kate nodded. 'I've heard of it happening.'

'Don't they tell the police when that happens to them?'

Kate gave a short false laugh. 'As if they give a fuck. They might do something if some bastard tops you, but otherwise forget it. Besides the punter normally pays a lot more especially once they realize what they've done and how much shit they're in. A wad of notes usually sorts the problem out.'

Sharman shook his head in disbelief. The things people will ignore for money. 'Ever been spreadeagled on a bed?'

Kate laughed. 'Most days, and nights if it comes to that.'

'I mean tied spreadeagled?'

Kate shook her head. 'Once, but not for long.'

'Sharman was intrigued, 'What do you mean?'

'Difficult to have sex. Not much movement, can't get your hips up, if you follow me. It's much better with your hands above your head and your legs free. Then the punter gets the restraint he wants, and at the same time can move you about for sex. No, spreadeagle's crap, worst position you could choose. Looks good, though,' she said mischievously.

Sharman lit them both another cigarette. 'These mates who've been burnt with fags, get me their names, can you?'

Kate glared at him. 'Are you taking the piss?'

'No. It might help with something.'

'What?'

'Can't say, but it's important.'

'Is it about that MP's wife? Heard she'd been cut up.'

Sharman sighed. 'Well, you heard wrong.'

'I thought you were off that case, anyway?'

Sharman wondered how many more people knew. It was all getting bloody ridiculous. 'I am, so it's obviously not that.'

Kate looked back up at the ceiling. 'I'll see what I can do. But you didn't get it from me, right?'

Sharman nodded. 'Right, thanks. What do I owe you, by the way?'

Kate remained motionless. 'Nothing, freebie. I enjoyed myself, thanks.'

This time Sharman felt for her hand and gave it a squeeze but she pulled it away. 'Let's not get too soft, Stan. I'll probably charge you extra next time.'

Adams looked at his watch. 6.28 a.m. He'd decided to go in at 6.30 so for the next two minutes at least everyone would have to wait. The tip-off had been a good one. More information than the usual 'helpful' punters gave. If there hadn't been he certainly wouldn't have organized the dawn raid. Whoever made the call knew enough about the murder that hadn't been released to make it worth listening to. Therefore the suspect named had to be taken seriously. If he could get this inquiry cleared up quickly, it would be a weight off his mind and he'd have the Chief Constable off his back. He was also glad he wouldn't have to appear on *Crime Watch*. He knew the programme did a lot of good, but for some reason on the two occasions he'd appeared he'd felt very uncomfortable. Not that he was sure John Clarke MP would feel the same. Since the murder of his wife he had appeared on just about every news and current affairs programme going, as well as making appearances in all the national and local newspapers. Grieving in public was obviously good for votes.

He looked around Victoria Road. Maddingly was a very attractive, middle class area. The kind of place you aspired to live when your life and career prospects improved. Handsome, expensive-looking houses fell back behind tree-lined roads, while on their drives only the very best cars were parked. BMWs, Mercedes, Jaguars and even, he noticed, a nice red Ferrari. It was the kind of place he'd love to live and perhaps one day would.

Adams looked at his watch again. 6.29. Christ, he thought, things seemed slow. He knew Graham Ward was there. One of the lads had called him with a 'wrong number' call at six and Ward had answered it. Odd how the old and well-tried methods of checking people out were often still the best. He turned and looked behind. The Special Operations van was in place with six eager and large uniformed lads awaiting his command. Chalky White was in the second car with two other detective constables, four scene of crime officers were in the van behind that, and he was in the lead car with Dick Meadows. Everything seemed to be set. As the final few seconds ticked by Adams' mind wandered to his current relationship with Sam. Something really would have to be done. He'd tried visiting her cottage but she was either never in or refusing to answer the door. Phone calls met with a similar response. The problem was, the current atmosphere had been picked up by just about everyone and he was rapidly losing credibility. It wasn't the kind of problem you wanted to cope with in the middle of a major murder inquiry, especially one as important as this. With the position of deputy chief constable coming up soon he really could do without a situation like this.

Meadows suddenly interrupted his thoughts, pointing to his watch. 'It's time, boss.'

Adams stared across at him for a moment, collecting his thoughts. 'All right, Dick, let's go.'

Dick Meadows picked up his radio and shouted the call sign, 'All units go, go, go,' and with that a dozen officers raced towards number 24.

Graham Ward was asleep when he heard the door go in. At first he thought there had been an accident on the road outside the flat but as the sounds began to be decoded in his head he realized that it wasn't the sound of crunching metal but the sound of wood and glass, cracking and smashing. Before he'd had time to recover himself properly, he found himself face down on the floor with three dark-suited police officers pulling his arms behind his back. The only thing he could think he'd done wrong was to run a red light the evening before whilst drunk.

They couldn't know anything about that though, surely, and this did seem a little bit of an overreaction. Finally he was forced to his feet and held securely.

Adams entered, 'Graham Ward?'

Ward glared at him. 'What the hell is this all about? I hope to God you realize who I am?'

Adams smiled at him. 'Oh, yes, we know who you are, Mr Ward, that's why we're here.'

Ward glared at him, curling his voice in anger as he spoke. 'Then perhaps you'd have the good grace to tell *me* why you're here?'

Before Adams had time to answer one of the Socos entered the room holding up a coil of white cord inside a clear plastic exhibit bag.

'Where did you find it?'

'Garden shed.'

'Is it the same?'

'Similar, won't know till later but it's been cut at one end.'

Adams nodded and walked across to the side of his bed where he picked up a box of cigarettes. 'Marlboro Lights. Your usual brand, are they?'

After the initial shock of the raid Ward was beginning to grow in confidence. 'I don't know what the fuck is going on, but you're in so much trouble, mate, it's untrue. I'm going to bury both you and your career. Do you understand? And if you want to ask me any more questions you'd better get my solicitor down here.'

He smiled arrogantly. Adams' face remained impassive. All the cards were his and he knew it.

'Graham Ward, I am arresting you on suspicion of the murder of Sophie Clarke between Monday the 14th of August and Tuesday the 15th of August. I have to warn you that anything . . .'

Ward never heard the rest. He could feel the colour draining from his face and then his legs buckled. If it hadn't been for the two men holding him up he would certainly have crashed to the floor.

Adams smiled, satisfied. Holding Ward's head up he looked into his eyes. 'Shall I call an ambulance, *sir*?'

Ward never replied, just stared back at him in total disbelief.

Adams left Chalky White to take Ward down to the station while he remained behind for a few moments to supervise proceedings. He called Colin Flannery across. 'I want it done by the numbers, Colin. Can't afford to lose this one on a technicality.'

Flannery felt quite insulted that Adams would even consider that they would do it any other way than strictly professionally. His department had never lost a case on a 'technicality' since he had taken over, and he'd have thought a superintendent of police would have realized that. Flannery was too annoyed to answer without being sarcastic so he nodded his understanding and walked away.

Meadows looked at his boss. 'Do you think we've got him for it?'

Adams was defensive. 'I wouldn't have gone out on a limb like this if I didn't. Information was good. He knew her so she would have let him in without suspecting what might happen. The cord we found in the shed is similar to the type used to tie her up, hopefully we'll get a match, and he smokes.'

'All a bit circumstantial, sir.'

Adams looked at him, 'Your cup's always half-empty isn't it, Dick?'

Meadows shrugged. 'Just pointing out the facts, sir.'

Adams looked back towards the house. 'It's early days, granted, but once we've had a go at him and got the DNA evidence I'm sure we'll have our man.'

'Let's hope we sort it out before the Deputy Chief Constable board, eh, sir?'

Adams looked at Meadows for a moment, clearly objecting to what he had just said, but remained silent. Meadows realized he'd gone too far and tried to put the matter right. 'You'd make a good Deputy, sir, about time we had someone up there that's done a bit of time on the streets and knows what they're doing.'

Adams looked at him. 'You think the current Deputy doesn't, then?'

There was an edge to Adams' voice that Meadows didn't like. 'I'm not exactly saying that, sir, it's just that, well he's a Bramshill man, what does he know about anything?'

'I went to Bramshill, what have you got against Bramshill?'

'Oh, er, nothing, but you've done some time at the sharp end as well.'

Adams, finally sick of the game, walked back to his car alone, leaving his inspector standing on the pavement concerned and confused.

CHAPTER THREE

Stan Sharman dragged himself into the incident room the following morning. A night out with Kate was more than he could really handle when he had work the next day. But when it came to Kate he didn't mind suffering a little. The incident room seemed quieter than he would have expected so early into a major inquiry and he wondered why. Sharman walked across to Chalky White's desk. 'Morning, Chalky, what's the crack? Everything's a bit quiet.'

Chalky looked up at him, irritated at having to look away from his paper. 'Don't let Adams find you here, mate, he'll have your guts.'

'Too late, bad curry had them last night.'

Chalky laughed. 'Yeah, know what you mean.'

'So where is everyone?'

'Surprised you don't know.'

'I've been busy.'

Chalky returned to his paper. 'So Vice Squad have been saying.'

Sharman was unhappy about the comment but let it go for now.

'They've got a suspect. Adams is going to interview him in a bit. Should all be over after that.'

'They're sure they've got the right man, then?'

'Adams made a big show of a dawn raid. So I guess so. He gave a DNA sample to the police quack, so even if he doesn't cough it we'll know soon enough. Funny, isn't it? Guilt or innocence can all be established by how hard you jerk your right hand. Progress, eh, who'd have thought it.'

Sharman was surprised how quickly Adams had got a result, and wondered how he had done it. 'Adams was a bit quick—'

Chalky, clearly equally unhappy with Adams' progress, cut in, 'Too bloody quick, if you ask me. There goes my overtime and my holiday in Spain. Back to a caravan in bloody Cromer again.'

Sharman persisted. 'So what happened? Suspect give himself up?'

Chalky continued reading while trying hard to remove something unpleasant from between his teeth, 'Anonymous tip.'

Sharman was suddenly very interested. 'Saying what?'

Chalky shrugged and examined what looked like a piece of overchewed beef he'd managed to extract from between his back teeth. 'Not being too senior in rank, Stan, I'm not really privy to that kind of information, but it must have been good otherwise Adams wouldn't have put himself on the line, would he?'

Sharman became thoughtful for a moment. 'Who've they got in for it?'

'Graham Ward, Clarke's political agent. You wouldn't think it to look at him. But then you never can tell.'

'When is Adams going to interview him?'

'Soon. He's keen to get it out of the way and take the pats on the back he feels he deserves.'

Sharman persisted. 'Have they got anything else?'

'They turned his place over good and proper yesterday, found some rope, cigarettes—'

Sharman cut in again. 'Same kind we found at the scene?'

Chalky shook his head. 'No idea, I wasn't there and they don't tell us anything anyway. Scared we might try and share their glory.'

'Anything else?'

Chalky didn't even bother looking up this time. 'Who knows? I'm sure they'll get around to telling us in time.'

Sharman put a hand on Chalky's shoulder; he really was the most miserable bastard he'd ever known. 'Do you know what, mate, you should have been in criminal intelligence.'

Chalky looked up and nodded, agreeing with Sharman's assessment of him.

'Then we'd all be fucked, wouldn't we?'

Chalky scowled and gave Sharman the finger before returning to his paper.

Sharman crossed the incident room to Meadows' office, knocking loudly on the door. Meadows' voice penetrated the door. 'Come in!'

Sharman opened the door and stepped into his boss's office. Meadows was searching through a pile of papers with the air of a man interrupted in the middle of dealing with important work. His demeanour suggested concentration and competence, both of which Sharman knew for a fact to be pure play acting. Meadows, like most of the other sods with rank, was good at sports, and that, next to being a Mason, was the easiest way to get promotion in today's modern police force. He'd played rugby and cricket for the force when he was younger, which meant, as it always did, that he spent very little time on the streets but a lot of time kissing the butts of senior officers in the bar after the game. Later, as he aged, it was golf. Like most of the idle bastards Sharman had been forced to work with over the years, he could lower his handicap by at least two during a major inquiry. It really was unbelievable.

As Sharman entered he looked up with a distracted air. 'Stan my boy, how's it going?'

Sharman shrugged and sat down opposite his one-time partner.

Meadows looked at him quizzically. 'So, to what do I owe the honour of this visit?' He leant back in his chair and smiled. 'No, don't tell me you've decided to join the Masons after all, and you want me to sponsor you?'

Sharman looked at Meadows with a blank expression. 'I'd rather stick red-hot needles in my eyes than join that bunch of trouser lifting toss-pots.'

Meadows leant forward across the desk and lowered his voice to a whisper. 'Most of our senior ranks are members, you know. So careful what you say and who you say it around.'

Sharman remained unimpressed. 'Issuing flared trousers to our braided ranks now, are we? Make it easier to lift them. If you know what I mean?'

Meadows leant back in his chair again. He knew he was fighting a losing battle. With all that talent, if Sharman only played the game a little he could do so much better for himself. He decided to move on. 'So how did it go yesterday? Sorry to stick you with it.'

Sharman gave a sarcastic laugh. 'I bet you were.'

Meadows ignored Sharman's sarcasm. 'There was no one else, Stanley. Adams has got everyone on this bloody murder inquiry. There was only you left. It was either that or see her former psychiatrist. I thought the body might be more interesting.'

Sharman stared at him for a moment taking in what he'd just said. 'She was seeing a shrink?'

Meadows nodded. 'Andy Herman. Been under him for about six months apparently, depression.'

'What the hell had she got to be depressed about?'

Meadows shrugged. 'We'll never know.'

Sharman leaned back. 'No, I suppose not. Got someone in for it, then?'

'We have, but it's all a bit circumstantial. Adams reckons he'll get a cough this afternoon, though.'

Sharman shook his head. 'Adams couldn't get a cough from a consumptive.'

'You ought to open a charm school, you. I think you'd do very well. So tell me about yesterday.'

'That's why I'm here. You've got another murder inquiry to deal with.'

Meadows suddenly shot bolt upright, his previously calm exterior and laid back attitude gone. 'What! I thought it was a dead junkie, overdose or something?'

Sharman smiled. He was enjoying the panic in Meadows' face. 'Well, you're right about one thing, who-ever it was is very dead but it was no overdose. I reckon whoever it was was murdered.'

Meadows was still struggling to control his emotions. 'What do you mean you "reckon"? I take it you've got proof?'

Sharman nodded. 'Enough.'

Meadows wasn't satisfied. 'What's enough?'

'Firstly, who covered the body over?' Sharman reached into his bag and pulled out an envelope containing the photos he'd taken at the scene. He handed them to Meadows. 'Have a look at those, Dick.'

Meadows began to skip through them. 'Where did you get these developed?'

Sharman looked at him, slightly confused by the question. 'Boots. They do them in an hour. I've still got the receipt, I'll put a claim in.'

Meadow shook his head in disbelief and horror. 'Boots? For crying out loud, Stan. These aren't exactly your bloody holiday snaps, are they?'

Sharman ignored him. 'Have a look at the stuff over the body. What do you think?'

Meadows skipped back several pictures and looked at three closely before shrugging. 'What am I supposed to think?'

Sharman pulled his chair closer to Meadows' desk. 'Look –' he pointed to various parts of the photograph to help illustrate his conjecture – 'someone has tried to hide the body. Either they didn't want it discovered, or didn't want it discovered too soon.'

Meadows looked at them again, unimpressed. 'Why didn't our killer just bury the body?'

'Because then it would have looked like a murder if anybody found it. This way we can't be sure.'

Meadows shook his head. 'Well, he was a clever bugger, then, because I'm not sure.'

'Then who do you think covered the body over? A friendly passer-by?'

'Druggies keep themselves out of the way, you know that. Probably took a fix and then crawled under there to sleep it off. Come on, Stan, for Christ's sake. You're trying to make something out of nothing here. I know you're not happy with Adams throwing you off the case, and for what it's worth I wasn't happy about it either, but this is ridiculous.'

Sharman could feel himself getting annoyed at Meadows' flippant approach to his theories and the questioning of his integrity. 'But why go out into the middle of bloody nowhere to get your fix?'

Meadows shrugged, skipping through the photos one more time, before handing them back to Sharman.

'It's not something they do in public, Stan. They do it in odd, out of the way places. You were on the Drug Squad long enough to know that.'

'Yes, I was. I was also on it long enough to know that they don't bloody well go too far from town to do it. Back alley, empty house, bit of waste ground – they have to think about their next fix. They don't walk ten bloody miles from their source, knowing they have to walk ten bloody miles back again to get their next fix.'

'Perhaps they came with someone?'

Sharman interrupted. 'Yeah, the bloody person that killed them.'

Meadows began to relax. Sharman didn't have enough. Even though, if he was honest, he thought he might be right, the last thing he needed right now was another bloody murder to deal with. The Clarke inquiry was only a few days old and already they were having to go cap in hand to the Home Office for more cash. Besides, how many druggies died each year? If they hadn't been murdered first they would probably have died of an overdose in the end. Most of them did. Let's be honest, he thought, who the hell cared.

'You'll have to bring me more than that, Stan, it's not enough, and you know it.'

Sharman stood suddenly, making Meadows lean back hard in his seat.

'Not enough! Bloody hell, Dick there was a time when we'd be on a case with a lot less than this. Or aren't you involved in solving crime any more? Not important to "New Policemen" any more, is it?'

Meadows remained tense, looking beyond Sharman for help should it be required. He'd seen Sharman in action and if he was honest he was frightened of him. 'I can't go to Adams with what you've got, he'll throw it straight out of the window.'

'Adams has just nicked someone on the word of a bloody unknown informant. How vague can you get?'

'He's got a bit more than that.'

'Like?'

'The cord found in the house, possible DNA.'

'All found *after* he made the decision to nick him. I'm sure we'll do the same. Come on, Dick, try being a policeman again. Roll your bloody trouser leg down for once.'

Meadows thought about it for a while considering what to do. Finally he relented. 'I'll talk to Adams if you like, I'll see if I can persuade him.'

Sharman snorted his derision at the suggestion. The anger in his tone forced Meadows to make an immediate decision.

'Look, I'll tell you what I'll do, I'll write you off to the inquiry for two weeks, OK? Bring me some more evidence; evidence that I can go to Adams with, and I'll see what I can do. Until then,' he raised his hands in the air despairingly, 'well, it's up to you now, Stan. You've got fourteen days to convince me, then I want you back at section doing your stuff, OK?'

Sharman stared at Meadows for a moment. 'Overtime?'

Meadows shook his head. 'Not a chance, all used up, and no time in the book either. I'll have half of bloody CID off next year if I keep giving time off in advance.'

Sharman sighed deeply. 'I thought the inquiry was finished?'

'Possibly. But the overtime allocation for this year has still gone. Don't forget this is the fourth major inquiry we've had this year, and it's only August.'

Sharman wasn't impressed by the offer. 'You always were a tight bastard, Dick.'

Meadows shrugged. 'Not me, the system. Sorry, mate, best I can do. Take it or leave it.'

Sharman knew he had no choice but to take it. Worse still, he knew Meadows understood that too. 'You've got me by the balls, Dick, and you know it.'

'Stan, I'm putting my neck out here if only you could see it.'

Sharman realized he probably was but was still not satisfied. 'Will you be in on the interview with Ward?'

Meadows nodded. 'Hope so.'

Sharman thought for a moment. 'Do me a favour . . .'

Meadows gave a little sarcastic laugh. 'What, another one?'

Sharman hesitated, annoyed by his unhelpful reply. 'OK, do yourself a favour. Ask Ward if he sails.'

Meadows frowned. 'If he what?'

'Sails. You know, with boats.'

'Is there something you're not telling me, Stan?'

Sharman shrugged. 'Remember the knots she was tied up with? Let me know what he says. I'll let you have my theory then.' With that Sharman turned and without another word stomped out of the office.

Meadows called after him, 'Two weeks, remember!' As far as he was concerned it was a result. Sharman was out of his hair and, more importantly, away from Adams. Sharman would have to come up with something bloody good to make him go to Adams right now. As good as he knew Sharman was, he felt confident that he wouldn't come up with enough. And what had sailing got to do with anything? He knew Sharman too well to ignore the request, however. Stan would get around to telling him in his own good time. He picked up the papers he had been reading before Sharman arrived, and began to study them again.

Since the excitement of the Clarke murder things had become mundane again. 'The bodies keep coming and we keep cutting,' as Fred was fond of saying. Nothing particularly interesting. Heart attacks, cancer, a couple of 'not quite sures'. Sam had completed the report on Sophie Clarke sooner than usual. She had Trevor Stuart camped in the office until it was complete, which was about as much incentive as she needed to get the report finished as quickly as possible. Not that she'd stated anything but the obvious. Cause of death, strangulation. Yes, she had been raped and sodomized, and quite clearly some instrument, perhaps a bottle, had also been used on her. She had also been tied and tortured for some time prior to death. Small cuts and burns covered her chest, lips, anus, vagina, and neck. Sam had managed to collect semen samples from the vagina but not the anus, where only some form of instrument had been used. It was an odd feeling to be pleased that someone had been raped. Not pleased for the victim's suffering, but pleased that at least that meant you could collect the evidence needed to convict the guilty person and not see them walk free. No more long, fruitless interviews with suspects, one small sample and you knew conclusively one way or the other.

She wondered how Ward would be feeling right now, knowing that there was scientific evidence that would either convict him or establish his innocence. He didn't really need to tell the police anything; the DNA evidence alone would almost certainly convict him. No wonder lawyers were running around like headless chickens trying to rubbish the science. They hadn't got a chance.

A quiet rapping on the office door broke her concentration and she looked up. Stan Sharman was standing by the door peering in, and by the look on his face it was serious.

'Hello, Stan, what can I do for you?'

'Can I have a word, Dr Ryan?'

'After travelling all the way across Cambridge to see me, it would be a bit hard of me to send you home now. If it's as serious as the look on your face, then you'd better come in and sit down.'

Sharman did as he was bid and sat down.

'Tea?' Sharman nodded and Sam called through to Fred. 'Fred, couldn't get us a couple of teas, could you?'

Fred didn't have to reply, he just put his thumb up and disappeared towards the kitchen at the back of the mortuary. Sam's concentration returned to Sharman.

'So, what is it that drags you away from the world of crime?'

Sharman gave a short false laugh. 'You know I'm off the Clarke case, I take it?'

Sam nodded.

'I don't think your friend Adams likes the way I do business.'

Although Sam sympathized with Sharman's situation she knew Stan only too well. Sharman was a good policeman but a difficult man. Clash of personalities, she suspected. She smiled across at him. 'I don't think he liked the way I smelt either.'

Sharman smiled broadly.

'So, if it isn't about the Clarke murder, what is it about?'

Sharman coughed nervously. He hated asking for favours, it put him at a disadvantage and he preferred to be reliant only upon himself, and this time he knew he was about to ask for a big one.

'There was a body, well rather, what was left of one, brought in yesterday. Found under a railway bridge off Hitchins Lane, on the Cambridge Road.'

Sam nodded. 'The drug addict. Overdose, wasn't it?'

Sharman eyed her, concerned. 'You've already done the PM?'

Sam shook her head. 'No, not yet, just repeating what I was told.'

Sharman leaned forward. 'Whatever you were told, Dr Ryan, was wrong. It wasn't an overdose, it was a murder.'

Sam felt a certain sense of surprise and the familiar flutter of interest. Sharman might have been many things but he wasn't a time-waster and he would not risk making himself look foolish. 'How did you come to that conclusion?'

'Gut instinct.'

'That should impress Superintendent Adams. I take it he knows about this?'

Sharman shook his head. 'No, not yet. Talked to Dick Meadows this morning.'

'And his opinion was?'

'I hadn't got enough evidence to proceed. Wants me to find some more.'

'And that's why you're here?'

'Yes.'

'Have you got anything else besides your "gut instinct"?'

'Position of the body. Let me show you.'

Sharman passed Sam the photographs he'd shown Meadows. She flicked through them quickly then went back and studied a couple in more depth. 'Looks like someone covered the body up.'

Sharman could have jumped up and kissed her. 'Precisely. The killer.'

After one more inspection Sam put the photographs back on the table. 'Doesn't mean she was murdered, though. Someone else could have been with her, panicked when she died and then tried to cover the body over so they could get away.'

'What about the location?'

Sam looked slightly bemused.

'Five miles from the city and miles from any village.

Why go there when there are hundreds of places much closer?'

Sam thought about it for a moment. Being an instinctive person herself she put a lot of store by Sharman's gut reaction.

'I can think of a hundred reasons without too much trouble.'

Sharman sat back in his chair despairingly and sighed. Sam took pity on him. She'd been in his position too many times herself not to be.

'OK, what do you want me to do?'

Sharman sat up at once, excited by her interest. 'The PM. Would you conduct it as if it was a murder inquiry?'

'That will be expensive. Soco teams don't come cheap. How much have you got in the kitty?'

Sharman sat back again. 'Nothing. Meadows has given me two weeks off to try and come up with something, otherwise that's it.'

Sam stared at him for a moment. 'What about a bank loan?'

It wasn't quite what Sharman had in mind but if that was what it took. 'If it would help, then—'

Sam cut him off mid-sentence. 'Joke. OK I'll do it but you'll have to assist, and we'll have to do it after hours, if you know what I mean?'

Sharman nodded. 'When do you think you can do it?'

Sam glanced at her watch. 'Now seems good. Hope you hadn't got anything planned?'

Sharman had. He was hoping to see Kate. But as ever, the job had to come first. He'd sort it out with Kate later.

Sam looked through her office door into the mortuary beyond. 'Fred!'

Fred appeared as if by magic from behind one of the stainless-steel fridges, two piping hot mugs of tea in his hands. He handed them to Sharman and Sam. 'Weren't doing anything tonight, were you?'

Fred thought for a moment. 'Well, actually I was—'

Sam wasn't really interested. 'Good, then how do you fancy some unpaid overtime?'

Before Fred could reply Sam moved on. 'It's the skeletal remains they brought in yesterday.'

'The junkie?'

'Yes, that's the one.'

Fred turned and disappeared back amongst the fridges. Sam stood. 'Do you have your camera with you?'

Sharman nodded, still taken aback at the speed of her response.

'Good, then we'd better get on with it. Fred will help you scrub.'

With that Sam marched out of her office with Sharman, searching desperately for his camera, following enthusiastically behind.

Adams watched Ward for a moment, trying to judge his man. This was one of the most important interviews of his life. He'd interviewed murderers before, but the political ramifications of this arrest went far beyond anything he'd ever dealt with. For the past few days every television station and newspaper had been full of the story. He'd had phone calls from the Home Office, the Home Secretary, and he'd lost count of how many times the Chief Constable had called. The media interest was intense and far beyond anything he or the force had ever witnessed before. Requests to appear on every news broadcast from the *Today* programme to *Newsnight* had come in daily. He'd avoided them all up to now, allowing the Chief and his deputies to handle the media. It wasn't that he was afraid to give interviews – he'd given them before – but none had been as important as this and he was afraid of being tripped up and making a fool of himself, with the effect that would have on his promotion chances. He was sure the arrest and conviction would be enough to secure his promotion to deputy chief constable and wasn't going to let anything or anybody get in the way of that. He switched on the tape recorder and commenced his interview.

'The time is now 3.35 p.m. on Tuesday the 22nd of August 2000. I am currently in Interview room number three. Present are Mr Graham Ward, his solicitor Mr Peter Appleyard, Detective Inspector Richard Meadows and myself, Detective Superintendent Thomas Adams. I have already reminded the suspect Graham Ward that he is under caution and both he and his solicitor have acknowledged that they understand that.' Adams paused for a moment to collect his thoughts. 'Mr Ward, you are aware you have been arrested in connection with the murder of Sophie Clarke?'

Ward looked at his solicitor, who nodded his approval of the question, and he answered, 'Yes, I am aware of that.'

Adams continued, 'Did you know Mrs Clarke?

Ward nodded.

'For the tape recorder, please, Mr Ward.'

'Yes, I knew her.'

'How well?'

'She was the wife of my employer, John Clarke MP.'

'How often did you see her?'

'She was sometimes around when I saw John. She hosted coffee mornings and I dropped into a few of those and we went to the odd function together. That was about it.'

'Were you attracted to her?'

Appleyard interrupted. 'Is that entirely relevant, Superintendent?'

Adams stared at Appleyard for a moment, annoyed at being interrupted.

'Given the circumstances of Mrs Clarke's death, yes, I think it is.'

Ward glanced across at his solicitor. 'It's all right, Peter, I don't mind answering.' He looked back at Adams. 'Yes, I was, she was a very attractive woman. A very nice one too.'

'Did you ever try to form a relationship with her?'

'No! For God's sake, man, she was my boss's wife. I liked her but that's as far as it went.'

'She was much younger than John Clarke. What were your feelings about that?'

'What the hell has age got to do with anything?'

'Twenty-one years is quite a lot.'

'John's got more about him than many men half his age. He's rich, powerful and has a wonderful lifestyle. I don't suppose there would be many women not attracted to him. By God, you should have seen them at the party conferences, they were dropping their knickers all over the place.'

'He was unfaithful?'

'I've no idea. The point I'm trying to make is that he could have been if he'd wanted. There are an awful lot of women after him. Many of them just as young as Sophie.'

'Was he a good husband?'

'She seemed happy enough.'

'Did they have a good sex life?'

Appleyard interrupted again. 'I really don't see how my client can possibly be expected to answer that.'

Ward shrugged. 'I really have no idea. Like I said, she seemed content.'

'What about your sex life. Do you have one?'

'If you mean do I have a girlfriend, then the answer's no.'

'But you have had girlfriends?'

'Yes.'

'Did you have sex with them?'

Ward nodded and Meadows pointed to the tape recorder again.

Ward sighed heavily and ground out his affirmation through gritted teeth.

'Straight sex?'

'Depends what you mean by "straight".'

'Did you like, say, tying them up before sex?'

Ward's face reddened and he snapped, 'No, I bloody well didn't.'

'What about hurting them? Did you enjoy that?'

Ward looked at his solicitor in desperation. 'Do I have to answer these sick questions?'

Appleyard looked across at Adams. 'Is this all necessary?'

Adams repeated, 'Given the nature of Mrs Clarke's death, yes, I think it is.'

Appleyard looked at his client and nodded curtly.

Ward looked back at Adams and, with a visible effort to control the level of his voice, answered, 'No, I didn't like hurting them, tying them up, dressing up as a vicar or even using a vibrator. Happy now?'

'Would you have objections to us speaking to some of your previous girlfriends to confirm this?'

Ward shrugged as if defeated. 'Suit yourself. They'll only reiterate what I've said.'

Adams looked at Appleyard. 'Perhaps your client would be good enough to let us have their names and addresses after the interview?'

Ward nodded at Appleyard.

'Certainly.'

Adams turned to Meadows, who handed him a clear plastic bag containing what appeared to be magazines.

'These were found hidden inside your shed. They're magazines about female bondage and sexual torture. I am now showing Mr Ward six magazines called *Bound to Please*, which were discovered in his shed. Exhibit number 4a.'

Adams showed them to Ward, who glanced at the front covers and almost shot out of his seat. 'They're disgusting! There is no way you found those in my shed. This has to be a fit-up!'

'They were found in your shed and your fingerprints were found all over the bag we found them in.'

Ward shook his head vigorously. 'No way, no way. This is a stitch-up. I don't . . . I wouldn't . . . buy filth like that.'

'Then how did your prints get on the wrappings?'

Ward shook his head in despair. 'I don't know, I really don't know.'

Adams continued. 'What about this?'

Meadows produced a length of cord, again wrapped inside a clear plastic bag, and showed it to Ward.

'I am now showing Mr Ward a length of white washing-line rope also discovered in his shed. Exhibit number 6a.'

Ward shrugged. 'What about it?'

'Is it yours?'

'I've no idea. Looks like washing line.'

'It's similar to the type used to tie Mrs Clarke up.'

'There must be thousands of yards of that stuff all over Cambridge.'

'Interesting that we found it in your possession, though?'

'What's odd about that? I hang my clothes out like everybody else. I bet if you searched Mr Appleyard's house you'd find something similar.'

Appleyard grunted nervously. 'We have a tumble-dryer actually.'

Ward looked at his solicitor in disbelief as Adams continued, 'Do you smoke?'

Ward glared sarcastically at him. 'As if you didn't know.'

'What brand?'

'Marlboro Lights.'

'Are they all you smoke?'

'Just about. If I'm desperate and can't get them I'll smoke something else.'

'Like?'

'Don't know, depends what I can get my hands on at the time.'

'Do you ever pull the filter tips off prior to smoking them?'

Ward shook his head and looked slightly surprised at the question. 'No, why should I?'

Adams shrugged. 'Make them taste better?'

'If I wanted non-filter tips I would buy non-filter tips.'

'It's just that several Marlboro Light cigarette butts were found at the scene of the murder. The tips had been pulled off all of them. Now why would our killer do that?'

Ward shrugged again. 'You're the detective, you tell me.'

Adams continued, 'They'd been used to burn Mrs Clarke prior to her death.'

Ward looked visibly shaken by this news. 'He tortured her first. Oh God, I didn't know that. I hope she didn't suffer too much.'

Adams raised an eyebrow at him, impressed by his acting ability. But then, he was a politician. 'I'm afraid she suffered rather a lot before she eventually died. I'm surprised you didn't know that.'

Ward became red in the face and began to shake with the effort of controlling himself. 'It's true, isn't it—'

Adams cut in. 'What is?'

'All coppers are bastards.'

Adams ignored the remark as Appleyard tried to calm his client down. 'Where were you between midnight and 6 a.m. last Monday night?'

'Asleep in bed.'

'Anyone confirm that?'

'As I don't live with my mum any longer, and as you know I don't have a current girlfriend, no, there's no one.' He thought for a moment. 'Look I'd had a very hard day, I was tired. I went home, watched some crap war film on the TV about a bunch of old men fighting the Second World War or something, had a large brandy and went to bed. I got up about eight and went to work.'

There was a sudden loud rap on the interview room door and a uniformed officer entered. 'Can I have a word with you outside a moment, sir?'

Adams was clearly irritated by the interruption but stopped the interview. 'Interview terminated at 3.55 p.m. for a short break.' After turning off the tape recorder he followed the PC out of the office.

As he did Meadows looked at Ward for a moment before asking, 'Do you still sail, Mr Ward?

Ward looked at him nonplussed. 'I've never sailed. What a pointless question. Why did you ask me that?'

Meadows smiled. 'Sorry, I thought you did. I have an interest in boats. Just making conversation. Wasn't trying to be clever.'

Appleyard and Ward exchanged glances. They clearly didn't believe him, but let the question go.

Adams glared down at the young constable who had interrupted his interview. 'This had better be bloody good, son.'

'The results of the DNA sample are back, sir. They match the suspect.'

Adams looked at him, slightly disbelieving. 'No doubt?'

The constable shook his head. 'No doubt. You've got him, sir. Well done.'

Adams had to resist the temptation to hit the air with his fist and shout 'Yes!' He had his man and he also knew that the promotion he so desperately wanted was in the bag.

As the remains were slowly and carefully laid out on the mortuary slab Sharman began to take his photographs. He'd seen it done enough times to know what he was doing, he also knew that if he missed anything Sam Ryan was bound to point it out. After he had finished taking all his pictures, Fred pushed the X-ray machine into place, and after they had all taken cover behind a lead screen he took several X-rays of the body. Anything that Sam missed they knew would show up later on the X-ray, including any old injuries that might not be apparent to the human eye, but might indicate signs of long-term abuse. Once that task had been completed Fred began to remove all the debris that still covered the body, carefully placing all of it into plastic exhibit bags. Small bits of rubbish, dead insects and maggots, bits of leaves and what looked like parts of a couple of wild flowers. This job would normally be done by a team of Socos but as there was only Fred, if the job was going to get done properly then they would all have to be patient. Once everything had been collected it would be labelled and sent to the laboratories in

Huntington for analysis. Sam knew a lot could be established from the debris that was found on the remains: the original location of the murder, time of death, even the general health of the deceased.

Once Fred had finished and Sam was convinced everything had been collected and bagged, she went over to the centre of the slab and moved her gaze slowly and carefully over the length of the body. She turned to Sharman. 'Come over here, Stan, stand next to me.'

Sharman did as he was bid.

'Now, my lad, let me give you some basic lessons in how to establish sex . . .'

Sharman grinned at her. 'I think I've already got some good ideas about that.'

Sam shook her head and frowned slightly before continuing, 'And hopefully the cause of death of the young woman we have before us.'

Sharman looked across at her. 'Young woman? How can you be sure of that? Is it because she's got her mouth open?' He immediately regretted his crass attempt at a joke. What an idiot he was making of himself.

Sam appeared to ignore the comment and continued, indicating to the head. 'Look at the skull. It's thinner, smaller and lighter than the male skull.'

Sharman nodded. He couldn't really see it, but he wasn't going to admit to his ignorance.

'So you see,' Sam continued, with a twinkle in her eye, 'men are much thicker than women, and there's your proof.'

Sharman was reminded why he had always like Sam Ryan. Not only was she one of the best-looking things around, but she also had a wonderfully dark sense of humour, just like his.

Sam continued, 'The brow ridges are also more prominent. See?'

He looked. If he had something to compare it with he was sure it would be obvious but there wasn't, so he just grunted his agreement. Sam moved down the body.

'The other strong indicator is the pelvis. On a woman it is wider and lower, just like this one. The deceased was also white. Again, you can tell this by examining the shape and size of the facial bones. So, already we know she was a white female.'

'Anything else?' Sharman asked.

Sam looked at him from under raised eyebrows. 'Give me a chance. Remember this is a freebie.'

Sharman put his hand up by way of apology, as Sam moved towards the skull again.

'The teeth appear to be healthy and intact with few fillings and no caps. From the eruption of the third molars I would estimate the age of this person to be,' she paused for a moment, warming to her role and wishing to add dramatic effect, 'in her early to mid-twenties?'

Sam then turned her attention to the height of the remains. Fred measured both the length of two of the leg bones.

'From the measurements of the femur and tibia I would estimate the height of the woman as between five feet six and five feet eight. It is also worth noting at this time that there are gnawing marks around several parts of the skeleton. Which I would assume, considering where the body was discovered, to have been made by rats.'

Sam then returned to the skull once more, picking up a pair of scissors on her way and cutting several strands of hair from the few that remained. 'Her hair appears to be brown, but it might have been dyed.'

She dropped the strands into a sample bag, which Fred held out for her. 'Put this in my office would you, Fred. I'll get Marcia to have a look at it later.'

She returned to the body. 'There are no obvious signs of injury to the body. The bones appear to be intact with no breaks.'

Then something caught her eye. Almost invisible, and situated between several marks made by the rats, was a small thin groove or chip in the bottom left-hand side of the ribcage. The mark was different and inconsistent with any of the other injuries she had observed on the body. She leaned over the ribcage for a closer look. 'Fred, bring the light over here, will you?'

Fred positioned the powerful mortuary light, making sure its shadows didn't interfere with Sam's work.

'There appears to be a scrape or groove mark on one of the lower ribs which is inconsistent with damage caused by a rat or other animal.' Sam put out her hand. 'Pass me the magnifying glass, would you, Fred?' Fred already had it in his hand and gave it to her immediately. She studied the groove carefully and for some time, measuring it, looking at the angle and depth of the indentation and getting Sharman to take several photographs. Then she examined the rest of the ribcage, convinced she must have missed several other similar chips. After a few minutes of careful examination she could, much to her surprise, find nothing. Although she examined several other indentations a little more closely they were definitely rat bites and not stab wounds. She returned her attention to the original mark and examined it again. Finally she looked up. 'Fred, get Colin Flannery on the phone, would you. I want him and his team down here at once. Explain the situation to him. If he wants any paperwork tell him I'll sort it out when he gets here. Tell him it's a favour for me.'

Fred nodded and disappeared towards Sam's office. Sharman, who had been watching her and wondering what the hell was going on finally exploded.

'Would someone mind telling me what the bloody hell is happening?'

Sam took his gloved hand and ran his nail through the inside of the cut. 'That, Stanley, is a knife wound.'

Sharman knew better than to argue with Sam but he was still interested. 'How do you know?'

'The shape of the mark, like a small V cut into the ribcage. The angle is low and upward. Our killer pushed the knife in from down here . . .' She put her hand by the side of her abdomen. 'And then pushed the knife upwards –' she gestured the movement with her hand again, pushing it upwards sharply from her side – 'inside her rib cage and into her lungs and heart, catching the edge of the rib on the way in, and leaving this telltale nick we see here.'

Sharman smiled broadly. Sam had proved his theory.

'Is there only one? Wouldn't it take more than that?'

Sam nodded. 'Yes. I would have expected to find more, I was lucky to spot that . . .'

Sharman knew that was false modesty. Sam was never 'lucky,' she was just good.

Sam continued, 'But there appears to be just the one. I've known a single stab in the right place to kill before. It's not that unusual.' She looked directly at Sharman. 'Well, Stan, looks like your instincts were well founded, this girl's been murdered. All we've got to do now is convince Adams.'

If he'd had the courage, Sharman would have lifted her off her feet. Instead he placed his hand awkwardly on her shoulder.

'Thanks for the trust, Dr Ryan.'

Sam smiled at him. 'No, thank you, Stan. You do have a habit of making life much more interesting. Are you going to tell Adams or shall I?'

Sharman smiled. 'If it's all the same to you, why don't we both go and tell him. Bit of mutual support. I'll take you for that drink after. Deal?'

'Deal. Let me just get out of these greens and I'll be right with you. Can't wait to see the look on his face.'

Graham Ward stood opposite Adams in the charge room at Cambridge's Central Police Station. Next to Ward stood a nervous-looking Mr Appleyard, his hands wringing the handle of his briefcase. Adams stared into Ward's eyes as he began to read the charge.

'Graham Robert Ward, you are charged that on . . .'

Ward had stopped listening. He began to hum 'Jerusalem'. He hummed it louder and louder as Adams continued to read the charge, trying to drown out his words. At the end Adams cautioned Ward and waited for a reply, there was none, just 'Jerusalem'.

Adams looked across at Appleyard.

'Does your client understand, Mr Appleyard?'

Appleyard took hold of Ward's arm. 'Graham, do you understand what you have been charged with? This is very serious.'

'Jerusalem' got louder and louder. Appleyard shook his head. 'I don't think he's well, Superintendent. Perhaps a doctor?'

Adams nodded and searched for Meadows. 'Dick, send for the police surgeon, then put him back in his cell. I want a man with him around the clock. Not outside the cell either, inside. Is that clear?'

Dick Meadows and the Station Sergeant nodded in unison. Satisfied with their response, Adams left the room. He knew it would be the DNA evidence that would finally clinch it. How Ward could continue to deny it when presented with that kind of evidence was beyond him. The circumstantial evidence was strong too. He was going down for life and Adams estimated with satisfaction that that meant at least twenty-five years.

When he reached his office he picked up the phone and dialled the Chief Constable. He felt a sense of elation. He always did after a good result, but this one was special. This was a bigger feather in his cap than usual.

'Chief Constable, please. Detective Superintendent Adams.' He waited, the Chief came on. 'Good afternoon, sir. Just thought I'd let you know that I charged Ward five minutes ago. No, there's no chance of a mistake. We've got a positive match on the DNA so we've got enough with that alone. We've also got a lot of circumstantial. We found a similar rope to the type used to tie Mrs Clarke up in his shed, together with a bag full of pornographic bondage books, with his prints all over them. . . . Thank you, sir. I thought I'd ring you first so you could pass the good news on to John Clarke, and of course the Home Secretary. I'm sure they'll both be pleased . . . Thank you, sir. Glad we got a quick result. No, sir, I haven't seen the papers today, been too busy if you know what I mean. Yes, sir, at once. Can you tell me what it's all about? OK, sir, I'll call you back in a few moments.'

Adams called through to his secretary. 'Emma, have you got a copy of today's paper?'

Emma entered the office nervously. 'I was going to show it to you earlier, but you've been so busy with one thing and another.' Dropping the paper on his desk she retreated quickly from the room.

Adams knew he was in trouble at once. There on the front page was a photograph of Sam with nothing more than a towel wrapped around her. Above the headline read, 'LOVERS' TIFF ON MAJOR MURDER INQUIRY.' Adams could feel his pulse begin to race. It took a lot to rattle him but this had. Sam had moved from being his closest friend and confidante to being a deliberate threat to his life, and more importantly his career. Something would have to be done and done quickly.

Sam and Sharman knew Adams would be in his office this time. They'd checked. They hadn't made an appointment, they felt they didn't have to. They were well aware, however, that had Sharman gone on his own he probably would never have got into the station, never mind the door. Having a VIP like Sam with him was a definite bonus, and opened most of the doors that would otherwise have been closed. Although Adams' secretary was surprised to see them when they arrived, she wasn't going to turn down a request from Sam to see her boss. She smiled sweetly at Sam, ignoring Sharman, whom she'd always disliked. 'I'll see if the Superintendent will see you.'

She knocked quietly on Adams' door and opened it. 'Dr Ryan and DS Sharman are here to see you, sir. Shall I send them in?'

Adams shouted past her, 'Come in, Sam, and you, Sharman.'

The two companions made their way past Emma and into Adams' office. He stood. 'To what do I owe this honour? Please sit down. Emma, can you get some coffee, please?'

Sharman and Sam sat down opposite him and waited as Emma left the room. Sam smiled across at Adams. 'We've come to report a murder.'

The news didn't excite or irritate Adams as Sam thought it might. He just leant back in his seat and smiled.

'Not the druggie?'

Sam nodded. 'Yes, how did you know?'

'Dick Meadows told me.' He looked across at Sharman. 'You're like a dog with a bloody bone, aren't you, Stan?'

'Well, bones actually, sir,' Sharman replied straight-faced.

Adams looked away, not appreciating the joke. 'Dick said you hadn't got enough evidence to start an inquiry. I take it you've come in here mob-handed with some more?'

Sam nodded. 'Yes. I conducted a forensic PM on the remains—'

'You did a what? With whose authority?'

Sam remained relaxed. 'Mine. Detective Sergeant Sharman came to me with some concerns, which I agreed with. As a result I conducted a PM on the remains and am satisfied that the young woman I examined was murdered.'

Adams leaned forward across the desk. 'Who paid for the examination?'

Sam smiled witheringly at his reply. 'I did it out of the goodness of my heart.'

Adams ignored the sarcastic tone of the response and continued, 'Prepared a report?'

Sam handed him the file.

'So how was she killed?'

'Stabbed with a sharp-bladed instrument.'

Adams flipped through the file, uninterested. 'You can tell this for sure from a few bones, can you?'

It's funny, Sam thought, he wasn't like this a few years ago. In those days the slightest inconsistency and he wanted to open a major incident room. How time and rank change people. She wondered what Harriet Farmer would have made of him now.

'Yes. It's what I do for a job, remember?'

'Well, what I remember from a recent conversation is that you simply report your findings and leave others to draw their conclusions from it!' snapped Adams. 'All right,' he sighed, 'leave the report with me and I'll let you know what I think.'

Sam was suddenly up in her chair. 'Leave the report with you? Aren't you going to do something now?'

'After I've had time to study it, I'll come to my own conclusions, I'm sure. I'll let you know in due course.'

'But this is murder. I think it needs a bit more of a response than "in due course". I've got Flannery and his team down there already.'

Adams slammed the report down on the desk. 'Then you'd better stand them down because I'm not going to pay for them. Next time get permission before you race in issuing orders that you have no right to give. Am I making myself clear?'

Sam glared at him. 'Crystal.'

Adams next turned his attention to Sharman.

'Who the hell gave you authorization to get involved in a PM without permission, and try and commence a murder inquiry without going through the proper channels? You are completely out of control, Sharman, this has got to stop.'

Sharman attempted to defended himself. 'Dick Meadows authorized it.'

'Inspector Meadows, I take it you mean?'

Sharman ignored Adams' pettiness and continued, 'He gave me two weeks to come up with additional information to prove my theory about the murder. That's what I have done.'

Adams stood and leaned across the table. 'You've

been around long enough, you know the procedures, Sharman . . .'

Sharman was having none of it. 'Detective Sergeant Sharman, don't you mean?'

Adams ignored him and continued, 'You've crossed far too many lines.'

Sharman shrugged, incensing Adams further.

'OK, until I can discover exactly what you've been up to you're suspended, subject to arranging a full disciplinary hearing. Do you understand?' Adams reached out his hand. 'Warrant card.'

Sharman, pushed beyond the limit, suddenly jumped up and pulled his fist back.

Sam grabbed his arm quickly. 'Stan, don't, it's just what he wants.' Sam's intervention calmed him long enough for him to reconsider.

'He's not worth it, Stan. Why give him the satisfaction?'

Adams smiled at Sharman. 'She's right, Stan, it's just what I want you to do. Then I could really have you.'

Sharman relaxed and put his arm down. Pulling his warrant card from his inside pocket he threw it on Adams' desk. Sam, still holding on to Sharman's arm, guided him out of the office. As they reached the door Sam turned to her former partner. 'You haven't heard the last of this.'

Adams looked at her passively. 'Nor have you. By the way, seen today's paper? Might be worth you having a look.' He showed her the front page. 'You're still looking good, Sam.'

Sam shook her head before throwing the paper across the room. She didn't like to think she was a vindictive woman, but if she ever had the opportunity to do the bastard a bad turn she would.

Sam took Sharman to the Eagle, her favourite pub in town. It was the place where the discovery of DNA was first announced and for that reason alone it seemed appropriate. Sam picked up the drinks despite Sharman's protests and took them across to the table. 'How are you feeling?'

Sharman took a sip from the large glass of Scotch that Sam had presented him with. 'Fine. It'll take better men than Adams to put me down.' He hesitated for a moment. 'Thanks for what you did, in Adams' office I mean.'

Sam shrugged. 'I didn't want to, believe me. Under any other circumstances I'd have willingly helped you.'

Sharman raised his glass to her. 'I'll hit him, you kick him.'

Sam raised her glass back. 'Deal.'

They drank together.

'Never been suspended before. Come close to it a few times, but it's never quite happened. Always been able to talk my way out of it.'

Sam suddenly felt quite sorry for him. 'What are you going to do now?'

He smiled at her and took another drink. 'Continue with the inquiry.'

'After what Adams just said? Isn't that asking for trouble?'

'What's he going to do, suspend me?'

'He could have you arrested.'

'For what, being nosey? I don't think so.'

'It could make things worse in the disciplinary.'

Sharman took another drink, longer this time. 'Unless I can prove conclusively that the girl I found was murdered I'm fucked anyway. So what have I got to lose? Mind if I smoke?'

Sam shook her head. She did mind, but wasn't going to object just this minute. Sharman pulled out a half-empty packet of twenty and lit one, drawing deeply on it.

'I might have a poke around the Clarke inquiry as well.'

Sam looked at him, interested. 'Why?'

'I think they've got the wrong man.'

'Really?'

'A feeling – instinct again, perhaps. Picked up a few bits from Chalky that didn't sit right in my head.'

Sam was becoming more intrigued. 'Did you tell him about the knots?'

Sharman shook his head. 'Did I hell. Let them work it out for themselves. I did ask Meadows to ask Ward if he was a sailor. If he can't take the hint then I'm not going to spell it out for him. Besides, Flannery knows, so I can't pull the "I know something you don't" trick for much longer.'

'Anything else?'

Sharman smiled at her. 'Maybe. I'll tell you later, when I've had a chance to pick up one or two more bits of information.'

Sam suspected that he was heading for trouble, but also knew that she couldn't stop him. 'Why do you always look for trouble, Stan?'

Sharman gave a look of false alarm. 'I don't. It always comes looking for me.'

'Stan, if you were in the middle of a bloody desert you'd find a problem.'

Sharman laughed. 'Well, perhaps so. I don't suffer fools easily.'

'You don't suffer anyone easily.'

Sharman laughed again. He was enjoying Sam's company. 'I suffer you, don't I?'

Sam took a sip at her tonic. 'Do you know, that's the closest you've ever come to paying me a compliment?'

'Make the most of it, it will probably be the last.' He turned to Sam, hoping to take advantage of her mood and the moment. 'I don't suppose you'd consider giving me a bit of a hand? Think I'm going to need all the help I can get.'

Sam shook her head. 'Sorry, Stan, would if I could, but I'm up to my eyes right now. Besides I don't particularly want to confront Adams again.'

Sharman turned away. 'Scared of him?'

It was an old ploy but could still be effective. Sam spotted it at once, however, and wasn't falling for it. 'Nice try, Stan, but no chance.'

Sharman emptied his glass and looked at Sam. 'Another?'

Sam nodded and Sharman began to make his way to the bar. 'I'll get them, my round, you sit tight.'

It wasn't often that Trevor Stuart sent for Sam quite so late in the day. They used to go out quite often for a drink or a meal, trying to relax after a full day in the mortuary. As the workload increased, however, this didn't happen as often as they would have liked. By the time Sam reached his office his secretary had gone for the evening and there was only Trevor left. Sam knocked on his door and entered.

'Evening, Trevor, you wanted to see me?'

Trevor, who was sitting behind his desk at the far side of the room, stood.

'Sam, I always want to see you, but you always seem so busy.'

'Name of the game. More rank, more responsibility.'

'Tell me about it. Have a seat.'

Sam sat down on the deep settee that Trevor Stuart had brought into his office. His rooms had begun to look more like a luxury suite at a top hotel than those of the Head of Department. As Trevor sat down, Sam saw a newspaper in his hand and suddenly realized what it was all about.

'I see you've been reading the paper, then. Didn't know you were interested in tabloid rubbish, Trevor?'

He looked down at the paper. 'I'm not, wouldn't touch it with a bargepole normally, you know that.'

'However?'

'However. When one of my senior people seems to be involved, then I become involved.'

'And in what way do you want to be involved? Concerned that the picture's on the front of the paper and not on page three?'

Trevor smiled and shook his head. 'No, no, not at all. I'm considering writing to the Press Complaints Authority about that. Absolutely disgusting.'

'I'm sure you'll have them all quaking in their boots, Trevor.'

He stared at Sam for a moment, unhappy at her flippant approach to what he considered to be a serious matter. 'It's more the contents.'

'As outrageous as the picture, surely, Trevor? I was hoping you were going to complain about that too.'

He stood and began to pace around the office. It was always a sign that he was nervous and uncertain of his ground. 'Well, I was going to until I had Tom Adams in here basically telling me it was true.'

Sam shot up. 'What! I hope you told him to bugger off.'

Trevor stopped pacing for a moment. 'I can't tell a superintendent of police to bugger off, can I?'

'So what did he say?'

'That because of your previous relationship your attitude towards him and therefore the inquiry was, shall we say, less than professional.'

'And of course you defended me?'

He started pacing again. 'It did end rather badly, Sam. Are you sure you're not letting your personal disdain for Adams cloud your judgement?'

Sam could feel herself becoming angry. 'I do not have any personal disdain for Adams. In fact I have no feelings for him whatsoever.'

He stopped pacing for a moment and looked at her. 'So you have let them interfere?'

'What!'

'Sam, people who say that sort of thing have nothing *but* disdain for those they're saying it about. You know that.'

'Was there anything wrong with the work I did on the case?'

'No, it's not about that.'

'Then what the hell is it about?'

'Adams feels you try to belittle him.'

'I don't have to try, he does that all by himself.'

'He feels it creates an atmosphere amongst the team that

doesn't help when everyone should be pulling together towards a common purpose.'

'And what's that, then? His promotion to deputy chief constable?'

Trevor looked suddenly surprised. 'I didn't know he was after that job.'

Sam glared at him. 'Well, he is, and that's what this is all about.'

'Do you think he'll get it?'

'Almost certainly. Especially after the Clarke case.'

'Well, we'd better watch ourselves, then. That will make him extremely important in the scheme of things.'

'Well, that's it then, Trevor. You'd better start believing everything he says.'

Trevor changed the direction of the conversation. 'He tells me you carried out an unauthorized PM. Is that true?'

'No. I carried out an *authorized* PM, but just took a little bit more care. Did a good job, too. The body in question had quite clearly met an unnatural end.'

Trevor began to pace again. 'I understand it was one of Sharman's cases?'

'So.'

'Sam, he's a bad lot. Did you know his girlfriend was a prostitute?'

Sam didn't know but objected to Stuart's line of reasoning. 'What the hell has that got to do with anything?'

'Adams tells me he threw him off the Clarke case for incompetence and this is Sharman's way of getting back at him. I understand he's been suspended?'

'For trying to do his job the best way he knew how. Even if Sharman was being vindictive, it doesn't stop the fact that I carried out a PM and am satisfied that the girl in question at the very least suffered a physical attack before her death.'

Trevor Stuart sat next to her again. 'Can you assure me categorically that you are not letting your personal feelings cloud your judgement over this?'

Sam leaned forward, in his face. 'Positive!'

He leaned back. 'He's asked me to conduct a second PM on the remains and see what my conclusions are.'

She looked at him quizzically. 'And of course you said no?'

'No. I said yes.'

Sam was fuming now. 'What! Are you questioning my judgement?'

Trevor, alarmed at her reaction, retreated behind his desk. 'No, I'm just going to give a second and unbiased opinion.'

'Really. Even though he's about to be made Deputy Chief Constable and therefore could be so important to the department?'

Trevor felt himself begin to get hot. 'Listen, Sam, I feel I have no choice in this. Please don't take it personally.'

Sam waited.

'I think it might be wise, for a little while at least, to keep out of Adams' way.'

'What are you doing, Trevor, suspending me?'

He looked aghast. 'Good God, no. Just giving you other assignments until things calm down a little.'

Sam stood up and marched towards the door. 'I'm going to take some leave.'

Trevor looked at her. 'Right now? We're up to our eyes.'

'I haven't had a day's leave for over a year. I've worked God knows what hours, without a penny in extra pay or time off. I've worked my weekends. Do you know I don't have a social life any more, I just work? The only man I have in my life is Fred. So I'm off, see you in three weeks.'

Before he had time to reply Sam pulled the door open and stomped down the corridor.

He called after her, 'And keep away from Sharman, he's a bad lot. He'll drag you down with him.'

Sam couldn't remember ever being angrier than she was right now. As far as she was concerned there was only one man to blame for her current mood and that was Adams.

If she'd considered refusing to help Sharman before, she certainly wasn't going to now. Any help he wanted he was going to get.

CHAPTER FOUR

Sharman didn't know why Sid Booth had chosen such a depressing location for the meeting, but it was Sid's call and he was doing him a favour, so who was he to complain? Sharman parked his car amongst the mourners and made his way into the cemetery. As he pushed through the crowds of people, a few of the faces seemed familiar and Sharman found several of them looking at him for longer than was strictly comfortable, indicating that they found him either familiar or unacceptable, or both.

Sid was standing at the far side of the cemetery watching proceedings from behind a large Victorian gravestone. Sharman walked across to him.

'Morning, Sid.'

Booth glanced across at him. 'Stan, long time no see. How ya doing?'

Sharman inclined his head towards the large burial service taking place a few hundred yards in front of him. 'Relative?'

Sid laughed. 'Sort of. Minnie Sitwell, she was everybody's bloody mother. Head of one of the biggest criminal families in the country. Gave birth to most of them as well. Thought I'd pay my last respects. Make sure the old lag was really gone.'

'What was your involvement with her?'

'Nicked her for murder when I was with the Met. She

did a London gangster called Black Harry about twenty
years ago. Smashed his head in with a metal bar when he
pushed in front of her at the local chip shop.'

'That'll teach him.'

'Gave him a bit of a headache. Charged her with
murder, she put her hands up to manslaughter, sentenced
to life. Out in five. East End had one of the biggest parties
it had seen for years. Even the twins sent cards.'

'How did she end up around here?'

'She retired a few years ago with cancer, wanted to live
her time out quietly. Bit like me, really.'

'I wouldn't have said working in Criminal Intelligence
was retiring?'

'Not like being on the squad, though. Now instead of
nicking criminals I tell others how to do it. It's not the
same, Stan. I miss the buzz.'

Sharman nodded sympathetically. He had an affinity
with Booth. He was a coppers' copper and one of the best
thief-takers he'd known.

'Do you know the old bitch has got a nephew at
John's?'

'Moving up in the world.'

'He's reading Economics. Expected to get a double first.'

'He'll be taking over the family business, then?'

Sid turned to him and grinned bitterly. 'Just like the
bloody Mafia. Drugs and prostitution, to property and
share holdings. Funny old world, isn't it, Stan? Criminals
become millionaires while we struggle on hoping for our
pittance of a pension.'

Sharman shook his head. 'Bloody hilarious, Sid.'

The two detectives moved back from the gravestone
and away from the funeral. They began to walk back
through the graveyard.

'I was the only copper that ever managed to get her sent
down. Always upset her, that, don't think prison went
down well. She threatened to come back and get me, you
know. She said if she had to crawl out of her coffin and dig
her way out she'd bloody well have me.'

Sharman looked at him seriously. 'That worry you, does it, Sid?'

Booth shook his head. 'Not at all. I bribed the funeral directors to bury her face down. I hope she likes Sydney.'

They burst out laughing and made for Sharman's car. As they settled down inside, Sid handed Sharman a brown paper envelope. 'There's a few things inside there that might be of interest.'

Sharman took the envelope and pushed it inside his glove compartment.

'So, why were you suspended?'

Sharman glanced at his friend. 'Thought you might have heard about that by now.'

Booth stared blankly into the graveyard watching the crowds of people making their way back to their cars. 'If the devil should cast his net.' Sharman followed his stare as Booth began to point out the more infamous characters. 'Half of gangland London are here. See that bloke over there?' He pointed to a middle-aged man in a smart black suit. 'One of the twins' nephews. Tipped to take over the empire, if he hasn't already. All very legit now, of course. Worth a fortune. I've heard several rumours, Stanley, mostly concerning your relationship with Kate.'

Sharman shook his head. 'I see the serious rumour squad's been hard at it again.'

Booth laughed. 'So what is the truth, then?'

'Adams.'

Booth nodded knowingly. 'Guessed as much.'

'Last thing he wants anyone to know is that he suspended me for doing my job.'

'I wouldn't worry about it too much. Word is he'll keep you on suspension until he's got the deputy's job, then all will be forgiven and forgotten.'

'By him, maybe, I'll not forget so easily. Anything in the packet I ought to know about?'

'Not much, I'm afraid. Most of the crime around the time you're looking at was straightforward enough.'

Sharman was disappointed. He wasn't sure what he

was looking for but was confident he'd know it when he saw it. He wanted anything that might help put a face and a name to the girl now lying on a slab in Sam's mortuary.

'By the way, just over a hundred young girls have disappeared from the general area over the last six months.'

Sharman was surprised at the number. He knew a few disappeared on a regular basis, but a hundred, that was a sizeable number. 'A hundred? Bloody hell. What the fuck's happened to them?'

'Run off to London, run off with their boyfriends, dead and buried, who knows? If you ask me, Stan, you're taking on too much without a team around you.'

Sharman shrugged. 'I know. But I'll have to make do. I can only do my best.'

'Fair enough. All their names and addresses are in the envelope. Try the Suzy Lamplugh Trust, I've found them pretty good in the past. Might take some of the pressure off you?'

'Thanks, Sid.'

Booth sucked his teeth for a moment. 'There is one thing in there that might be of interest, although it's a bit of a long shot.'

Sharman looked across at him.

'There was a car found burnt out in a wood about two miles from where the body was discovered.'

Sharman shrugged. 'OK, but that must be a fairly regular occurrence?'

'Sure, but this one was slightly different. There were unusual circumstances around it. The car was never reported stolen and no insurance claim was ever made on it.'

'Owner?'

'Previous owner told DVLC he'd sold it about two weeks before.'

'Who to?'

'Local plods checked that out. Whoever bought it gave a false name and address. So what would that be all about, then?'

'Was it used in a crime – you know, a robbery or something, the get-away car?'

'Nothing reported.'

'Anywhere?'

'Not anywhere we could tie it in with.'

'OK, that is odd. I'll check it out.'

Sid Booth began to climb out of Sharman's car. 'Got to go, Stanley, I could lose my job for being seen with the likes of you. Going to have a bite with the family. Tell them how wonderful I thought the old bitch was.'

'That will stick in your throat.'

'Maybe, but I'll wash it down with all that free drink.'

Sharman laughed. 'See you, Sid, have one for me, and thanks again.'

Booth wandered off towards the mourners, disappearing into the crowd of black-suited criminals.

Sam looked around the desolate spot where the body of the unknown girl had been discovered. It was a dirty, unpleasant situation and not the most desirable place in the world to end your days. The hot weather had made everything so dull. The grass along the railway embankment looked brown and parched, and the soil in the fields, instead of being a moist, rich, dark brown, had been baked hard and crumbled to dust in your hands. She glanced across at Marcia, who was surveying the tip with a certain amount of distaste. Although she enjoyed being a forensic scientist, there were some things she could never quite get used to.

'I hate doing rubbish tips, you can never be quite sure what's lurking inside them.'

Sam smiled at her old friend. As usual she had only needed to ask Marcia once. When she had explained the circumstances surrounding the case, and more importantly what Adams was up to, Marcia was at her side in a trice. The two of them were like sisters, insult one and the other took immediate offence.

Marcia looked at Sam. 'Well, where do you want me to

start? Remembering I've only taken one day's leave and they complained about that.'

Sam squeezed her arm affectionately. 'Don't think it's not appreciated, Marcia.' The two women smiled at each other. 'Have a root around the rubbish, see if you can spot anything that might be of interest. At this stage I'm not sure what we're looking for . . .'

'But I'll know it if I see it?'

Sam nodded.

'As clear and precious as ever, Sam.'

Marcia pulled on her white protective suit and shoes, and made her way into the centre of the tip.

Sam walked across to Sharman, who was standing at the bottom of the embankment looking across the fields towards Cambridge. 'What are you thinking about?'

Sharman looked at Sam. 'I was just wondering why she was here. Why here?'

Sam looked around. 'Yes, me too. This is more than just a quiet place to do drugs, there're any number of those which could be reached much more easily. There has to be more to it. She could have been meeting someone.'

Sharman nodded. 'Her killer. But who?'

'Her dealer?'

'Bastards won't travel unless there's a lot of money involved.'

'Perhaps there was. Perhaps she crossed him over a deal and this was the outcome. It happens all the time.'

'Maybe, but I'm not convinced yet.'

'If we knew the reason, Stan, we'd have the case cracked. Think how bored we'd be then.'

'That's true.' He looked across at Marcia, who was carefully gathering samples and dropping them into exhibit bags. 'How's your friend getting on?'

'OK. She'll do her best, but I'd be happier with Colin Flannery and his team down here to do a proper job. Mind you, Marcia's a useful ferret when she gets going. I did think about asking Colin, and I think he'd do it for me—'

Sharman cut in. 'Fancy you, does he?'

Sam's reply was sharper than she had intended. 'I was thinking more of professional courtesy than anything else.'

Sharman looked at her. He was beginning to realize that there wasn't much she was going to let him get away with.

'Besides,' Sam continued, 'the fewer people who know what we're up to the better. Especially Adams.'

Sharman nodded. 'I expect you're right.' He looked at Sam. 'I appreciate what you're doing. I know you're out on a limb for me.'

'Yes, I am.'

'What changed your mind?'

Sam thought about it for a moment. 'Justice, and the look on your face.'

She was lying, but the truth was hard to admit, even to herself, it was unbecoming and so petty. The trouble was she suspected that Sharman knew she was lying. She was ashamed of herself but it was too late now. She was committed and her curiosity was roused. She would see this through to the end no matter what.

'Finished!'

Sharman and Sam looked up to see Marcia emerging from the tip. They walked across to her. Sharman looked at the handful of exhibit bags in her hand.

'Find anything?

Marcia shrugged. 'Rats, lots of rats. Horrible ugly bloody things. The things I do for you, Sam.'

Sam winced. 'Sorry, Marcia.'

Sharman continued. 'Besides rats, anything else?'

'Don't know yet.' She looked into her exhibit bags. 'There might well be something lurking about in here. But at this stage everything's a bit subjective. Who knows?'

Sharman was confused. 'Meaning?'

'Unless you can find me something to compare my samples with, then they might be a waste of time. If you see what I mean?'

Sharman nodded. 'We'll have to see what else we can find, then, won't we?'

Marcia smiled and looked back towards the old drums around the edge of the tip. 'I'd be interested to know what's leaking out of those drums. There might be something to investigate there.'

Sharman glanced at the brown ooze dripping slowly from several of the upturned cans. Something to look into another time, perhaps. Collecting his thoughts together he looked across at the two women. 'Ready to move on to the next location, ladies?'

'You sound like a cheap movie producer, Stan, not an out-of-work detective.' Sam could have bitten her tongue the moment the words were out but it was too late. 'Sorry. I didn't . . .'

Sharman gave her a cold look for a moment, then burst into laughter. 'Sorry for what? Speaking the truth? You'll never have to apologize to me for that, Dr Ryan. Christ, and I thought I was blunt.'

He walked away towards his car still laughing, leaving Sam feeling awkward and embarrassed.

It took no longer than ten minutes before Sharman was turning off the main Cambridge road and on to a wooded dirt track. Sam, who was sitting in the front passenger seat, glanced mischievously at Marcia, who was perched on the back seat leaning forwards with her head stuck between Sam and Sharman. 'Detective Sharman, why are you taking us into this isolated wood? I'll tell the vicar.'

Sharman's response was immediate. 'Madam, I am the vicar.' Despite the age of the joke all three companions fell about laughing.

Approximately a quarter of a mile along the track the path suddenly narrowed and Sharman was forced to stop. He turned to the two women. 'We have to walk from here.'

Marcia frowned, 'Can't we get any closer. The nicked car did?'

Sharman laughed, 'That's just it, it was nicked, the

driver didn't care how much he smashed it around. I do, so grab your boots.'

If nothing else, years of experience struggling through dark, muddy, isolated fields, had taught them to be well prepared. They certainly needed no prompting to bring suitable footwear.

After walking approximately two hundred yards along the track they came to a small clearing, at the centre of which was the burnt-out and blackened wreck of what appeared to be a saloon car. Sam and Marcia followed Sharman across the clearing to it. Sharman stopped by the side of the car. 'I think this might have been the car our killer used.'

'Not that you're one for long shots, eh, Stanley? I'll grant you it's close to the murder scene, so it's worth checking it out.'

'It's never been reported stolen, and it was bought by a man who gave a false name and address.'

'How do you know all that?'

'Engine number. Whoever dumped the car took the plates and- the fire did the rest. He forgot the engine number, though.'

Sam walked around the car checking the charred remains. 'There might be a thousand explanations as to why he dumped it. People dump things all the time. Maybe they didn't want to pay the road tax. Or had a string of outstanding fines to pay. Might even have been used in some other crime?'

Sharman shook his head. 'No, checked all those out, nothing, and who's going burn their own car to avoid paying a parking ticket? Besides, even old cars are worth something to a scrap yard. Why not sell it? No, this is it, all right, I'm convinced.'

'What have we got here, then? An amateur who thinks he knows a bit?'

Sharman nodded. 'Exactly.'

'Then we're in with a chance. Whoever our killer is, he's making mistakes.'

'You'd have thought the council would have moved it by now,' Marcia said indignantly.

Both Sharman and Sam looked at Marcia, who suddenly felt very awkward. 'Well, you know, it's such a pretty spot and the council have had months to get it shifted.'

Her two companions burst out laughing again, infecting Marcia, who felt obliged to join in. When things calmed down Sam finally looked across at Sharman. 'OK, what do you want us to do?'

'Much the same as before. Need to search the area as best we can.'

Marcia looked around the glade. 'Any idea of a search pattern?'

'Marcia, if you take the area from the road to here. Pay some attention to the pull-in where I've parked my car. Whoever dumped this one must have had another to get them back to town, or wherever they went to after they dumped the car. Probably parked their vehicle in the same place I have.'

Marcia nodded. 'I'm on my way.' She handed a pile of exhibit bags to both Sharman and Sam before disappearing back down the path and into the wood.

Sharman shouted after her, 'Back here in an hour?'

Marcia raised her arm in acknowledgement as she strode away.

Sam looked at Sharman. 'Where do you want me?'

Sharman smiled wickedly at her. Sam pointedly ignored him. 'If you take the far side of the wood and move around in a half-circle back to here, I'll take the other side.'

'What am I looking for?'

'Anything out of the ordinary?'

'Oh good, that narrows it down, then.'

They parted and the search began.

Sam thought she knew Cambridge well but she'd never been here before. It was a beautiful spot. Full of wild flowers, insects and other wildlife. As she looked around, marvelling yet again at the glories of nature, she forgot for a moment what she was there for, and had to concentrate her mind. There was nothing obvious, although she couldn't help wondering what Flannery and his team would have discovered by now. As much as she despised him, they might have to consider getting Adams on board if they were going to make serious progress. Looking through the trees she saw Sharman searching the ground around the car. Every now and then he would stop, crouch down, and pick up some object which he would drop into an exhibit bag before moving on. An instinctive person herself, she felt closer to Sharman's world and alienated from Adams.'

'Over here!'

Sharman and Sam made their way quickly towards Marcia. She was standing about twenty yards in front of Sharman's car, pointing to something lying at the bottom of a bush.

'I think that might be something?'

Sam and Sharman looked in the direction Marcia was staring. Just in front of her was a small white sock, which carried a dark stain over two-thirds of it.

'I know I could be wrong and will have to do some tests, but I think that's blood?'

Shaman looked at Sam, who nodded. 'I think so too. Just depends on whose.'

Sharman could feel himself becoming excited. 'Can we get a match with our girl?'

'Difficult.' Sam looked concerned.

'Why?'

'We can match the blood but that won't be seen as conclusive. Might be a common type. I would have to do a DNA match to be sure and that's expensive.'

Sharman felt a sense of despair creeping over him. 'Don't you know anyone who would help?'

'A few, but it's not the kind of thing you can do for free without anyone noticing. Especially as we're not even sure that the sock belongs to our victim.'

Sharman began to feel depressed.

'Look, let me ask around, I might be able to do something.'

Marcia also chipped in. 'I'll try and call in a few favours too. I'm sure we can do something.'

Sharman looked at them both. God knows why they were helping an old lag like himself, but they were, and he was grateful.

'OK, ladies, let's get it flashed and bagged, as the Americans would say, and I'll buy you both a drink.'

Sam looked at Marcia. 'Last of the big spenders.'

Sharman wasn't good at having a partner, he was a loner and liked to do things his way. However, these were extraordinary circumstances and he'd have to make allowances. Marcia had made her way back to the lab to start work on the sock and see if she could call in a few favours. As much as he appreciated her commitment, he wasn't optimistic. With the forensic science service already under strain, favours would be hard to find.

As Sharman finally pulled up outside a small semi-detached house not far from the city centre, Sam turned to him. 'What are we doing here?'

'This is the bloke that sold the car we saw earlier. Thought I might have a quick word.'

'Hasn't he already talked to the police?'

'Couple of plods who didn't know their arse from their elbow. They got the basics, I want a bit more.'

'Like?'

'Is he telling the truth, or is he our killer? If he is telling the truth, then let's see if he can remember enough to give us a description of the man who bought his car.'

They climbed out of the car and walked along a small concrete path between two sides of an unkempt garden before Sharman knocked loudly on the front door. Sam looked around. The house was shabby and in need of a lick of paint. A few hours in the garden wouldn't go amiss either. A large overweight man in his late forties wearing a stained grubby vest answered the door. Sam

couldn't remember seeing a beer belly quite as large
before. She wondered how his heart was coping and
how much longer it would be before she would see him
again.

'Who are you?'

Sharman stared hard into his eyes. 'Police. Jim
Clements, is it?'

The man wasn't convinced. 'Might be, where's your
warrant card?'

Sharman reached into the inside pocket of his jacket and
pulled out, much to Sam's surprise, his warrant card. 'DS
Sharman. Like a word about the car you sold.'

'Couple of your lads have already been around, told
them everything I know.'

'Perhaps they forgot to ask you a few things. Can I come
in?'

With that Sharman pushed past the man before he had
chance to reply and made his way inside. The man
followed him in with Sam bringing up the rear.

The inside of the house was no better than the outside,
dirty and scruffy, with what looked like yesterday's
breakfast on the table. The man also smelt, and that was
one thing Sam could never abide.

'I don't remember asking you in?'

Sharman turned sharply and seemed to lean over the
man. 'We're not going to have any problems, are we, Jim?
This is an important investigation involving the death of a
young woman. I'm sure you'll be keen to help?'

'Well, if that's the case I'll try and help as much as I can.'

Sam could see the fear in the man's eyes. His sudden
public-spiritedness had more to do with the look on
Sharman's face than any desire to help.

'Would you like to sit down?'

Sharman and Sam took one look at the state of the chairs
and decided to stand.

'No, it's all right, sir, we won't be long. You can sit
down, though, if you want.'

With that Sharman put his hand on the man's shoulder

and forced him into one of his own chain. Sharman liked to stand over his interviewees, it gave him the authority he needed to get the information he wanted.

'How long did you have the car before you knocked it out?'

'About a year. It still had a few weeks' tax on it, and a month's MOT.'

'Why d'you sell it?'

'Bit short on the rent.'

'What did you get for it?'

'Three hundred. It was worth more.'

'What did you ask for it?'

'Three.'

'But you would have taken less?'

'I'd have probably gone down to two.'

'Did he try and knock you down?'

'No, and he paid cash.'

'What was he like?'

'All right. Didn't say much. "Yes . . . No . . . here's three hundred notes." I like a man that's to the point.'

'What did he look like?'

'Average.'

'So, describe average?'

'Quite tall, thinnish.'

'Colour of hair, eyes?'

'Hair was black, don't know about the eyes, he had sunglasses on.'

'How did he speak?'

'He was quite posh, considering what he was.'

'What do you mean by that?'

'He was a mechanic.'

'How did you know that?'

'He was wearing mechanic's overalls – you know, blue and stained, oil and stuff.'

'Shoes?'

'Didn't notice.'

'Anything else?

Jim Clements shook his head. 'No, nothing.'

Sharman leaned down and put his face close to Clements' face. 'Are you sure? It would be a shame to miss anything out.'

The man was unnerved but as Sam watched he managed a feeble shake of his head in response to Sharman's question before gathering himself to say slyly, 'Well, the memory's a funny thing. Sometimes it needs a bit of encouragement.'

Sharman stood straight again and moved casually away from the man. 'OK, thanks for your time.'

The man stood up sharply. 'Is that it? Nothing else?'

Sharman nodded, refusing to take the hint, and began to make his way towards the door. Sam, however, had pulled out two twenty-pound notes from her purse and handed one of them to the man. He looked at the second. Sam smiled at him, keeping the second note pressed firmly in her hand.

'Are you sure there was nothing else? Nothing at all?'

Clements looked at her, his mind clearly racing. 'Maybe there was something else.'

Sharman stopped at the door and looked back while Sam continued the interview.

'What?'

'I think he was wearing a wig.'

'What made you think that?'

'It wasn't a very good fit. I could see his real hair underneath.'

'What colour was it?'

'Fairish, light brown.'

Sharman was across the room in a flash. 'Why didn't you tell me that in the first place?'

'I had trouble concentrating with your bad breath in my face!'

Sharman glared at him as Sam handed over the second twenty-pound note.

Once outside Sharman took Sam by the arm. 'Impressive. Where did you learn that trick?'

Sam smiled, pleased by the compliment. 'Years of

hanging around with you lot. You can't help picking up a thing or two.'

Sharman laughed. 'Better watch myself, you'll be after my job next.'

'I couldn't live on what they pay you, Stan.'

'Isn't that the bloody truth.'

The two climbed back into Sharman's car.

'Where to now, Batman?'

'Grantchester.'

Sam was concerned. 'Are you sure that's a good idea?'

Sharman nodded. 'Oh, yes.'

To save time and effort, Sharman and Sam decided to go their separate ways. Sharman would drive to Grantchester to speak to the Clarkes' handyman and cleaner while Sam made as many enquiries as she could with Marcia Evans, who should, they hoped, by this time, have returned to the forensic science laboratory in Huntingdon and come up with something useful. Sharman dropped Sam off at her cottage first. She wanted to change from her outdoor working clothes into something a bit smarter. Sharman admired her home. 'Nice place, must be making it pay.'

Sam hated that expression. It gave her the feeling that she was getting something for nothing. 'Thank you, I worked long and hard to make it pay.'

'I'm sure you did, but then so have I, and I couldn't even come close to a place like this.'

'Never had you down as a socialist, Stan?'

'I'm not, just wish I had a bit more to show for my sweat and toil than a two-bedroom flat on the down side of town.'

Sam suddenly felt the familiar stab of embarrassment she had often felt with members of her family who had made it clear that they thought she had ideas above her station, but she had always been driven to work hard and had been ambitious. Over the years she had learned to accept that her success, both financial and professional, had been hard won and deserved and that she had no reason to feel awkward about it.

'Want to come in, I'll make a brew?'

'Are you inviting me up for coffee, Dr Ryan?'

Sam could feel herself blush. 'No, Stan, I'm inviting you in for tea, now do you bloody well want some?'

Sharman smiled, pleased that he was at least able to make the good doctor blush. 'No, thanks, Dr Ryan. It's getting on and I've still got a few things to sort out.'

Sam found herself both relieved and surprised at Sharman's refusal.

As she turned to go inside he asked one last question. 'Do you know a doctor called Andy Herman?'

Sam nodded. 'Very well. He was a psychiatrist at the Park. Got his own practice now. Doing very well I understand.'

'He was Sophie Clarke's psychiatrist.'

Sam was surprised. 'She was seeing a psychiatrist? Why?'

Sharman looked at her out of the corner of his eye. 'I was hoping you might find out.'

Sam thought about it for a moment. 'That's asking rather a lot.'

Shaman shrugged. 'Will he talk to you? Because he sure as hell won't talk to me.'

Sam really wasn't sure, but realized she was up to her ears in it, so could hardly say no. 'I'll see what I can do. No promises, though.'

Sharman nodded. 'Understood. There is one thing you could do.'

Sam looked at him inquisitively. 'How many more things, Stanley? What is it this time?'

Sharman opened his glove compartment and reached inside, retrieving an exhibit bag, which he handed to Sam. Holding it up to the light, she looked at it for a moment. It was a watch, an expensive-looking one at that. She looked across at Sharman. 'Is it all right to take it out?' He nodded and Sam pulled back the strip at the top of the bag and dropped the watch into her hand. It was a modern gold Rolex. Sam moved around in her hand. There was nothing particularly unusual about it, except that the back of the watch had been filed down to obliterate the engraving that had once been there. Sam looked back at Sharman.

'As I'm not coming up to retirement, I take it there is a good reason for giving me this watch?'

'Found it under the girl's body.'

'How do you know it's hers?'

Sharman shrugged. 'I don't, but it's a good bet. It's a woman's watch, and let's be honest, no one throws watches like that away.'

'Might have been stolen?'

'It was stolen, all right, and I reckon our victim was probably the thief.'

Sam still didn't understand why Sharman was showing it to her. 'So what do you want me to do with it?'

'Give it to Marcia. See if she knows a way of finding out what was written on the back. Might give us the biggest clue we've had to date. At least we might be able to find out who she was. Then we might be in with a chance of picking up her killer.'

'And embarrassing friend Adams.'

Sharman smiled. 'My main motivation. So, can you do that?'

'I can give it to Marcia. Whether she can do anything with it is another question.'

'We all do what we can in this life, that's all we can ever ask.'

'Philosophy before tea. This is more than I can stand. I'm off before you start quoting poetry.'

Sharman laughed. 'Not a chance, unless you like limericks?'

'Not the type you'll know, Stan.'

As Sam turned she noticed Sharman admiring her and was surprisingly flattered. 'I'll see you later, Stan. Give me a call?'

'Will do. Let me know if Marcia turns anything up, won't you?'

Sam nodded. As she began to walk across to her front door Sharman sighed. She really was very attractive. But, like her cottage and lifestyle, she was way out of his league.

Sam showered and changed quickly. She called Marcia before driving off towards Huntingdon, so they'd get their stories straight in case anyone asked any difficult questions. Fortunately, with so much going on Sam could think of a million reasons for visiting the labs and for seeing Marcia, so they should be safe.

It took her just over an hour to reach the laboratories. This was longer than normal. There had been a small bump on the motorway, and the entire county seemed to have ground to a halt. Sam wasn't sure how many hours she had been locked into traffic jams but it was a lot. Over the years she had discovered that she had begun to resent drivers who crashed and held her up. Especially when the accidents were stupid, or could have been avoided. She actually found herself scowling at the two drivers who had been involved, as her car passed the scene of the collision.

On reaching Huntingdon, Sam parked her car in her usual spot and made her way inside. Fortunately, there wasn't a glimmer of interest in her from anyone. She was in and out of that place so often that she'd almost become part of the furniture. Familiarity breeds contempt, she thought. She made her way through the endless corridors until she finally reached Marcia's lab. Sam peered through the glass door. She was in luck, Marcia was on her own. Tapping quietly, she entered.

'Any luck?'

Marcia looked up from her microscope. 'Yes and no.'

'An absolute maybe, eh? What have you found?'

'Well, firstly the cigarettes that were found at the scene were Marlboro Lights and they were export only.'

Sam stared at her friend. One cigarette looked to her, like most people, much the same as any other.

'How do you know that?'

'They're longer, for a start, more of them. Then there's the blend. Did you know that there are well over a thousand different blends of tobacco?' Sam didn't but didn't want to get into a debate about it right now so she kept quiet and let Marcia continue. 'The paper's different too. Anyway I checked the blend in the cigarettes we found at the scene with the various manufacturers and it came back as being from Marlboro Lights, export cigarettes only.'

Although Sam was impressed, she couldn't really see the relevance and wanted to get on. 'What about the sock you found?'

'There is enough blood on the sock to do a DNA analysis, but I can't find anyone to do it.'

Sam peered through Marcia's microscope. 'That's not like you, Marcia.'

Marcia sighed. 'Listen, I've tried everything, believe me. Everyone's either too busy, or aren't willing to put their necks out.'

Sam pushed herself on to a stool, disappointed. 'Why?'

'The word's out, I'm afraid.'

Sam was alarmed. 'What word?'

'About the fallout you've had with Tom Adams and the fact he wanted you off the case. People are surprisingly nervous of Adams.'

Sam scowled. 'With good reason.'

Marcia replaced Sam at the microscope. 'Anyway, all is not lost, there was one interesting thing I managed to lift from the sock.'

Sam moved closer to her friend. 'What?'

'Do you remember those drums of brown yuck that were lying about the tip?'

Sam nodded.

'Well, I took samples, and that brown yuck was bitumen.'

Sam was getting anxious. 'And your point is?'

'I found traces of bitumen on the sock.'

'Brilliant. Well done.'

Sam was concerned that Marcia didn't look as happy as she had hoped.

'Well, like I said, yes and no. Yes, I did find traces, the trouble is it's quite a common chemical and could have got there from a number of sources.'

'Bit of a coincidence, though.'

'Don't get me wrong, it's her sock all right. You know that, I know that, but it's about convincing Adams, and from what I understand he's looking for a way out.'

Sam shook her head despairingly. 'Fair enough, Marcia. But at least we know, which means were on the right track. Was there anything else?'

Marcia nodded. 'The hair and maggots were interesting.'

Sam sat up, interested again. 'You found something?'

Marcia shook her head. 'No.'

Sam sighed. 'This isn't a time to be playing games, Marcia.'

Marcia smiled at her friend's gloomy face. 'The point is I should have done.'

'Ah, so what *didn't* you find?'

'There was no trace of heroin, or any other drug for that matter, in either the hair samples you sent me or the maggots.'

'So it seems she wasn't a drug addict of any kind?'

'Nothing, she was a clean-living girl. Her hair was black, by the way, she'd coloured it brown, and only recently too.'

Sam became thoughtful. 'Someone has gone to a lot of trouble to cover this murder up. I wonder who and I wonder why?' She sighed. 'All I have to do now is convince Adams to treat this as a murder investigation.'

'Who would have thought that was going to be the difficult bit?' Marcia gave her depressed friend a hug. 'We'll sort it out, don't worry.'

Sam gave a short sarcastic laugh. 'Will we? I wonder. This one might well have us beaten.'

As if hit by inspiration, Sam suddenly dived into her handbag and handed Marcia the watch Sharman had given her. 'What do you make of this?'

Marcia looked at it through the clear plastic of the exhibit bag. 'Are you trying to tell me I'm ready to retire?'

Sam smiled. 'Already said that. Sharman gave it to me, he found it under the body of the girl. He's certain it was hers.'

'Around her wrist, was it?'

'No, under her bum.'

'Odd place to wear it.'

'It's possible she might have been trying to hide it.'

Marcia nodded. 'Possibly. Do you think her death might have involved a robbery?'

'It's not possible to say for sure, there were certainly no particular belongings of hers recovered from the scene.'

'What do you want me to do with it?'

Sam turned the watch over in Marcia's hand. 'Look at the back, there, where someone's tried to file off an inscription or something. I was wondering whether there was any chance of bringing the inscription back up so we can read it. Might give us a bit of a clue?'

Marcia examined the back of the watch closely. 'Maybe, I'll have to see. I'll try a bit of ultraviolet first, see what that brings up.'

'And if it doesn't bring up anything?'

'There's a few other things I can try. Might mean selling my body, though.'

Sam feigned shock. 'Marcia, how could you?'

Marcia looked at her friend. 'Don't you want me to, then?'

'Of course, if that's what it takes, just don't do it too cheaply.'

The two women burst out laughing and for once since the inquiry began felt an inkling of hope.

*

The frantic activity that had surrounded the Clarkes' house only a short while before had died down, although the evidence was everywhere. Black and yellow marker tape fluttered loosely in the breeze, and hung from poles and branches. The police cones he had given the young constable such a hard time about were still there. Sharman smiled to himself. Perhaps he had been a bit hard on him. Still, it wouldn't do him any harm. Might even instil a little respect into the cocky bastard. Something he thought was sadly lacking in today's force.

He parked his car on the drive in front of the house, and pulled out a sheet of A4 paper from his briefcase, examining it carefully. Michael John Rogers. Born 11th November 1960, London. Six feet one inch tall, fourteen stone six pounds. Blue eyes, brown hair. National Criminal Records number 4356/78. Sharman was impressed by the man's list of convictions. According to the list he'd had a record since he was eighteen years old, although Sharman suspected he'd been at it a lot longer than that. Theft, burglary, car theft, fraud, grievous bodily harm, actual bodily harm, but the two convictions that interested Sharman the most were the ones for indecent assault and further two for unlawful sexual intercourse. What Sharman couldn't understand was what a man like this was doing working for a nob like Clarke.

He stepped out of his car and walked around to the back of the house, where Rogers had his flat. As he emerged into the back garden he looked back at the house. It really was an impressive place. It was the second time today he'd seen something he liked but couldn't afford. Then he remembered watching Sam walk back to her cottage. OK, three things he liked but couldn't afford. He reached the flat at the back of the house and knocked. The door was quickly opened by a man fitting Rogers' description, who glared at Sharman.

'What do you want?'

Sharman forced a smile. He really didn't like this man

and it was harder than he thought. 'John Heep, *Daily Mail*. I'd like to ask you a few questions, if you don't mind?'

Rogers leaned forward till his face was inches from Sharman's. 'Piss off, I ain't talking to any press.'

It was all Sharman could do to restrain himself, and not punch him senseless. Despite these overriding feelings, however, he remained calm. 'I am empowered to offer you fifty thousand pounds for your story.'

Rogers' expression and posture suddenly changed. 'How bloody much?'

Sharman knew he'd got the greedy little sod. 'Fifty thousand.'

Rogers thought for a moment. 'What do you want to know?'

'Can we talk inside?'

Rogers nodded and invited Sharman in. 'How do I know you're telling the truth about the money?'

Sharman reached inside his briefcase and produced a receipt. 'All you have to do is sign this and the cheque will be paid out to you this week.' Sharman had prepared the receipt earlier and done an impressive job. He never went into situations like these without being totally prepared. Rogers signed the slip eagerly. Sharman gave him the bottom copy and put the top copy in an envelope addressed to the Chief Accountant at the *Daily Mail*. He never missed a trick.

He sat down in a large easy chair and Rogers sat opposite him.

'Thought you were another copper when you came to the door. If I see another one of those I'll kill one of the bastards.'

'Really, whatever made you think that?'

'You look like a copper. Smell like one, too.'

'Investigative journalist. Same job, I suppose, only I can't arrest anyone.'

'You're all bloody snoopers.'

'True, but we pay better than the police.'

Rogers laughed. 'That's true enough.'

'Is that what the tattoo on your arm means, A. C. A. B.?'

'All coppers are bastards. That's true too.'

Sharman noticed a plaster in the crook of his arm above the tattoo. 'Cut yourself?'

Rogers looked at it. 'What? Oh, that. Had to give the coppers some blood. They're going to DNA test me too. That'll be a first. Anyway, what do you want to know?'

Before answering Sharman looked around the flat. It was a dirty scruffy place with no sense of permanence. It fitted Rogers' personality however. The one thing that did surprise him was the collection of *Star Trek* videos. There were about ten lined up next to the video recorder. He didn't seem like the 'Trekkie' type. He looked at Rogers. '*Star Trek*? I love the show.'

Just for a moment Rogers looked nervous, his arrogance and aggression disappearing into controlled fear. For Sharman it was enough.

'Yeah, it was a great show. Bit of a fan.'

Sharman nodded and smiled desperately, trying to control his own emotions. This kind of interviewing was like playing cards, where no one dare show their emotions for fear of losing.

'How did you and Clarke meet?'

'Prison. He was a prison visitor for a while.'

'What were you doing there?'

'Doing a three-year stretch for burglary and assault.'

'So what happened when you got out?'

'He wrote to me while I was in there. Offered me a job when I got out.'

'And you took him up on it?'

'Bloody right. Money was OK, got this flat and the work wasn't too much.'

Sharman smiled and nodded. 'I take it you have an alibi for the night in question.'

'With my record I had to have. I was in London. Hotel confirmed I was there. They turned my place over, too. Didn't find anything, though, so you don't have to worry. I'm in the clear.'

'What were you doing there?'

Rogers shrugged. 'Like visiting the West End.' He winked at Sharman. 'If you know what I mean.'

Sharman winked back, understanding the implication of the gesture. Suddenly he exploded into a fit of coughing. Rogers looked genuinely alarmed.

'Are you all right, mate?'

Sharman stuck out an arm. 'Water, can you get me a glass of water?'

Rogers quickly disappeared into the kitchen. As soon as he was out of sight, Sharman leaned across and quickly removed one of the tapes, pushing it inside his jacket. Rogers returned from the kitchen with a large glass of water, handing it to Sharman. Sharman sipped it for a few moments before putting it down, and recovering quickly.

'Thanks, sorry about that, don't know where that came from. Too many fags I expect.'

After giving himself a few moments, for show's sake, he continued, 'What do you do?'

'Handyman stuff mostly, fixing things, bit of gardening, bit of security.'

'Did you know Mrs Clarke?'

'Yeah, nice woman. I've pulled a few strokes in my time, but fucking hell what happened to her was bloody awful.'

'Great tragedy,' Sharman agreed. 'Bit of a looker, wasn't she?'

'Very. Fuck knows what she was doing with a bloke like Clarke.'

'He's looked after you.'

'Fair enough. But there was a twenty-year age gap. Don't know how he handled her.'

'Money and power are wonderful things. More important than looks for most women.'

'True enough.'

'Reckon she was playing away then?' Sharman winked at him knowingly.

Rogers hesitated just long enough for Sharman to realize that what he was about to say was a lie. 'Not a chance. Faithful type.'

Sharman pressed home his advantage. 'Are you sure? As you said, she was a lot younger, it wouldn't be the first time that kind of thing's happened?'

Rogers nodded but again there was the hint of hesitation. 'Positive.'

He was definitely lying. All Sharman needed to know now was why.

Sam slammed the receiver down hard as Jean entered the office.

'Not a problem, I hope, Dr Ryan?'

Sam sat back in her seat, shaking her head. 'The amount of favours I have done that man, and now I want one back he's told me to sod off.'

Jean put Sam's coffee down on the table. 'What man and what favour?'

'Dr Sydney Joyce.'

'I doubt Dr Joyce told you to sod off. He's much too much of a gentleman to say that.'

Sam relented. 'Well, no, but words to that effect. Just one small favour, after all the years we've known each other.'

As much as Jean respected Sam she knew she could be unreasonable when determined to get her own way. 'So what favour was this, then?'

'Remember the young girl we had brought in the other day?'

'What was left of the poor thing, yes.'

'We haven't identified her yet and I wanted Joyce to do a facial reconstruction on his computer. If we could have got an image of her then we might have stood a chance of getting her identified.'

'Doesn't seem much to ask, on the face of it.' Jean smiled broadly. 'If you'll pardon the pun.'

'He said that it's too expensive and he hasn't the time. The truth is, Tom Adams has had a word with him.'

'You don't know that.'

'Oh, yes I do.'

Jean wasn't convinced. 'How?'

'He told me,' Sam did her best impersonation of Joyce. '"I'm not sure Superintendent Adams would approve, considering what's happened recently." I'll probably get a call in a minute telling me my bridge night's been cancelled because Superintendent Adams wouldn't approve.'

'Well, let's not get too paranoid about Superintendent Adams' powers,' Jean scowled. 'Anyway you could always do it the old-fashioned way.'

'How do you mean?'

'With an artist.'

'It would still cost, and is there anyone locally who still does it that way?'

'There is one. The young man who's always in the paper. The one doing his Ph.D. at Trinity. You know he makes masks from the faces of dead people then get his models to walk around wearing them. He did that exhibition, "Bring back the dead". All very odd. Now what was his name? Peter Hudd, that was it, Peter Hudd. Didn't he win some big art prize for turning skulls into faces again? The Montague prize.'

'It's had some odd winners, that one. It might still cost us a fortune, his masks sell for thousands now apparently.'

'But he could do it, and if he's as arrogant as he seems in the press – I think he is – he might do it just for the kudos.'

Sam pondered the idea for a moment. It was certainly worth a shot. After all, what had she got to lose? She smiled warmly at her assistant, she was optimistic again. I'll try it.'

Jean shook her head. 'And what about the time you were going to take off?' she asked, amused at Sam's enthusiasm.

Sam laughed. 'Time off? I'm far too busy.'

Sharman fingered the *Star Trek* tape he'd stolen from Rogers' house. The idea that a moron like Rogers enjoyed a show like *Star Trek* still didn't sit right. Trekkies were like train-spotters, wet and eccentric. It didn't seem to fit Rogers' character. Pushing the tape into his machine he waited. After the BBC 2 logo, an early episode of *Star Trek* appeared. For a moment he could feel a sense of doubt creeping through his body. He picked up the remote control and pressed fast forward. The video raced through the episode before finally running the end credits. The picture then went black and fuzzy. Sharman was just reaching for the stop button when the picture returned. This time it wasn't a *Star Trek* episode, but something far more sinister.

The film had obviously been shot by an amateur on a hand-held video camera. It was also a second- or third-generation tape. Despite this, the content was clear enough; four men were enacting a vicious rape on a young woman. At one point the woman clearly passed out. One of the men disappeared from shot, returning with a bucket of water, which he threw over her to wake her up. Once they had finished with her one of the men picked up a cord from a table at the side of the bed and strangled the still-struggling woman to death, to the cheers of his friends.

Sharman watched the video twice. It was a sad and sick scenario and he had seen a lot of similar stuff when he was on Vice. He was never sure whether the snuff movies were real or just well acted with a few special effects. The men looked Eastern European, while the woman was young and attractive and Sharman had to admit looked genuinely frightened and in pain. Before he made a move against friend Rogers, however, he decided to show the tape to his old friend DI Panna in Vice. No matter how you looked at it, it wasn't a pleasant tape, but if it was the real thing then a homemade one of Mrs Clarke's unpleasant demise might well be mixed in with Rogers' collection. Although he was pleased they hadn't, he was also surprised that the local plods had missed them when they turned his place over. New policemen, he thought cynically. Everyone had to be nice and understanding. The job was going to the dogs.

Sam parked in New Court next to two very old and battered Mercedes cars. Walking past the roundabout with the giant horse chestnut tree at its centre, Sam made her way into Neville's court and to 'I' staircase. She loved the old wooden staircases, worn smooth and indented by thousands of feet over hundreds of years. She often wondered what great people had come before her and climbed exactly the same steps. One thing about Cambridge, and especially Trinity College, was its sense of history. Reaching I5 she knocked firmly on the door.

'You sound like the police, you'd better come in.'

Sam pushed the old oak door open and entered. Sitting in the centre of the room sketching one of the reconstructions he had just finished was Peter Hudd. He looked up.

'You must be Dr Ryan. Come in, I'm intrigued.'

Hudd was shorter than Sam had expected, around five feet six inches tall, slim, very attractive, with a crop of long fair hair, blue eyes and a pleasing smile. He was also typical of his class. Public-school educated, confident with his world and life mapped before him.

'Please sit.'

Somehow when people from Peter's background invited you to do something it often came out as an order, and Sam always found this irritating. She bristled but did as she was bid, after all, she was about to request a favour.

'So, Dr Ryan—'

Sam cut in, 'Sam.'

Hudd continued drawing, not looking up for a moment. 'Sam, then. So, *Sam*, what is it you want me to do?'

'Help me to identify the remains of a dead girl.'

'Don't the police normally do that sort of thing?'

Sam hesitated, not sure how much to tell him. 'Normally yes, but they don't think she was murdered—'

This time it was Hudd's turn to cut in. 'Murdered? My,

this is getting more interesting by the minute. You say the police aren't dealing with this. Might one ask why?'

Sam decided to come clean. 'They don't believe me and won't treat it as a murder.'

'Considered using computers? I understand they are very efficient.'

'Yes, but their time has to be accounted for on the budget, and I don't have a budget.'

For the first time since Sam had entered the room Hudd stopped drawing and looked up her. 'So, you are expecting me to offer my services for free?'

Sam nodded. 'Art meets crime, I thought it might be of some interest to you. If we manage to prove my theory it would certainly be very high profile publicity for you.'

He smiled at her. 'It might. Tell me more.' He returned to his drawing,

'The body of a young woman was discovered a few days ago under an old railway bridge. I believe she was murdered – stabbed to death. Because of the state of the body we don't have too many clues to her identity. If you could do a facial reconstruction, then it would help us enormously.'

'Why do you believe she was stabbed?'

'There is a mark at the bottom of her ribcage which I know was made by a knife.'

'Anything else?'

'We believe our killer was very careful. The body had nothing on it to identify her and there was a burnt-out car a short distance away which we believe the killer used to destroy the evidence.'

'If all the evidence was destroyed how can you be sure someone else was involved?'

Sam was beginning to get irritated by his questions and was concerned about giving all this information away. However, she overcame her reluctance as she realized that she had little choice.

'We found a sock with a chemical on it that matched chemicals present at the scene of the murder.'

'Lucky. Is that all?'

'Just about.'

Hudd continued drawing for a few more moments before turning to Sam.

'I'll play.'

Sam could feel a wave of relief flow through her. 'Thank you. I'm sure you won't feel it to be a waste of time. I'll need to take you down to the mortuary at some point.'

'Tomorrow OK?'

Sam nodded. 'What time?'

'Shall we say about two?'

Sam nodded and stood. 'That's fine.'

As she got up Hudd rolled up his drawing and gave it to her. 'Thought you might like to have that. Show you I'm a real artist and not simply a technician, as I've been called in certain unscrupulous newspapers.'

Before Sam had a chance to thank him there were several quiet raps on the door. 'Come in, Fiona.'

A beautiful young woman of about twenty entered the room. Hudd put his arm around her.

'Sam, this is Fiona, my sometimes girlfriend.'

Sam shook hands with her. 'Sometimes?'

'Sometimes. Because sometimes I drive her so mad that she walks out on me and sometimes she comes back. Anyway. Dr Ryan. I must get on, see you tomorrow.'

'Yes, see you tomorrow.'

As Sam wandered back down the stairs towards Neville's Court she opened up the drawing she had been given. Instead of the drawing of a reconstructed head she'd expected, the picture was of her, and more alarmingly she was in the nude. So he did have an imagination, after all.

CHAPTER FIVE

Fortunately for Sharman the Vice Squad office was situated quite a distance from the force headquarters, and therefore from Adams and his sycophantic cohorts. Detective Inspector Maurice Panna had been in charge of the unit for almost three years, and although he had run the squad successfully he was due for a move. For once Sharman's luck was in, he hadn't moved yet. Panna had the unusual and useful talent of truly understanding people and their motivations, which most policemen, despite their commonly held belief to the contrary, did not.

Maurice Panna was waiting for Sharman as he pulled into the car park. As Sharman climbed out he greeted his friend. 'Stan!'

'Maurice. Long time no see.'

'And whose fault is that?'

'Sorry, Maurice, but you know how it is. How's Jill and the kids?' Sharman knew Panna's family were the way through to his heart.

'Fine, Rebecca's just got into drama school.'

'Star in the making. Perhaps she'll be able to keep her dad in the style he's become accustomed to?'

Panna laughed. 'That shouldn't be hard. Still seeing Kate?'

Sharman nodded briefly.

'She's still on the game, you know?'

Sharman nodded again. 'I know.'

Panna shook his head. 'Give it up, Stan, she isn't going to change for you. I've told the lads to leave her alone for a while to give you a chance, but I think you'll be struggling to change her.'

Sharman acknowledged his friend's advice. 'I know, but I've got to give it my best shot. I love her.'

Panna laughed. 'You love her body, her youth.'

Sharman had to admit that there was a great deal of truth in the observation. 'Both. But there's a bit more to it than that.'

'Forever the optimist, you, Stan.' Panna put his arm around Sharman's shoulder. 'Come on up, the coffee should be ready by now.'

He guided Sharman through the doors and up the stairs to his office, where coffee had already been prepared. The men sat opposite each other.

'I hear you're not officially one of us any more?'

'No, suspended on full pay until further notice.'

Panna had heard that phrase too many times before. 'Or until Adams has got enough information to stitch you up.'

Sharman grinned ruefully. 'You know how the system works, then?'

Panna sipped at his coffee. He disliked Adams as much as his friend did, but knew how to play the game better. 'The little shit did his CID attachment under me. Didn't like him then and my opinion hasn't changed since.'

Sometimes Sharman found Panna hard to understand. 'If you didn't like him why didn't you kick him off when you had the chance?'

'Farmer. He had her protection, and she wasn't the kind of woman you crossed if you wanted to keep your balls attached.'

Sharman laughed. 'Yeah, I remember. Good copper, though.'

There was a moment's pause as the two detectives remembered a fallen friend.

Panna broke the silence. 'So, Stanley, as I don't imagine for a moment that this is a social call, and bearing in mind I could get suspended for being seen with you, what's all this about?'

Sharman reached into his bag and pulled out the video, handing it to Panna, who examined it quickly.

'Very nice, but I'm more of a *Superman* fan myself.'

Sharman glared at his friend. 'Just play it, Maurice, and you'll see what I've come about.'

Panna slipped the tape into the video machine and the opening credits began. 'Don't tell me. This is the episode where Spock does it with a dog from Mars, and you thought I might be interested?'

'I've heard you've done it with a few dogs, why should Spock be any different? Now spin it on and let's get to the point.'

Panna pressed the fast forward button and after a few moments began to view the snuff movie at the end of the tape. The jokes stopped as the two men watched. After the video had finished Sharman turned to his friend.

'Well, what do you think?'

Panna shrugged. 'Snuff movies.'

'But are they real, or just acted?'

Panna stepped over to the video and popped out the tape before turning the machine off. 'Can I ask where you got it from?'

Sharman shook his head. 'Not yet, later. So are they real or not?'

Panna sat down again. 'Who can say?'

'You can. Come on, have an opinion.'

Panna thought for a moment. 'I think they're real.'

'So we've just witnessed a brutal murder?'

'Yes,' he nodded.

'So what are you going to do about it?'

Panna shrugged again. 'Nothing, there's nothing I can do except hand it over to the Bosnian war crimes investigators in the Hague.'

Sharman was confused. 'Why?'

Panna hesitated for a moment. The existence of these tapes was almost a state secret and he wasn't sure if it was safe to tell his old friend. Finally he made his mind up. He'd known Sharman a long time.

'Hundreds, probably thousands, of these tapes have flooded Europe. Interpol have traced the tapes to Bosnia. During the war hundreds of young girls were raped and murdered on both sides. Some enterprising bastards decided that there might be a few bob to be made from it. So not only did the young women have to endure torture, rape and murder, someone filmed it happening and made a small fortune on the pornographic market.'

Sharman had always prided himself on having heard or seen just about everything, but this was the limit.

Panna continued, 'The only chance we have is to hand the tapes over to the War Crimes Tribunal and hope that some of the faces are recognized.'

'What about the distributors?'

'Same thing, only less chance of finding them. When you're ready to tell me where you got them, we can try and trace the videos back to their source. Trouble is most of them are picked up through the Internet, so we're struggling from the very start. Do you know if your source has got any more?'

'Maybe.'

'If you can get me the rest, I'll do my bit. These tapes need stopping.'

Sharman stood. 'Give me a day or two and I'll see what I can do.'

Panna hadn't finished. 'Has this got something to do with the Clarke murder case?'

Sharman hesitated for a moment, unsure what to say. Realizing, however, that Panna had just trusted him he knew there was no point lying to his old friend. Besides, Panna already knew the truth, he just wanted con-firmation. 'Yeah.'

'Thought so. Be careful, Stan, I don't like Adams but he's a dangerous bastard. You're already in too deep, don't make it any worse. The word is he's after you and won't let go until he's brought you down.'

Sharman acknowledged the concern of his friend. 'Thanks, Maurice, but I'm more than aware of Adams' plans for me.'

'It's a no-win situation, Stan. Even if you survive this time, he's too well connected, you'll still lose in the end.'

Sharman knew his friend was right but couldn't help himself. If he was going down, he'd go down fighting.

Sam had arrived early at the Park, to try and keep pace with the growing amount of paperwork she needed to get through. Jean had stacked the files in order of urgency. She wouldn't have minded but most of it was routine rubbish which seemed to serve no purpose other than to allow pen-pushers in the hospital to justify their existence. Jean came in at nine and made coffee. Sam was always pleased to see her friend. Since her sister Wyn had moved out of the cottage there were times when she felt lonely. Wyn came to see her quite regularly, but it wasn't the same. She was normally self-sufficient and with repairs to the cottage, most of which she did for herself, gardening and the village choir her time was usefully employed. But in her quieter moments, mostly in the evenings, she did feel the need for a companion and missed not having one. Mulling the day and her problems over with Jean was always relaxing. Although her assistant didn't have her scientific mind she had oceans of common sense, which Sam listened to and often acted upon. There were times when she really didn't know what she would do without her.

At two there was a light tap on Sam's office door and Jean entered. 'Mr Hudd's here to see you, Doctor. Shall I send him in?'

Sam considered this for a moment. She was doing well. Another twenty minutes and she would have cleared most of the important backlog. On the other hand was it worth keeping Peter Hudd waiting? He might take offence and walk out or worse still draw Jean in the nude. This final thought made Sam's mind up for her. 'Ask him in, Jean.'

Jean beckoned him into the room. 'Coffee?'

He looked at Jean, surprised. 'I'm trying to avoid poisoning my body. Got any water, bottled, that is?'

Jean looked a little taken aback. 'I'll see what I can find.' Disgruntled, she turned to Sam. 'Coffee for you, Doctor?'

Sam nodded. 'Yes, please, Jean. Extra poison.'

Jean left the room and Hudd sat down opposite Sam, looking around her office with that air of superior confidence that only public school and Oxbridge can develop. He finally looked at Sam and smiled. 'Do you smoke?'

Sam shook her head. 'No, why? Would you like one? I'm sure Jean will be able—'

Hudd cut her short. 'No I don't smoke, I just wondered if you put any other poisons into your system.'

Sam smiled back at him. 'Just enough to keep me sane.'

Hudd continued. 'You would have thought that doctors and pathologists would have avoided anything that might have a negative effect on them. I mean seeing the damage it does at first hand, if you take my meaning.'

Sam found his remarks patronizing but suspected that he was oblivious to their effect. 'I do indeed take your meaning. In my experience people in the medical profession are the worst.'

This time it was Hudd's turn to look alarmed. 'Really, you do surprise me.' Then, almost as if he was bored with the conversation, he moved on. 'Where is the mortuary?'

'In the basement. I'll take you there in a minute. There's just one or two things I'd like to discuss with you—'

He cut her short, not interested in Sam's 'one or two things'. 'Do you have many bodies in at the moment?'

Sam was about to warn him about the state of the unknown girl's body but was so disgruntled by his

behaviour she decided to let him find out for himself. The
sights alarmed most people, but the smells tended to
alarm everybody. The aroma of a decomposing body
could be so pungent it often drifted through the entire
hospital, causing offence to everyone. 'Full house. It's that
time of the year.'

Hudd laughed. 'What a strange description for a
mortuary, "full house".'

Jean arrived with a coffee and bottle of still water. Hudd
took it without a word of thanks and examined the label.
As Jean's face reddened with anger he turned to Sam,
'That'll do. Shall we go down to the mortuary now, Dr – I
mean Sam?'

Fred had everything arranged by the time Hudd and Sam
reached the mortuary. Fred had left the girl's body on the
slide tray that allowed the bodies to be pulled in and out
of the fridges easily. Despite the sub-zero conditions the
smell of the still slowly decomposing body was strong,
and Fred didn't fancy the idea of moving it too far from
the fridges. He wanted to try and control the smell and not
let it drift around the mortuary and out into the hospital.

Sam looked towards her assistant. 'Everything ready,
Fred?'

Fred nodded. 'As instructed, Dr Ryan.'

Sam returned her attention to Hudd. 'When you're
ready, just say.' She could see by the look on his face that
the smell was already getting to her artistic friend. She
was still annoyed with him and decided to remain silent.
Hudd tried to maintain his confident air but Sam could
see he was struggling. He finally nodded towards Fred,
who slowly pulled back the sheet covering the remains.
As the body was revealed Hudd's eyes seemed to flicker
and widen. His colour changed, from a healthy pink to a
insipid white, and he began to shake. Sam gestured to
Fred, who moved around the body quickly and took hold
of Hudd's arm, while Sam took his water bottle off him,
opened it, and offered him some. After taking a large

mouthful and swallowing hard, he handed the bottle back to Sam. His air of superior indifference had now all but disappeared.

'Thank you, I'll be all right in a minute. Bit more of a shock than I thought it would be.'

Sam nodded understandingly but was secretly pleased she'd managed to dent his arrogance.

'I thought you would have been used to seeing bodies. I thought it was all part of your art?'

Hudd shook his head. 'Not like this. I deal with skulls. Old and smooth-boned. Nothing like this. I just didn't expect . . .'

Sam began to feel a tinge of real sympathy for him. 'Would you like to go out and get some air?'

'No, it's OK, I'll be fine in a minute. It's just the smell.' Hudd shuddered, but refused to accept defeat.

Fred slowly let go of his arm as he began to compose himself. Finally he put his hand up and Fred stepped away. Sam could see it was a mammoth effort for him, but Hudd slowly pulled his head back and looked down upon the remains of the girl. This time he didn't look away, but when he spoke his voice was still shaky. 'I'll need to take some sketches.'

Sam admired the effort he was making to pull himself together. 'That's fine. I can let you have some photographs if that will help?'

'No, I'll need to sketch. I'll be as quick as I can.'

Sam nodded. She was becoming increasingly impressed by Hudd. Perhaps he wasn't simply the arrogant little sod she had first thought. Perhaps much of it was show. Just like the rest of the Oxbridge lot.

'Can I suggest you wear greens? The smell tends to stick. You'll carry it everywhere on your clothes otherwise.'

'Like cigarette smoke?'

'Just like cigarette smoke,' Sam agreed.

Hudd suddenly seemed to lose interest in both Sam and his surroundings, concentrating instead on the girl's face.

Then, much to Sam's surprise, Hudd stretched out his hands and placed them on to what was left of the girl's head and face. Sam very quickly stepped forward and tried to restrain him with a hand on his forearm. She offered him the use of rubber gloves, which he refused saying that it would dull his sense of touch. Even when Sam pointed out the risks and the need to be protected under Health and Safety Regulations he still refused, asserting that it was his risk and his choice and that he would take full responsibility.

He stroked the girl's forehead and cheeks, his fingers occasionally running under the thin layers of skin that still hung desperately to her face. He ran his hand through the remaining strands of hair trying to replace them as they pulled away and got attached to his fingers. Fred looked across at Sam and raised an eyebrow, but Sam ignored him, completely absorbed and fascinated by Hudd's performance. He moved his hand from her hair to the edge of her face, feeling the line of the jaw and neck. His fingers then moved slowly across to what was left of her mouth. Part of her lips finally gave way under the light touch of Hudd's fingers and fell inside her skull. Sam looked up and searched his face trying to see what he was thinking. Much to her surprise his eyes were closed tightly, as he tried to memorize everything by touch. Finally his hands reached her eye sockets. He first ran his fingers slowly around the rims, then stopped, as if the horror of what he knew he had to do next was too much, even for him. Then, summoning up what courage he had left, his fingers began to crawl slowly inside her eye cavities, feeling slowly around the skull's dark, rancid interior. The bone inside was rough, broken up occasionally by bits of rotting flesh. Finally, pulling his fingers out of her eye cavities he placed them gently against each side of the girl's cheeks, leaving them there for a moment as if trying to extract her very essence. Then, as quickly as he had begun, he removed his hands. He looked at Sam. 'Have you got anywhere I could wash?'

Sam directed him to the scrub room, where he washed and scrubbed his hands for some time. He looked across at Sam as he was doing it. ' "Out, damn spot." I'm not sure my hands will ever be clean again.'

Sam smiled sympathetically. 'Why did you have to feel her face in the way you did?'

Hudd turned back to the sink, still scrubbing. 'I had to know her. If I'm going to do her justice I need to know her. It was the only way.'

Sam had to admit that she still didn't fully understand. 'Couldn't you have just drawn her?'

'I will, but it wouldn't have been enough. I want to know every line, every bump on her skull, I couldn't do her justice unless I knew her face properly.'

'There wasn't that much left to feel.'

Hudd looked back at her. 'There was enough. I have her soul now.'

Sam wasn't sure if he meant it, or was just being 'arty'. It was probably a combination of the two. 'So what happens now?'

'I'll finish my sketches and then start work on the reconstruction.'

'How long will it take?'

Hudd thought about it for a moment, considering the question. 'A week?'

Sam winced. It was too long. 'Any chance of having it sooner?'

'It won't be easy, I'll need time if I'm going to get it right. Might be able to do it in four days?'

She winced again but Hudd wouldn't budge. 'Sorry, but it's the best I can do, and remember, I said *might* be able to do it in four days.'

She shrugged. She wasn't happy but what could she do?

'If that's the best you can offer, that'll be fine. Just make a good job of it. I'd like to know who she was too, you know?'

He smiled broadly at her. Discovering the dead girl's

identity was becoming almost as important to him as it was to Sam.

'Don't worry, it will be my best work to date. Now I really must get on or you'll never get to see her, will you?'

After showing Peter Hudd out, Sam made her way back up to the office, her mind still full of what she had just seen. Jean was waiting for her.

'I wasn't very sure about him, doctor?'

'You know what these arty types are like, Jean.'

Jean gave Sam a knowing look. She was far too practical to countenance the likes of Hudd. 'Head in the clouds, most of them.'

Sam smiled at her friend. She was right, but Sam had rather taken to this particular arty type. 'Sounds like your average Cambridge student to me.'

Jean huffed. 'Sounds like your average student, Cambridge or otherwise. Was he any good?'

'I won't know for sure until I see his work, but I'm very hopeful.'

'How long will it take before we get a look?'

'Three or four days. With luck.'

Jean looked sceptical. 'We'll see. What are you up to now?'

Jean's pessimism made Sam nervous. 'Thought I might try and finish some more of the backlog.'

'But you're supposed to be taking a few days off.' Jean was indignant.

Sam indicated the pile of paperwork on her desk. 'This lot won't get done by itself, Jean. I'll feel happier when it's done.'

Jean nodded, still slightly indignant. 'I suppose so. Coffee?'

'Please, Jean, that should keep me going for a bit. I've got to cover the afternoon list after this lot.'

If she had been indignant before this fresh piece of information incensed her. 'Afternoon list? But that's Dr Dixson's!'

Sam shrugged. 'He's been called back to court, someone's got to do it.'

'Yes, but why you?'

'I'm the only one left standing apparently.'

'What about Dr Stuart?'

'Chairing a conference.'

Jean shook her head. 'What, another one? He'll be opening supermarkets next.'

Sam laughed at her friend's displeasure.

'How many have you got?'

Sam examined a sheet of paper in front of her. 'Nine.'

'I'm afraid it's ten now.' Jean showed her yet another sheet of paper.

Sam stared at her despairingly. 'What?'

'Middle-aged man died, apparently of a heart attack, on his way to work this morning.' Jean examined the sheet of paper again. 'Didn't live far from me. Don't recognize the name, though.'

She handed the sheet to Sam who took it and examined it quickly. 'Ten it is, then. Seems straightforward enough.' She knew she would regret saying that.

A loud rap on the office door stopped their conversation. Jean answered it. As she did, she turned to Sam, confused and surprised, unsure what to do next. 'Superintendent Adams. Shall I . . . do you want—?'

Sam cut her short, recognizing the confusion in her voice. 'It's all right, Jean. Come in, Superintendent.'

As Tom Adams walked past Jean she eyed him suspiciously.

'Morning, Jean.'

Jean didn't reply. As far as she was concerned any enemy of Dr Ryan's was an enemy of hers.

Sam looked across at her. 'Better make that coffee for two. Thank you, Jean.'

Jean nodded, sniffed loudly and left the room. Sam didn't stand to greet Adams as she normally would, but remained seated watching him as he crossed the room and sat down opposite her desk. She leaned forward, trying to sound as professional as she could.

'What can I do for you, Superintendent?'

Adams smiled at her. 'You can cut the crap for a start, Sam, we know each other too well.'

Sam remained grim-faced. 'So well, in fact, that you feel you can go behind my back and try and get me thrown off a case.'

Adams leaned back in his seat. 'That was nothing to do with your professional competence as you well know, but about our relationship—'

Sam cut in, unconvinced. 'I didn't know we had one.'

This time Adams leant forward in his seat. 'According to the tabloids we do.'

'Don't flatter yourself.'

Adams shook his head. 'I'm not, they are. How could you have allowed yourself to be photographed like that?'

Although she was irritated by Adams' comment Sam knew he was right, it had been stupid. 'I didn't do it on purpose. How was I to know he had one of his photographers hidden in the bushes waiting his chance? It's not only coppers that are bastards.'

Adams leant back in his seat again. 'Look, I'm sorry about what happened to us, I truly am. Maybe in retrospect I could have handled it better, I don't know. The truth remains the same, however; at a time when I wanted someone in my life, you didn't want to be there.'

Sam stared at him but didn't reply.

'If I, or anyone else for that matter, try to come between you and your bloody career, the result will always be the same.'

Sam sprang to her own defence. 'That's not true.'

'Yes it is, and if you're honest with yourself you'll admit it.' Adams was adamant.

Sam knew, had always known, he was right. It wasn't that she wouldn't admit it. She couldn't. It was like confessing that perhaps you weren't the perfect human being you'd always thought you were. People never like to think ill of themselves and Sam was no exception.

Adams continued, 'The only reason I asked to have you removed from the inquiry was because neither of us is over it yet and it shows. I felt undermined by your attitude at the Clarke murder scene and you know it. No matter what we might be feeling personally we have to keep our private lives separate from our professional ones.'

Sam eyed him for a moment. 'I thought I was,' she lied.

Adams shook his head. 'No, you don't. Sam, I think about you every day. It's not easy for me either.'

Sam could feel herself getting upset. 'Only you've got someone to go home to, talk your troubles over with. Who the hell do I have?'

Adams looked at her steadily for a moment. 'You're living with your own decisions, Sam. You don't have to live alone, there are plenty of people who want to share your life with you. Including me, once.'

Sam pondered what he was saying. He was right but she was damned if she was going to admit it.

'Is that all you came to see me about?'

Adams hesitated for a moment. 'Not all.'

'So what was the real reason?'

He hesitated again, unsure of his ground. 'I was wondering how you were getting on with that unknown dead girl?'

Sam shrugged. 'Fine.'

'Discovered any fresh evidence? I really would like to help if I can.'

He was lying. He wasn't worried about helping at all. He couldn't afford another major inquiry, but had to watch his back in case she came up with something and he was left looking ridiculous.

'When's the board for the Deputy Chief Constable's job?'

Adams took a deep breath. He was beginning to lose the calm he had been so determined to maintain. 'It's got nothing to do with that, Sam. I'm just here to try and help.'

'Like hell you are. You're here to watch your back, terrified that I might come up with something that will take the gloss off your shiny reputation and damage your chances of getting that all-important promotion.'

Finally losing his composure, Adams stood. 'That's not true, and it's bloody unfair.'

Sam stared at him, hostility written all over her face. 'Isn't it, Tom? You have the nerve to come in here and accuse me of putting my job and career before anything else. What do you think you are doing? Talk about throwing stones at glasshouses. If I am able to prove to everyone's satisfaction that the poor kid found under the bridge was murdered, you'll be the last to know. Trust me.'

'Withholding information is a criminal offence, Sam.'

Sam was on her feet now. 'Don't you bloody well threaten me, you bastard. I won't withhold anything, I'll just let the Chief Constable know first, and put a complaint in at the same time.'

'For what?' Adams had now completely lost his composure.

'Neglect of duty. That should help dull the image, don't you think?'

He glared at her but didn't reply. Finally, red-faced, he turned on his heels and stormed towards the office door. Sam called after him, 'How is Rebecca, by the way?'

Adams stopped and turned to face her. 'Pregnant!'

The harshness of his voice showed the comment was intended to hurt and it did. Short of being punched in the face it couldn't have hit Sam harder, but she was determined not to show it. Adams paused for a moment searching for an indication that he'd got through to her and won the conflict. Sam stood there emotionless, leaving him unsure of his success. Finally, tired of the game, he marched out of the office and past a surprised Jean, who had just opened the door with two coffees in her hand. She looked across at Sam, who was still on her feet with her arms crossed in a defiant gesture.

'Just one coffee, then, is it?'

Sam nodded, trying hard to fight back the tears.

William and Betty Waddam lived in a small, but smart, semi-detached house on the Darwin Estate. It was well maintained with PVC double-glazed widows and doors, a recently painted fence and neatly kept front garden. It stood out like a shiny new pin in an otherwise scruffy street, where most of the gardens were overgrown or had rotting car shells sitting in the middle of them. Sharman wasn't surprised then to see a 'For Sale' board outside the house. If he lived around here he would have been glad to get out too.

As he emerged from his car he eyed the small gang of kids sitting on a low wall on the opposite side of the road. He beckoned the ringleader over. The boy dragged himself across the road reluctantly and stared up at Sharman. As big as Sharman was compared to the boy, there was no fear, no concern, or for that matter respect, in the boy's face.

'You the leader?'

'Who wants to know?'

'I'll give you a quid to look after my car while I'm inside.'

The boy looked at him considering the offer. Then looked across at his friends. 'Fiver.'

Sharman shook his head. 'Too much.'

The boy shrugged. 'Can't guarantee your wheels will still be there when you get back, then.'

'Two pound fifty?'

The boy considered again. 'Three . . .'

Sharman got in quickly. 'Done.'

The boy hadn't finished. '. . . . Fifty.'

Sharman reached into his pocket and gave the boy the money. 'If there's so much as a mark on the paintwork when I get back I'll step on you. Understand?'

The boy nodded his understanding and walked back to his friends to share out his ill-gotten gains. Sharman shook his head. Instead of giving him money he should have been giving him a bloody good hiding. Society had apparently moved on since he first joined the force and that sort of treatment was now out of the question. Instead, gangs of kids like these were allowed to run amuck on council estates, smashing and kicking the shit out of anything and anyone they didn't like. Funny, Sharman pondered, how all the people who made the laws protecting these kids lived on nice middle-class estates far away from the problems that their policies caused.

Having secured his car Sharman opened the gate to number 47 and made his way to the door, and rang the doorbell. Bill Waddam answered the door.

'Whatever you're selling we don't want any.'

Sharman pulled his warrant card out and showed it to him. 'DS Sharman. Wonder if I could ask you a few questions?'

Sharman knew it was a risk but he considered it worth taking. Although he had been forced to hand over his warrant card to Adams when he was suspended, he had several, collected over the years for just such an eventuality. All he had to hope now was that the Waddams didn't ring the control room to ask about him.

Mr Waddam didn't seem very impressed. 'More questions? Bloody hell, how much longer is this going to go on for? We saw and heard nothing. We've already told you that. And made a statement.'

Sharman smiled as sweetly as he could. 'Just a few things I'd like to go over with you. Routine stuff, but it has to be done.' Bill Waddam sighed loudly before standing to one side and directing Sharman into the sitting room.

As he entered, Betty Waddam, who was sitting on the settee, knitting, stood up and looked at him curiously.

Her husband was quickly reassuring. 'It's OK, love, this is . . .' He hesitated as if he'd forgotten his name. Sharman helped him out.

Putting out his arm he took Betty's hand. 'Detective Sergeant Sharman. Sorry to bother you again, but there's just a few more questions.'

Betty Waddam looked across at her husband. 'We've already made a statement.'

Sharman interjected again. 'I realize that, Mrs Waddam. As I was saying to your husband, it's just routine.'

She sat down again. After Bill Waddam had directed Sharman to a chair he sat down next to his wife and took her hand. Sharman couldn't help noticing how drawn and nervous she looked. 'Are you OK, Mrs Waddam?'

Her husband answered for her. 'She's still getting over it. She was very fond of Mrs Clarke. Although she worked for her they were friends, you know?'

As Sharman nodded Betty Waddam lit up a cigarette and began to smoke.

Bill Waddam looked at him. 'Would you like a cigarette?'

Sharman shook his head. 'No, thanks.'

'Tea, then?'

Sharman shook his head again. 'No, really, I'm fine.' He returned his attention to Betty Waddam.

'You found the body, didn't you, Mrs Waddam?'

She nodded. 'It was awful. The poor girl, how she must have suffered.'

'What time did you find her?'

Mr Waddam cut in. 'It's in the statement.'

Sharman smiled sweetly again. 'I know, but with so much going on I've forgotten.'

Mrs Waddam looked at her husband reassuringly before returning her attentions to Sharman. 'Just before six, I was a bit early that day. Didn't sleep well the night before so I thought I might as well get on. Odd me not sleeping well that night. I usually sleep like a log.'

Sharman nodded in encouragement and turned his attentions to her husband. 'You dropped her off?'

He nodded.

'You didn't hang around at all?'

He shook his head. 'No, just dropped Betty off and then made my way back home.'

'What do you do for a living?'

'I'm a van driver now. I was a porter at King's for over twenty years. That's where I met Betty, she was a bedder.'

Sharman smiled. He had to keep the interview friendly for everyone's sake. 'Very romantic.'

Waddam gave his wife's hand a squeeze.

'How did you find out about the murder, Bill?'

Bill Waddam nodded towards his wife. 'She called me on the mobile. I came right back. She was in a terrible state. Mark you, after I'd seen the body I wasn't too good either.'

'What happened next?'

'I rang the police. They turned up pretty quick. We kept out of the way then. Well, until they wanted a statement and some blood from me for a DNA check. Just for elimination, they said. Suppose you have to be suspicious of everyone in your job?'

Sharman nodded. 'It's one of the drawbacks.' He continued, 'Did you touch anything or see anyone?'

They both shook their heads, but just before they did there was a glance between them. It was only for an instant but long enough for Sharman to realize that they were covering something up. Why they would lie or about what he had no idea, but lying they were. He pressed on.

'Was Mrs Clarke a good boss?'

Mrs Waddam nodded vigorously. 'The best, she was delightful. For someone to have done that to her, they must have been sick.'

Sharman persisted. 'Did she know Ward?'

'Yes, he came around to the house with Mr Clarke sometimes. Didn't like him, too full of himself for my liking.'

'Did Mrs Clarke like him?'

Sharman noticed the Waddams glance at each other again before Mrs Waddam answered, 'I don't know. I don't think so. I hope he rots in hell.'

'Did he ever come to the house when Mr Clarke wasn't there?'

Mrs Waddam cracked back, 'No, never. I never saw him there without Mr Clarke, never. She wouldn't have had anything to do with a man like that.'

The answer was too quick, too rehearsed and too adamant for Sharman's liking. Someone had briefed Betty Waddam and he needed to know who.

'Like what, Betty?'

Mrs Waddam realized that her answer had not been careful enough and tried to backtrack. 'She was a happily married woman. She would never have had anything to do with anyone except her husband.'

The interview was becoming tense so Sharman changed tack. 'I see you're moving?' He indicated through the window to the 'For Sale' board beyond.

Mr Waddam followed Sharman's stare. 'Can't stand to live around here any more. We've had years of it. It was all right when we first moved in. Lots of good working-class people, but now, just scum. We try and maintain standards but it's hopeless.'

'Where are you moving to?'

'We've seen a new bungalow in Histon we like.'

Sharman nodded. 'Very nice. It'll be different from here. I like Histon, bit pricey for my pocket.'

Bill Waddam nodded. 'I retire next month. I'm going to use some of my lump sum pension money and it looks like they're going to take this place in part exchange. We'd have never got rid of it otherwise, I don't think. Not round here.'

Sharman smiled. 'I expect you'll have to use all of it to live there.'

'Yes, I expect so, worth it, though. Betty's got a bit . . .' Bill Waddam nodded nervously as Betty shot a glance at him that silenced him at once.

Sharman decided not to react to it, and called it a day. 'Well, that's it. Shouldn't be any more questions. I'll try and keep the rest of the squad away from you. Give you some peace.'

The couple nodded and Mr Waddam shook Sharman's hand. 'Thanks for that. It's Betty's nerves, she's not been good since she found the body. She could do with some peace.'

Sharman shook Betty Waddam's hand. 'And I'll make sure she gets it. Good luck with the move.'

With that he showed himself out.

The boys had disappeared by the time he returned to his car. He walked around it to make sure it was still intact. No marks and the wheels were still there. Money well spent, he considered. Starting the car he pulled slowly away from the Waddams' house. As he did he looked across to the living-room window. They were both watching him leave. As soon as they saw him looking they pulled the curtains back across the window. They were hiding something, all right, and he had a good idea what.

Fiona Herbert lay naked across Hudd's bed, gently playing with her fair hair. She normally enjoyed watching Hudd work but right now all she wanted him to do was make love to her, and if she was being honest, she couldn't work out why he wouldn't. She'd promised him anything if he would just step across the room and lie with her. He never normally refused, in fact if anything she had trouble fending him off. She had been convinced at one time that he would have done it every hour on the hour seven days a week and she wasn't sure even that would have been enough. He really was insatiable most of the time. She looked down at herself to make sure she hadn't put weight on or there was some other awful defect that might be putting him off. There wasn't. Her body was long and slim. Her breasts were firm and high, and her legs the longest in the college. So why wouldn't he come over to her, even if it was only for a few minutes? She tried to entice him over again. Gently rubbing her body with her hands she called him, 'Peter, why don't you come over here, just for a minute or two, come on, I really am gagging for it, you know.'

Carefully studying two of the photographs that Sam had sent him and remembering his episode in the mortuary he continued working. 'Fiona, back it up, I'm working.'

She leant back across the bed arching her back so her body was stretched out. 'It's never stopped you before.'

That was certainly true, but somehow the work he was doing at the moment seemed far more important than lovemaking. He'd never felt that way before, in fact he would have said he was addicted to sex, and he was certainly addicted to sex with Fiona. Not only was she beautiful, with one of the finest bodies he had ever seen, she was wonderful in bed and a right screamer. Hudd always liked women who weren't afraid to vocalize their enjoyment.

'I've never had a job as important as this before.'

Fiona wasn't the kind of girl to give up easily. 'Come on, five minutes, aren't I more important to you than some dead girl?'

Hudd continued adding clay to the head without turning to see what she was doing, fearful that his resolve might weaken.

'Fiona, it's never five minutes with us. Five hours, more like.'

'Perhaps I can bring you inspiration?'

'I've already got that from Dr Ryan, thanks.'

She finally gave up and sat up on the bed. 'So you prefer an older woman to me?'

Hudd shook his head. 'No, although I have to say she was very attractive, didn't you think?'

Fiona began to dress. 'Can't say I noticed,' she said petulantly.

'I think she must work out. I mean you're not going to keep your body that good unless you do something, are you?'

Fiona finished dressing and made for the door. 'I'm going to try and find someone who appreciates my talents.'

Hudd finally looked up. 'Look, why don't you come back in an hour or so when I've done as much as I can with this? Keep yourself on the boil until then. What do you say?'

Fiona pouted by the door for a few moments. 'I'll stay the night, if you like?'

Hudd nodded. 'OK, but it's lights out at twelve, I've really got to get this finished.'

It seemed a little early to her, but she was sure she could extend the limit when she got her hands on him.

'OK, you've got a deal,' she lied, 'but it'd better be good or else I'll be using one of your knives for more than just applying clay.'

She made a cutting action in the air with her hand, making it quite clear what she meant, but fortunately he had returned his attentions to his work again.

With the distraction of Fiona's naked and wanton body out of the room and his view, Hudd began to concentrate more deeply. He'd never done anything quite like this before and had become fascinated, almost obsessed by it. Just by feeling the girl's features in the mortuary he knew she was beautiful, he just didn't know how beautiful and he was desperate to recreate that beauty through his work. Even now at this early stage it didn't seem quite right. He had sculpted hundreds of heads but that was just for his art and the fulfilment of his desire to become famous enough to be allowed to live within the world he loved, but this was different. This one had to be right. Through his hands this girl had to live again, he had to bring her back and see what she was like.

He stopped for a moment and stood back, judging and measuring what he'd done. Compared to the photographs he had in front of him it looked good. He closed his eyes and touched the edges of the head with the tips of his fingers, running them carefully over each ridge, line and bump. It felt different, it just wasn't the same. He needed and wanted more from this sculpture. Within this portrait he needed to catch her very essence, her soul. This couldn't just be another bust that might or might not look like the original person. This girl was relying on him to bring her back, it had to be right or it wasn't to be. He looked at the outline one more time before picking up a nearby knife and smashing it hard into the top of the head.

Sam arrived early at the forensic science service in Huntingdon hoping to see Marcia before the rest of the work force turned up. Although she always had a ready excuse should anyone question why she was there, it still helped if as few people as possible knew they were working together. The last thing she needed was to be summoned to Trevor Stuart's office again. As she pulled into the car park, she was beginning to regret starting so early. She'd had one of the worst nights she could remember. After she had returned to the privacy of her cottage she'd started to cry and hadn't really stopped until a few hours before she'd left to see her friend. She pulled down the vanity mirror in her car and examined her face. Try as she might there was no way of disguising her anguish. Her eyes were puffy and red and she seemed to have more tramlines than San Francisco. Applying more make-up around her eyes and face, she wondered if Marcia would notice.

After signing in she made her way along the corridors to Marcia's lab. She was expected and Marcia had a mug of coffee already made.

'You look like shit, if you don't mind me saying. Hard night?'

Sam nodded. 'Rebecca's pregnant.'

Marcia handed her the coffee. 'How the hell did you find that out?'

Sam looked knowingly at her and Marcia realized at once.

'No, don't tell me, he felt the need to come and tell you in person?'

'It wasn't quite like that, but yes.'

Marcia took a large mouthful of coffee and shook her head. 'And to think I once liked that man.'

Sam was contrite. 'It wasn't entirely his fault.'

Marcia would have none of it. 'It is in my book, dear. You'd be better off with Stan Sharman.'

Sam smiled. 'I don't charge for it.'

Now it was Marcia's turn to smile. 'Perhaps you should, probably make a killing. At least he's honest and straight-forward.' Marcia thought about what she'd just said for a moment. 'Well, for a copper, anyway.'

The two women laughed gently and Sam began to cheer up. She didn't know what it was about Marcia but she always managed to lift her mood. That was probably why they'd been friends for so long.

Sam sipped at her coffee as Marcia produced the watch, waving it in the air by its strap.

'Anyway, the good news is we're in luck with the watch.'

Sam became concerned about the careless way Marcia was treating the evidence. 'Be a bit more careful, Marcia, that's exhibit one right now, and the only tangible evidence we've got to help identify the girl.'

Marcia smiled. 'Nag, nag, nag.' She took the watch over to the bench and laid it face down before she began her commentary.

'I tried ultraviolet light first and got a few bits but not enough. Watch . . .'

Marcia manoeuvred an ultraviolet lamp over the top of the watch and turned it on. She pointed to a series of letters that hadn't been visible before. 'See those?' She showed Sam a PRE, which became visible on one side of the watch and an SA, which became visible on the other. Working her way down the watch looking at both sides a C and an M became apparent as well as an E and R. The same pattern emerged all along both edges of the watch. Finally after showing Sam all the visible letters she stood back. 'Well, what do you think?'

Sam looked at her friend curiously. 'Great, but it doesn't

really take us any further forward. It's just a jumble of letters.'

'I haven't finished yet. Realizing that it was just a jumble of letters,' she gave her friend a knowing look, 'I took it to Malcolm Brown across the way and he put his new X-ray machine to work.'

Sam was impressed. 'For free? That was good of him.'

Marcia nodded in agreement. 'It's still in its experimental stage so he was keen to try it on something real. If you know what I mean. We were lucky really, if it had failed it would probably have destroyed the watch.'

Sam was aghast.

Marcia grinned. 'Joke.'

Sam shook her head in despair at her friend.

'As I said, we were lucky. The inscription on the back had been impressed in with a stamp of some sort. If it had been engraved we would have been out of luck.'

'What difference does that make?'

'When you impress something, it cracks the metal below it, in the same shape you made on top. When you engrave something it doesn't do that. Engraving just scratches the surface. Anyway, Malcolm put his machine to work, and bingo, came up with the goods. He was very pleased with himself.'

'Well?'

Marcia stared back, wondering what was wrong, then realized. 'Oh, sorry.' She turned a photograph over that had been lying face down the table. 'Here it is. I hope it helps.'

Sam examined the photograph. It clearly showed the inscription on the back of the watch in its entirety.

'Presented to Sally Anne Cromer, on her retirement from Beaver and Sons, 26th March 1999.'

Sam leaned over and hugged her friend. 'Brilliant, I knew I could count on you.'

'Thank you, fans, thank you. All we need to do now is

find out who Sally Cromer is and we could be cooking on gas.'

Sam picked up the watch and examined it. 'Let's hope so, Marcia. This case could do with a decent break.'

Sharman knew he was taking a big risk by talking to Meadows but he couldn't see what option he had. If this case was ever going to get cracked then he needed Meadows' help. Besides, Meadows already realized he knew more than he was saying, and if he was ever going to get the credit for cracking this particular case, he was sharp enough to realize he was going to need him. Promotion was never a driving force with Sharman, unlike with Meadows, and he could use that fact to his best advantage.

They agreed the incident room wouldn't be the best place in the world to be seen together and they finally decided to meet in the Eagle in central Cambridge. Although it was a busy pub Sharman had enjoyed his last visit with Sam and it was convenient. The two men arrived together and on time. Meadows got the first round in and they settled themselves down in a corner out of the way.

After swallowing a large mouthful of ale, Meadows came to the point. 'So, Stanley, what's with the cloak-and-dagger stuff?'

Sharman took a long drink from his own glass before answering. 'You want help with the inquiry?'

Meadows shrugged. 'Not really, got our man bang to rights.'

Sharman hated the smug look on his face and was looking forward to wiping it off. 'Has he admitted it yet?'

'Doesn't have to, forensics are strong enough to convict him on their own.'

Sharman took another long drink. 'Are they? What if I was to tell you he didn't do it and I can prove it?'

Meadows was about to take a drink, but stopped himself midway and looked hard into the face of his old partner. Sharman wasn't the kind of man to say that kind of thing lightly. He obviously knew something he didn't. 'How can you do that?'

Sharman sat back and looked at Meadows over his beer glass. 'Let me interview him and I'll show you.'

Meadows almost choked on his drink. 'Are you out of your mind? He's on bloody remand in Lincoln. Adams would have both our jobs.'

Sharman gave a sarcastic laugh. 'He's already got mine.'

Meadows paused. 'Maybe, but he's not having mine as well.'

'He doesn't have to know. You arrange the interview at Lincoln and I'll just come along for the ride.'

Meadows shook his head. 'Only one snag with that, Stan, I'd have to book you in too.'

Sharman shook his head despairingly, his mind racing. 'What about Dr Ryan?'

Meadows laughed out loud, but controlled himself when he suddenly became the centre of attention. 'Adams reads the log every day. What's he going to think when he sees his former girlfriend's name on the visitors' list? I don't think so.'

Sharman grabbed his arm. 'Let me talk to her, I'm sure we can come up with a legitimate reason for her to be there.'

Meadows stared at him for a moment, trying to decide whether he was still sane or not. 'You mean you haven't asked her yet? How the hell do you know she'll do it?'

Sharman had never been more sure of something in his life. 'She'll do it, trust me.'

Meadows still wasn't convinced. 'What about his solicitor? He'd have to be there as well.'

'We tell him we think we have information that will get his client off the hook. I'm sure he'll cooperate then. Come on, what do you say?'

Meadows took another long drink. 'It's bloody dangerous, that's what I say. What's in it for me, anyway?'

'You stop both Adams and the force looking like a bunch

of fools. Think of that third pip, it's bound to come then.'

'If this goes wrong, Stan, I'll fucking kill you.'

Sharman smiled across at his friend. 'What can go wrong?'

'If I had a pound for every time I'd heard that one I'd be a rich man by now.'

'When are we going to do it?'

Meadows thought for a moment. 'You'd better make sure Ryan will do it first.'

'And if she will?'

'Give us a couple of days. I know some of the lads in Lincoln, I'll see if I can get her in without booking her. That way I can cover my back if the wheel comes off.'

Sharman smiled and finished off his drink. 'That's my boy.'

'By the way, that question about sailing?'

Sharman stared at him for a moment his interest renewed. 'Yeah?'

Meadows shrugged. 'He doesn't.'

Sharman smiled. 'Didn't think he did.'

Meadows knew there had to be more. 'Don't suppose you feel like telling me why you asked the question?'

Sharman shook his head. 'Get us into Lincoln and I'll see what I can do.'

Meadows knew there was no point in pursuing the matter. He did have some further information of his own, however. 'Did you know that John Clarke is funding Ward's defence?'

Sharman was stunned. 'He's what? After everything that's happened?'

Meadows nodded. 'I know, unbelievable isn't it? He's convinced of Ward's innocence, apparently. So you're not on your own.'

'I'm surprised the papers haven't picked up on it.'

'All very hush-hush. Men like Clarke buy their privacy, like their justice.'

Sharman put his thoughts to the back of his mind for a moment. 'What're you drinking?'

Meadows looked at his empty pint glass. 'Double Scotch.'

'You'll have a pint and like it. Rank's beginning to change you, do you know that?'

CHAPTER SIX

The outside of Lincoln prison reminded Sam of a medieval castle. A giant gate supported on both sides by high walls and turrets made it one of the most imposing buildings in the region. She was no prison reformer, but this place did have a darkness to it that made her shudder. There were worse places, of course, but the idea of being confined twenty-four hours a day, seven days a week, in such surroundings sent a tremble down her spine.

Meadows had picked her up at seven for the two-hour drive to Lincoln. She had never managed to warm to him and she knew he didn't like her much, so the majority of the trip was undertaken in silence, with just the occasional word for courtesy's sake. When Sharman had asked her to take the trip, her first reaction was to say no, but then after she'd had time to think about it she realized how important getting to Ward was, and if they did have Meadows' tacit agreement then it might work. It was certainly a big risk, but that fact alone seemed to excite her. The only thing that didn't excite her was the fact that she would have to go with Meadows. A day with him was not going to be a barrel of laughs.

Sharman was pleased when Sam finally agreed to do it and offered to take her out for dinner afterwards. She wondered, wickedly, if she would have to wait on a street corner wearing only a red dress and stockings. She really would have to find out why a man like Sharman used prostitutes.

As they waited for the warders to let them in Sam observed the faces of the long line of family and friends waiting to visit inmates. She wondered how far some of them had come, and how long some of them had been waiting. They were the ones who really suffered when their partner, father or son was sent down. Did the inmates ever realize the pain they caused their family and friends, or did they live in their own fantasy world where they were never in danger of getting caught?

Sam noticed quite a few of the visitors looking back at her, many with disdain. They probably thought she was a police officer. She didn't look like one, but Meadows certainly did, so as far as the visitors were concerned it was guilt by association. A few moments after Meadows rang the bell a dark-suited prison warder answered the door and let them in.

The interior of the prison was darker than the exterior and Sam hoped they wouldn't be there long. After Meadows filled in the log, and they were searched, they were taken through the prison and up several flights of stairs to the interview room. Meadows had left her name off the log when he signed in. He'd told her that's what he was going to try and do, but she was surprised how easily he got away with it. Wheels within wheels, she pondered.

When they reached the interview room Peter Appleyard was already waiting. He looked up nervously as they entered. 'This really is most irregular, you know?'

Meadows nodded and assumed an air of composed confidence. 'I realize that, Mr Appleyard, but we are doing this in the best interests of your client.'

His comments failed to completely reassure Appleyard. 'Well, I'm reserving judgement and I won't hesitate to advise my client to terminate the interview immediately if I consider it prejudicial to his case.'

He turned his attention to Sam. 'I'm surprised you have become involved in all this, Dr Ryan.'

'I am confident that it is a useful and necessary undertaking in the cause of the pursuit of justice, Mr Appleyard, otherwise I can assure you that I would *not* be here.'

Appleyard shook his head despairingly. 'I wish I could be so assured, I fear we must all be mad.'

Sam walked across and sat next to the anxious solicitor. 'We're all on the same side, Peter. We believe Graham is innocent and we're here to help prove it.'

Meadows suddenly cut in from somewhere behind Sam. 'Most of this interview is off the record. Is that understood? I'm only here to ask some basic questions to sort out a few ambiguities. They are the only questions that will be taped. Other than that you'll have to trust me.'

Appleyard looked at Sam with an expression that suggested that although he trusted her, Meadows was a different matter. He wouldn't trust Meadows if his life depended on it. He finally nodded. 'OK let's get on with it. The sooner I'm out of here the better.'

Meadows nodded to the prison warder, who had remained in the room with them. 'Ready when you are, John.'

His familiarity with the warder spoke volumes for the informal way he was able to get people in and out of the prison without having to register them.

When Ward entered the office Sam couldn't help notice how pale and drawn he looked, the darkness around his eyes emphasized by the paleness of his skin. He seemed to have aged and looked haunted and haggard; almost a different person from the photographs she had seen of him in the newspapers. He had the appearance of a man who had already been tried, convicted, and sentenced to some awful punishment. Which, given the gravity of the crime, and the public outrage surrounding it if he was found guilty, he would be. He made his way slowly across to the hard metal chair and slumped down opposite them. Meadows gestured to the prison warder, who left the room. Appleyard looked surprised and more than a little taken aback at the ease with which Meadows seemed to be able to control the situation.

For a moment there was an awkward silence while the occupants of the dismal room watched each other and tried to establish each other's mood and motivations. Meadows broke the silence. 'Want a cigarette?'

Ward nodded and Meadows handed him a fresh packet of Marlboro Lights. He opened the packet and took one, handing the rest back to Meadows, who put his hand up. 'Keep them.'

Ward nodded his thanks. 'Got a light?'

Meadows passed him a box of matches and Ward sparked up. A further silence followed, while the group allowed Ward to enjoy the first few draws before the questioning began. The act of smoking seemed to calm him and Sam observed a slight relaxation of his features.

Once again it was Meadows who broke the silence.

'We need to ask you a few more questions about the murder.'

Ward looked at his solicitor. 'Shouldn't they be taping this or something?'

Appleyard nodded. 'Normally yes, but they're here to help. It's all a bit unofficial.'

Ward stared at his solicitor for a moment in disbelief. 'I hope you're not playing games with my life, Mr Appleyard?'

Appleyard shook his head. 'I am still here to represent you and keep an eye on things. I think having Dr Ryan here speaks volumes for their intentions, Graham.'

Ward turned to Sam. 'Is that right, Dr Ryan, are you here to help or just act as a police stooge?'

Sam resented being called a police stooge but controlled the quick rebuttal which sprang to her lips out of consideration for the pressure he was under. 'I'm here to help, Graham, if you'll let me.'

Sam could see him considering the merits of her offer. She didn't blame him, if her life was on the line she'd think hard about it too. He finally made up his mind. 'OK, I'll cooperate.' He glanced across at Meadows. 'But I'll only talk to her not you. Is that understood?'

Meadows nodded. 'Fine by me.'

Ward returned his attention to Sam. 'So what do you want to know?'

Sam thought for a moment. She wasn't a police officer, had no training in interview techniques, and to be honest, wasn't at all sure what to say. This was going to be harder than she thought.

'I know you didn't kill Sophie Clarke. I just need your help to prove it.'

Ward took another draw on his gradually diminishing cigarette before answering. 'Well, that makes two of us.' He glanced across at his solicitor. 'Because I don't really think Mr Appleyard here really believes me either. Do you, Peter?'

Appleyard looked flustered and confused by the challenge and tried to defend himself.

'I can assure you, Mr Ward—'

Ward cut him short. 'Don't go on, Peter, I was only kidding.'

Appleyard stopped his defence and relaxed back into the chair.

'So why do you think I'm innocent, Dr Ryan? I thought the evidence against me, thanks mostly to the scientists like yourself I understand, was overwhelming. You don't even need my confession. So what is it that has you convinced of my innocence? Women's intuition?'

Sam found herself really not liking Graham Ward. But then, she considered, these were very trying circumstances. Besides, what did it matter if she liked him or not? The truth was still the truth. She chose not to rise to Ward's challenge but instead launched in with the first question.

'Were you ever a Boy Scout?'

Ward leant back in his seat and eyed her, unsure if she was being serious or not. He decided to compromise. 'No, but I've had a few Girl Guides in my time.' He was being facetious and defensive but Sam ploughed on.

'What about sailing? Ever sailed?'

Ward and Appleyard glanced at each other before they looked at Meadows, remembering his question from earlier. Ward smiled at Meadows. 'Hello, sailor?'

Sam felt her anger rising. 'It's a serious question, Graham, just answer it.'

He stared at Sam for a moment before dipping into the packet Meadows had given him and lighting up another cigarette.

'No, I've never been sailing. Hate boats, can't swim. Any more stupid questions, or shall I get DI Meadows to finish the interview off?'

Sam decided she should explain before the whole undertaking was thwarted by frayed tempers.

'Whoever tied Sophie Clarke to the bed knew about knots. The one he used was a round turn and two half hitches. Sailors use it almost exclusively. You would have to learn how to tie one, it isn't a knot which a person without the detailed knowledge would use.'

As Appleyard's eyes widened Ward drew again on his cigarette before replying. He knew now she wasn't playing games, and for the first time since he had been arrested he felt a sense of hope. 'Sorry.'

Sam took her opportunity. 'Were you having an affair with Mrs Clarke?'

'No.'

He was lying, Sam was sure, but how to convince him to tell the truth was another matter. 'I understand that John Clarke is paying for your defence?'

Ward looked at Appleyard, who shrugged in an attempt to proclaim his innocence.

'What if he is?'

'It's a very generous gesture to make.'

Ward looked up and blew a cloud of smoke high towards the already nicotine-stained ceiling. 'Yes, I suppose so. He's a generous man.'

'So you wouldn't want to do anything to upset him. Like admit to an affair with his wife?'

Ward thought for a moment. 'No, but then as I wasn't, it's not an issue, is it?'

Sam sat back and thought for a moment. 'It's not going to be enough, Graham.'

He looked at her. 'What isn't?'

'The small matter of the knots. You're facing the rest of your life behind bars. That would be a daunting enough thought for anyone. For an intelligent man like you, it will be a living hell.'

Sam could see by his face that she had got through to him. There was a difference between a police officer making the comment and an independent outsider. The police have to say it; it's in their armoury of interview techniques. If, however, someone else says it, someone with nothing to gain, then it has more of a tendency to hit home.

Ward looked at Appleyard, who remained impassive. He turned back to Sam. 'Is there really no other way?'

Sam shook her head and pressed home at his uncertainty. 'No, I don't think so. Were you having an affair with her?'

He drew in another lungful of smoke. 'This will hurt John. Is there any way of avoiding that? It's just that he's always been a good friend.'

Sam looked at Meadows, who shook his head deliberately. 'If it forms part of your defence he's bound to find out. Sorry.'

Ward sat back in his chair searching for inspiration, a way out of his predicament. He knew there wasn't one. If admitting to the affair was going to help his chances, then given the choice between hurting a friend and doing a life sentence he'd have to choose the former. He looked back towards Sam. 'OK, yes. I was having an affair with Sophie.'

Sam sat back. She wanted to smile. It felt a little like a victory but sadly it was a hollow one.

Sharman decided to call Sid Booth in the local intelligence

office this time, using an assumed name, rather than meet at yet another bloody funeral. He gave him the name and other details that had been lifted from the back of the watch they had found at the scene, and asked him to check them out. There was always a chance of finding out where something came from when it could be identified. Not always a great chance, but at least a chance. Sid agreed to do the work happily as long as there was a 'drink' in it, as Sid always liked to call a bribe. Sharman agreed willingly, as long as it wasn't a large one. Nothing came free any more. Not even from friends and colleagues. Whatever happened to loyalty and commitment, he wondered.

Much to Sharman's surprise, Sid came back in less than two hours with a reply. He called him at home from a paybox. Sid Booth was never one for taking chances.

'I've got a lead on that inscription you gave me.'

There was a pause as if he was waiting for Sharman to jump up and down and scream thank you down the phone. He didn't, this was just business.

'It came from a job in King's Lynn. Nasty one too, a man died.'

Sharman began to get excited. 'Go on, Sid, don't keep me in bloody suspense.'

'It was a burglary in a little village called Bridgford that went wrong. The owner came down in the middle of the night and caught whoever was it doing his drawers. He had a go and got beaten up with his own poker for his trouble. Died a couple of days later.'

'Did they get anyone in for it?'

There was a pause as Booth read the information sheet in front of him. 'No, but they had an idea who'd done it.'

'Who?'

There was another pause as Booth turned the page. 'A traveller named Alex Johnson, otherwise known as Spade. Nasty bastard, got form for just about everything, but mostly violence.'

Sharman could feel himself chafing at the bit. 'I'll come around and get his sheets.'

Booth gave a short laugh. 'No you bloody well won't. I'll meet you in Tesco's car park in thirty minutes and you'd better have a big drink for me.' By which, Sharman knew, he meant a hundred pounds.

'I'll be there, Sid, just make sure you are.'

As Sharman was about to put the phone down Booth shouted to him he hadn't quite finished. 'The DS dealing with it is Bill Flemming. He might be worth talking to. Have you still got the watch?'

Sharman lied, 'No, it got destroyed when we were checking the engraving.' With that he put the phone down and made for his car. He wanted Booth's information urgently.

After everyone had taken a few moments to take in what had just been said Sam continued, 'Why have you never told anyone before?'

Meadows eyed him suspiciously as Sam asked the question.

'Wanted to protect her memory and John's reputation. He's just become a cabinet minister.'

Sam nodded. 'I know. Surely his reputation isn't worth your life? It's not as if it was his fault.'

Ward smiled as he lit up his third cigarette. 'Public don't quite see it like that. Older man, young wife making a fool of him behind his back. "No fool like an old fool." You know what they are going to say. John's worth more than that.'

Sam sympathized but wasn't satisfied. 'Then why have the affair in the first place?'

He shrugged. 'Attracted to each other. It was no big deal. We weren't going to run off together. Just seemed right at the time and we were very careful. It wouldn't have lasted that much longer.'

'When was the last time you saw her?'

He hesitated for a moment looking at Appleyard for permission to speak then, looking back, made his own mind up. 'The night she was murdered.'

Meadows shifted awkwardly in his seat, it was all becoming very difficult. Sam continued, 'Why then?'

'John was at some party at the Commons. It was Roger's – the handyman's – night off, I think he was in London, so we had the place to ourselves. It was nice.'

Meadows suddenly cut in, feeling a little left out and unhappy at the way things were going. 'Did you tie her up before sex?'

Ward glared at him. 'If you interrupt again I'll walk out.'

Sam turned and put her hand up to silence Meadows before he ruined everything. She returned to Ward, who still looked annoyed by Meadows' interruption.

'Did you have sex?'

He nodded before looking past Sam to Meadows. 'And it was good old one-to-one stuff, no extras.'

Meadows looked at him impassively and without further comment.

'Did you come inside her?'

Ward took his fourth cigarette and began to light it. Keeping his eyes fixed on the packet of cigarettes on the table, he replied, 'Yes, more than once.'

Sam knew it was a difficult question but it had to be asked.

'Wasn't that a bit dangerous?'

Ward looked at her suspiciously. 'Why should it be?'

'Didn't you practise safe sex?'

'She was on the pill, and neither of us seriously felt we posed a threat to each other. Besides it's nicer without.'

'I thought Mr Clarke was hoping for children?'

Ward shrugged. 'He was. She wanted to have his children, just not quite so soon. Like I said, it wasn't a long-term thing.'

'What time did you leave her?'

'About midnight.'

'What was she like when you left her?'

He thought about the question for a moment as if remembering what it had been like.

'She was fine. Bit nervous, but happy enough.'

'Was the handyman back?'

He thought about it again. 'Don't know, didn't see him. Can't remember any lights.'

Sam continued. 'Was she dressed?'

Ward shook his head. 'No, she was wearing a silk pyjama top . . .' He paused for a few minutes, his mind once again wandering back to the night in question, his face softening with the memory. 'She looked wonderful.'

Sam waited, thinking what to ask next. 'Are you sure there was no one else around when you left the house?'

He shook his head slowly his mind scanning around what he had seen that night, like a video camera in slow motion searching through time for the right picture. There was nothing. He shook his head firmly. 'There was nothing and nobody.' Then, as if something had just occurred to him, 'There was one thing . . .'

Sam jumped in quickly. 'What?'

Ward paused, unsure of his ground and wondering whether it was worth saying anything. 'Something was bothering her, bothering her a lot.'

'Like what?'

He shrugged. 'I don't know, but I got the impression she was nervous of something.'

'Her husband?'

Ward shook his head vigorously. 'No, it wasn't him. John couldn't hurt a fly. He's all mouth and trousers, if you know what I mean. No, it was something or someone else.'

Sam sighed deeply. 'But you have no idea what?'

He shrugged again. 'If I did I'd tell you.'

She knew he was telling the truth. She also wondered what it was. Perhaps her trip to see Andy Herman, her psychiatrist, would reveal something later in the week. At least now she could explain finding the DNA in her system. Now all she had to do was prove it was consensual and that Ward was telling the complete truth.

If the journey to Lincoln had been bad the trip back was

worse. Sam picked up a magazine from the paper shop so the conversation was likely to be even more limited than it was before. She'd even asked him to take the sealed plastic cover off it. Allergic to plastic or some such nonsense. Meadows, however, was relieved at the silence. He didn't need anything to occupy him, he already had enough to worry about. He felt as if he was caught between two worlds. The information Ward had given Sam was interesting and explained the DNA in her system, but then he could be lying. He'd had time to think it up during the long days he was spending in his cell, people, especially the Wards of this world tended to do a lot of thinking in their cells. He'd probably received some advice from the other lags too. Trouble is, it did help form his defence and he was responsible for it. What the fuck was Adams going to say? Meadows began to regret the day he'd ever listened to Sharman. He had doubts now though, serious doubts about Ward's guilt, which hadn't been there before. It wasn't just the DNA evidence, it was the information about the knots too. That's what Sharman wasn't telling him. At least he wouldn't have to go back cap in hand to that bastard to get any more information and he was grateful for that.

Sam's voice suddenly invaded his thoughts. 'Where were the rope and magazines found?'

Meadows looked at her, unsure whether to reply, she was after all the enemy. On the other hand she already knew enough to hang him, so what the hell. 'In his garden shed.'

Sam looked surprised. 'What, both the rope and the magazines?'

Meadows nodded and Sam persisted with her questions.

'Was the shed secure?'

Meadows shrugged, trying to remember whether it was or not, but he couldn't. 'I've no idea.'

'So anyone could have got in and planted the stuff. If it wasn't secure that is. I take it the shed wasn't broken into?'

'It wasn't.' Meadows began to wonder where all these questions were leading.

'So the stuff could have been planted there?' Sam was beginning to sound like a defence counsel.

'Could have been but it wasn't. Don't forget the prints on the bag containing the bondage books. They were definitely his.'

'Were there any prints found actually *on* the books?'

'No, he was too clever for that. He forgot the cover, though. I've seen similar things happen before.'

Sam nodded her interest. 'Have you ever read any women's magazines?'

'Do I look like the kind of man who would read them? Do me a favour,' Meadows sneered.

Sam smiled and showed him the wrapper he'd taken off a copy of her favourite magazine. 'But your prints are all over this glossy cover. So you must read it.'

Meadows looked at her impressed and aghast all at the same time. If she ever wanted to leave the medical profession, he thought, she'd make a great advocate.

After three days of almost continual work Peter Hudd had finally finished. It was an unusual one in every sense. Normally he would build his reconstruction around the original head, but without the opportunity to do that, he had to do it from memory and feel. As the bust began to materialize, he would stop occasionally and feel the clay beneath his fingers, trying to imagine her skull and the way it felt. The only major problem he really had was Fiona. First she came around and never stopped complaining, then she stopped coming around and just made silly little phone calls telling him who she was with and what they might do later. It was all bollocks, he knew her far too well for that. She liked to talk the talk, but couldn't walk the walk. He let her have her bit of fun, however, and pretended to be annoyed or jealous. It seemed to satisfy her.

He was surprised how much time and energy he had put into getting the bust completed. Hardly stopping to eat or sleep, he just kept on working determined to get it finished and see what the girl at the mortuary really looked like. At first he thought it was about coming in on time for Dr Ryan, she had seemed so keen about it, but then as time went on and he became more obsessed with his work he realized he was really doing it for himself. Perhaps Fiona had sensed that. She could be a little volatile at times, but her behaviour at the moment was very uncharacteristic. She was normally so laid back. Perhaps, he considered, she had become jealous of his relationship with the unknown girl. He'd never really looked at another woman since he'd been with her. But now there was another woman in his life – well, part of one anyway – and she was taking all the attention away from Fiona. He didn't want to lose her, however, so he decided to make it up to her later. With the bust finished he would have more time for her and his new mistress would be banished back to Dr Ryan's mortuary to see out her days until they discovered who she was.

A few more strokes with the knife and she was finished. Hudd stood back and admired his work. He walked around the bust, tidying it up here and there, trying to get this right or that in proportion. He wanted Dr Ryan to be pleased with what he had done. More than anything, however, he wanted to be pleased with what he had done. The trouble was, the more he looked at it the more dissatisfied he became. There was something missing, he wasn't sure what, but like the stories of Winnie the Pooh, the more he looked the more it wasn't there. Still, he was sure it was a good likeness and that it would at least help identify the poor girl. She really had been a looker. What a waste. He knew that there were certain things that not even his genius could achieve and he wondered about her. What colour were her eyes, how long and thick was her hair, what was her smile like?

He began to wonder about her personality too. Was she a happy, easygoing person? Who did she love and who loved her? She was a similar age to him too. Could he have loved her in life? He had no doubt he could. But could she have loved him? Most women did, it was the artist in him, he knew that. Well, that and his boyish good looks of course. As bizarre as he knew it was, Fiona had been right. He was falling in love with this girl, this dead girl. Like a man possessed by a picture he was in love with an image and he couldn't get it out of his head. Before covering it with a damp cloth he picked up his camera and photographed the head from every angle he could think of. If the head did eventually have to go to Dr Ryan at least he would have a record of it. He might even make another based on the pictures. But then he'd only have the same problem. How did art capture the essence of a person? Within that answer he considered, was the difference between the average and the genius. Finally, satisfied that he had all the pictures he wanted, he picked up a damp cloth and threw it over the bust, before walking downstairs to call Sam from the staircase phone.

Meadows dropped Sam back at her cottage. As they pulled into the drive they noticed Sharman's old Ford parked by the door. Meadows looked across to it then back to Sam.

'Want me to come in? Make sure Sharman behaves himself?'

Sam stared into his car through the back window. It was his car all right but there was no sign of him, and she wondered where he was. She looked across to Meadows. 'No, it's OK, I'm more than capable of handling the Stan Sharmans of this world.'

Meadows nodded. 'Well, if you're sure.' He was secretly pleased about Sam's decision. The last thing he wanted right now was to confront Sharman.

'I am. Thanks for today. Hope it wasn't all too much for you. I know you took a risk.'

He smiled at her. It was the first time Sam could ever remember Meadows smiling at her. 'You have certainly given me a few things to think about, Dr Ryan. Things seemed so much simpler before.'

Almost a compliment, Sam considered. 'Going to tell Adams?'

Meadows nodded. 'Have to. I'll just mull it over for a while first. Make sure I tell him in the right way. If you know what I mean?'

Sam did. 'Good luck.'

He nodded his thanks as he stepped out of the car and made her way to the front door. Waiting until she was safely inside, Meadows finally drove away.

Once inside, Sam fed Shaw before he bit her foot off and then made her way into the back garden to find Sharman. He was sitting at the top of the garden on her favourite wooden bench looking out over the fields. He heard her coming. 'I do love your house, wonderful views over the fields.'

Sam sat next to him. 'Thank you, I love the view too. One of the reasons I bought it.'

Small-talk finished, Sharman came to the point.

'How did it go? Meadows behave himself, did he?'

'Impeccably, and it went very well.'

Sharman looked towards her slowly. 'So what did you find out? You're looking pretty smug?'

Sam was smug but she was alarmed that it showed. She tried to control her emotions. 'Ward admitted he was having an affair with Sophie Clarke, and that he slept with her on the night she was murdered.'

Sharman looked back across the fields.

'Was he? I half-guessed that. Doesn't mean he didn't kill her, though, does it?'

Sam agreed, with some reservations. 'No, it doesn't, but it explains why we found his DNA inside her. I'm sure he's innocent.'

Sharman grunted. 'Me too, but we're not the ones who need to be convinced, are we?'

'He doesn't sail either, and he was never a Boy Scout.'

Sharman nodded. 'I know that.' Sam looked at him quizzically. 'Meadows told me. Anything else?'

'I think I persuaded Meadows that the rope and magazines could have been planted in Ward's shed.' Sharman nodded, content. 'And there is something else, which I didn't tell Meadows.'

Sharman returned his gaze from the fields and turned it towards her. 'What?'

'I suddenly realized when I was talking to Ward why the ends of all the cigarettes we found at the scene had been pulled off.'

Sharman didn't reply, just waited impatiently for Sam to tell him.

'He didn't want his DNA picked up from the tips, so he took them with him. Especially as his DNA would be different from the stuff we found inside Sophie's body, which would have alerted us to the involvement of another person.'

Sharman looked at her for a moment then leaned across and kissed her on the cheek. Sam was surprised and flattered and found herself blushing slightly.

'Did you discover anything?' she asked, trying to cover her confusion.

'Only that the watch was stolen by a man called Spade, who is now wanted in connection with a murder regarding its theft.'

Sam's eyes widened. 'Christ. Nothing's straightforward with this one, is it? Any chance of finding this Spade character?'

'I've put a few feelers out, might get a result. Trouble is it all happened just outside King's Lynn, bit off my patch.'

Sam was increasingly intrigued. 'Since when's force boundaries bothered you?' Anyway, what kind of feelers?'

Sharman was coy. 'I know a few travellers who owe me a few favours. We'll see.'

He seemed to know lots of people who owed him a few favours. Sam often wondered if he was exaggerating. But he probably wasn't.

'Anything else?'

'Isn't that enough? Oh yes, there is one more thing. I had to pay two hundred quid for that information. If this really is fifty-fifty, you owe me a ton.'

'Fine, got a receipt?'

Sharman scowled at her. 'Just joking.'

As they sat, lost in thought, the phone suddenly burst into life. Sam marched quickly down the path to the kitchen and picked it up. It was Hudd. When she'd finished talking to him she marched back up the path to Sharman.

'It was Peter Hudd. The bust's finished. Want to come with me to have a look?'

With traffic as bad as ever in Cambridge it took Sharman and Sam just over an hour to reach Trinity. Sam still had a good relationship with the head porter and he gave her permission to park the car in New Court. As they made their way towards 'I' staircase a voice suddenly called to them from the other side of the court.

'Hey, hang on. I'll come up with you.'

The two companions turned to see Peter Hudd running towards them, a sandwich in his hand.

'Sorry I wasn't here, I went to get a bite to eat. Well, do you want to see it?'

Sharman remained indifferent while Sam nodded almost excitedly. 'Thanks for doing it so quickly. Are you happy with it?'

Hudd began to lead the way up the staircase. 'Delighted. It's one of my best works, I think.'

Sharman cut in. 'Congratulations, but does it look like her?'

Hudd reached the door and pushed his key in. 'This is not an exact science, of course, but I think so.'

Opening the door he stepped inside. As he entered, a gasp, followed by a scream, emanated dramatically from his throat. 'Who the fuck has done this?'

Sharman and Sam pushed past him into the room. As they did they saw the reason for his distress. Lying on its side, the face cut to pieces with a clay knife, was the bust, not enough of it left to be of any use for recognition.

As Sharman watched, clearly annoyed by events, Sam knelt down by the side of the distressed Hudd.

'Any idea who might have done this?' She could see he was almost in tears.

He shook his head. 'No, none.'

'Was your room locked when you went out?'

He nodded. 'You saw me unlock it when I came back.'

'Who else has got a key?'

Hudd shook his head again, his hands picking up fragments of clay, pulling them through his fingers before dropping them back on the floor again.

'No one. No one at all.'

'What about Fiona?'

Hudd stood, pulling up his stand and trying to get the remnants of the head back on to it. Sam helped.

'She wouldn't do this. I know she can be a bit of a flake, but she's not malicious. Besides, she hasn't got a key.'

'Are you sure? Is it possible you've lent her one in the past and she hasn't returned it?'

'Yes, I'm sure. Look, I have a lot of nude models up here. I didn't want Fiona getting the wrong idea.'

Or the right one, Sam thought cynically.

Sharman started to walk around the room. 'Anything else gone?'

Hudd looked around. 'Nothing obvious.' He stepped across to a large easy chair at the far side of the room and removed a red pillow, which had been sitting in the corner of the chair. Beneath it was a good-quality camera with what appeared to be a state-of-the-art lens attached 'The camera's still here, that's good.' He looked at Sam. 'I took some pictures of the bust before I covered it up. They should still be in here.'

Sam pulled the camera off him almost instinctively, fearful of losing its valuable contents. 'I'll get them developed, is that all right?'

Hudd nodded. He could do little else as Sam was

determined to keep the camera and its film.

Sharman stared around the room again. 'Are you sure nothing has gone?'

Hudd followed his gaze. 'Positive.'

'Then whoever it was came in here just to destroy the statue and for nothing else. Looks like someone's on to us. We need to find out who.'

Hudd looked a little disturbed by Sharman's rather blunt information. 'I'm not in danger, am I?'

'Not any more. Whoever it was has done what they came to do. It's a good job you weren't here, though, they might well have done you too.'

Hudd sat down suddenly as the full realization of the possible consequences of this incident dawned upon him and turned his legs to jelly.

Sharman continued, 'Good job he didn't know about the photos or he might have hung about. Then we'd have been scraping you off the floor with the clay.'

Seeing Hudd's increasing distress Sam turned on Sharman. 'That's enough, Stan, give him a break. He's done us a favour, remember?'

Sharman put his hands up and relented.

Sam crossed the room and sat next to Hudd. 'Listen, take no notice of the big black monster over there, you're in no danger at all. If whoever it is is after anyone, then it's me and Stan and let's hope he gets Stan first.' Sharman grinned at her. 'By failing to achieve what he came to do he might also have given himself away so I doubt he will be back. Let's get these photographs developed and see how they have come out. Perhaps we can make some progress in identifying the girl and then we will be closer to identifying her killer too.'

Hudd looked across at her. 'Would it be all right for me to have a set?'

Sam nodded. 'Not a problem.'

Hudd hadn't finished. 'If you do find out who she is and there are pictures, I'd like to come with you to see them.'

Sam saw Sharman shaking his head wildly out of the

corner of her eye but ignored him. 'Of course you can. Let's hope it's sooner rather than later.'

As they drove slowly over Trinity Bridge towards the Backs, Sam looked to her left and the wonderful view of St John's College. From this angle Sam had often thought it was the most beautiful college in Cambridge. No wonder Hitler wanted to use it as his headquarters after the invasion of England. But then, she thought, most of the Cambridge colleges had at least some small part which could not be described without the use of superlatives. All were beautiful and evocative in their own way. As she continued to admire John's through the tree-lined lane, Sharman's penetrating voice cut short her thoughts.

'Did you believe him?'

Sam looked across at him, puzzled for a moment as to who he was talking about. Then, as she focused her mind, she realized.

'Yes, I believed him. Why shouldn't I?'

Sharman was clearly less certain. 'Just seems odd. Who the hell would know that he was doing the bust for us, and have the knowledge and determination to break into his room and destroy it? Even then they must have known it was only going to slow us down?'

'Who knows? But I don't think Hudd had anything to do with it, otherwise why take the photographs – it's really all we need?'

Sharman nodded, still unsure. 'I suppose so. Still doesn't sit right, though.'

As they made their way slowly to the Park, Sharman suddenly took a different turn to the one Sam expected and headed away from the hospital. She turned to him, confused. 'Where are we going?'

Sharman replied without turning, 'My flat.'

'Might I ask why?' Sam hoped she didn't sound as alarmed as she felt.

'Don't worry, doctor, I know my place, you'll be quite safe.'

Sam tried to look indignant. 'That's not what I meant!'

'Oh, yes, it bloody well was. The reason you're going to my flat is so I can show you something that might be of interest. I wanted your view.'

She nodded but Sharman could sense she was still unsettled.

'Believe me, Sam, considering your background and where you live, I'm only taking you back to my place because I think it's important. I wouldn't otherwise leave myself open to this close scrutiny knowing I will be found wanting.'

The reply made Sam feel ashamed. 'OK, let's see what you've got.'

The trip to Sharman's flat took less than ten minutes. The contrast between the opulence of the colleges and the rather dreary council estate she now found herself in was marked. Parts were still pleasant enough, but though there were pockets where the residents had clearly made an effort to make the place look as decent as possible, no matter how hard they tried they could not entirely rid the area of an overriding sense of environmental decay which seemed to hang everywhere.

Sharman's flat was on the third floor of a block of flats called Martin Luther King Towers. It was in one of the better residential areas of the estate and was guarded by a twenty-four-hour security guard and a host of video cameras. The flat was smarter and more interesting than Sam had expected. Sam judged most policemen to be monotonous and lacking in any imagination or appeal, and assumed that their homes, like their lives, would be the same. Sharman's wasn't. The flat was light and airy, with coordinated paper, carpets and curtains. There was modern art on the walls, interesting pieces of glassware and porcelain on the shelves and over a dozen cookbooks in the kitchen. By far the most interesting items, however, were the dozens of small and large painted soldiers which were arranged in regiments all around the flat. There were also numerous cups and plaques commemorating different painting competitions from Britain and almost every country around Europe. Sharman walked into the kitchen and put on the kettle. 'Coffee?'

Sam looked up. 'Please!' She decided to be mischievous. 'I didn't know you played with soldiers, Stan. You seem a bit old for that?'

Sharman walked back into the room. 'I don't *play* with them, I leave that to the wargamers. I paint them. I find it calms me down. Relaxes my mind.'

He walked across to the bookshelves where many of them were situated and picked up a particularly attractive cavalry officer. He handed it to Sam.

'He's quite beautiful, no wonder you win so many cups.'

'Seventeenth Lancers, 1854. Charge of the Light Brigade. One of the greatest military disasters suffered by a British cavalry regiment, yet the most glorious and remembered.'

'Half a league, half a league, half a league onward, into the valley of death rode the six hundred.'

'Tennyson?'

Sam was impressed. 'See, you do know some poetry.'

Sharman began to walk back to the kitchen. 'Only if it's war poetry!'

'Some of the world's most powerful poetry comes out of the horrors of war.'

Sharman re-emerged from the kitchen with two piping hot mugs of coffee in his hand. 'Here, dead we lie, because we choose not to live and shame the land from which we sprang.'

He handed Sam her mug while she tried to remember the author of the words. Finally she gave up. Sharman was secretly pleased that he'd managed to catch her out at last.

'Thought you would have known that one, Sam. A. E. Housman, an old Trinity man.'

She smiled at him. OK, so he had one up on her, but she was impressed enough to be pleased. She sipped at her coffee mug.

'As I presume it wasn't just your soldiers you brought

me here to see, what is it you want to show me?'

Sharman walked across to the video recorder and pushed in the tape he had stolen from Rogers' house.

'Thought you ought to see this. It's not very nice, I would brace myself if I were you.'

As Sam watched, the worst pictures of rape, sodomy, torture and finally death appeared before her eyes. So gross and awful did she find it that she had to look away and ask Sharman to turn his machine off.

'Was that real?'

'I'm afraid so. The videos are coming out of Eastern Europe. Vice thinks they were made in Bosnia during the war. Plenty of captured women, no one to stop the excesses.'

'What about the UN?'

Sharman shook his head. 'Don't make me laugh.'

'How many of these things are there?'

'Thousands, involving hundreds of women. Someone's making a fortune out of this.'

Sam took a large mouthful of her now cold coffee. 'Where did you find this one?'

Sharman stood and picked up Sam's mug, intending to make her another. 'The Clarkes' handyman. He had them at his flat. I only managed to steal one, but there were plenty of others.'

Sam called through to the kitchen, 'Where's he getting them from?'

Sharman shouted back, 'Not sure yet, need to pay him another visit. I'm sure he'll cooperate if I ask him nicely.'

Sam knew exactly what 'asking someone nicely' in Sharman's terms meant, but she didn't protest. If anyone deserved a kicking then it was Rogers. She couldn't remember being so horrified by something in her life, and people were making money out of it. What the hell was happening to the human race? Sharman re-emerged with two refreshed and steaming mugs of coffee.

'Are you OK?'

Sam nodded, but she wasn't, she was deeply shocked

and horrified by what he had shown her. As she took the mug from Sharman's hand there was a knock on the door. Sharman answered it. A young and attractive girl strode into the room and looked menacingly down at Sam. 'Who the fuck's this, another of your tarts?'

She glared up at Sharman. Sam felt taken aback and confused whilst Sharman seemed amused by it all.

'Kate I'd like you to meet Dr Ryan, who I've told you about. Sam, this is my friend, Kate.'

Sam stood and put out her hand. 'Pleased to meet you, Kate. I think.'

Kate began to blush. She put out her hand and took Sam's.

'Sorry, Dr Ryan, I just thought, well you know what I just thought. Sorry.'

Sam put her coffee down on the table and turned to the still smirking Sharman. 'I'll leave you two alone, then. Let me know when you've seen Rogers and what the outcome is, won't you?'

Sharman nodded. 'Will do, sorry about Kate, she can be a little volatile and forthright at times.'

Sam looked at the still embarrassed girl. 'Being with you she'd have to be.'

Sharman had to wait for just over half an hour before Rogers finally returned to his flat. He had parked his car at the far end of the avenue so he had a clear view of the house without its occupants being able to see him. After Rogers had got home, he waited for a few moments to let him settle down, before pulling on to the drive and parking behind his Range Rover. Stepping out of his car he walked across to the half-open door and knocked. Rogers was at the door almost at once, glaring angrily at him.

'I wondered if you'd come back. You're no fucking journalist, I rang the paper.'

Without waiting for a reply, he pulled back his fist and threw a punch towards Sharman's face. Side-stepping the punch Sharman countered with his own fist, catching Rogers just below the ribs and knocking the breath from his body. Rogers crumpled to the ground, holding his stomach to catch his breath. Sharman picked him up by the back of his jacket and dragged him across the floor into the sitting room, dumping him on the carpet before going back down the corridor to close the door.

Returning to the sitting room, Sharman found Rogers trying to pull himself to his feet by grabbing hold of the coffee table. A short kick just behind his right kidney put paid to that effort and sent Rogers crashing back to the floor holding his back and screaming in agony. As he lay there Sharman put his foot hard across the man's neck, cutting off his air supply and choking him. He left it there for a few moments pressing down hard and making it difficult for the already exhausted Rogers to breathe. Once he was satisfied that he had learned his lesson, he eased his foot back.

'I'm going to ask you a series of questions, Mr Rogers, and how hard I'm going to press my foot down on your throat depends entirely on your answer. Do you understand?'

Sharman increased the pressure on Rogers' neck. Still choking, Rogers tried futilely to push Sharman's foot away. Finally, conceding defeat, he indicated his acceptance. Sharman smiled down menacingly at him.

'Where did you get the tapes?'

'What tapes?'

Sharman increased the pressure on Rogers' neck before waving the tape he had stolen in front of his face. 'Shall we try again?'

Rogers looked desperate. 'The Internet.'

'Wrong answer.'

He pressed down hard again. Rogers answered again choking as he did,

'I did, I'll give you the Web page address, you'll be able to see for yourself.'

Sharman eased his foot off slightly. 'How many of the tapes have you got?'

'Six, they're all over there, look, take them. I didn't realize what I was getting. I thought they were a bit strong, too, I never watched them all.'

Sharman looked across the room and saw them propped up against the video machine. 'Are you sure that's all of them?'

He pressed down gently again, just to remind Rogers who was in charge.

'Yes, yes. Look that's the lot. Who the fuck are you, anyway?'

Although Sharman ignored the question he was satisfied with Rogers' reply. Taking his foot off Rogers' neck he crossed the room and picked up the tapes. As he did, he ran his hand instinctively under the cabinet the TV and video sat on. Sure enough there was a concealed tape. He pulled it out and looked at it. Despite the pain he was in Rogers was watching him closely, a tenseness in his body.

'Leave that one, that's not one of them.'

Sharman put it with the rest.

'If it's not, then you won't mind me watching it, will you?'

Once he was satisfied he had all the tapes, he ripped a sheet of paper from his pocket book, pulled a pen from his top pocket and threw them on the floor next to Rogers. 'Write down the address I need.'

Rogers complied at once. Handing the note back to Sharman he collapsed back on to the floor. Sharman leaned over him.

'If anything in this note is wrong, I'll be back. Understand?'

Rogers nodded.

'Good. So I won't be seeing you again then, will I?'

Rogers shook his head. With that Sharman turned his back on the prostrate figure on the floor and left.

When Sharman returned home he decided to view the tapes at once. The sooner he'd seen them and made sure there was nothing of particular interest on them he could hand them over to Panna in Vice, with Rogers' name and address, and leave it with him to do the rest. He hoped Rogers went down for years. He was supposed to be seeing Kate that night but called her on her mobile and put her off. She wasn't happy about the decision, but was prepared to live with it. It was Sharman's unpredictability that she liked most, so she could hardly complain now. He made himself a coffee and slotted in the first tape. It was much the same as the rest. Young girls being attacked, raped, tortured and then killed in various ways. The tapes reminded Sharman of the *Friday the Thirteenth* films, only this horror was real. By the time he had reached the fourth tape he was feeling nauseated by it all. He stood up to switch the machine off, accepting that the rest of the tapes would be much the same, but he was suddenly and unexpectedly rooted to the spot. As this tape finished, instead of the black fuzziness that usually followed the video began to show pictures of the late Sophie Clarke. They were clearly photographed in secret from behind bushes and walls. Some showed her in her bikini swimming in the pool or just sunning herself in a deck chair. Others had her walking around the garden with her husband or Ward or just gardening on her own. The ones that were of most interest to Sharman, however, were shots clearly taken from the top of a tree outside her bedroom window. The video first showed her undressing – she really was very beautiful, Sharman considered and then a man entered the room. He recognized him at once, it was Ward. The couple began to make love, and continued until the tape ended about fifteen minutes later. Their love making although gentle was passionate and Sharman, much to his surprise and self-disgust, found himself becoming aroused by its contents. He raced through the other tapes to see if there was anything else, but he was disappointed. The key to this entire case was clearly held by Rogers. He would have to go back and see him and quickly. This time he would have to jog his memory a little harder.

After dropping six of the videos off at Vice with a covering note for Panna, he took the one with Sophie Clarke's pictures on around to Sam's, calling first to make sure she was in. Much to his surprise she'd invited him around for dinner. Although this would delay his confrontation with Rogers, and interview he was keen to conclude, it seemed much too good an opportunity to miss. Besides it was an excellent chance to show her what he had discovered, and talk it through with her before returning to Rogers' house to beat the truth out of him. The security light flashed on and Sam's cat raced out of the shadows into a clump of bushes on the far side of the drive as he parked. He tried to call Shaw across but, like his owner, he was an independent cat with his own ideas and he ignored Sharman.

Sam appeared at the door before Sharman had time to knock. He smiled warmly at her before presenting her with a bottle of wine, a video and a carefully wrapped surprise gift.

'What's this? There really was no need.' She was pleased and had to resist the temptation to kiss him on the cheek. 'Come in, but don't think for one moment that I can be easily impressed by gifts.'

Sharman smiled as he crossed the threshold. 'Perish the thought.'

Sam had prepared carefully. From the amount of cookbooks on Sharman's shelves she assumed that he enjoyed cooking good food for himself so she didn't want to be found wanting, especially by a man. Sharman ate it all, and seemed genuinely appreciative, and they had a pleasant evening. At the end of it he picked up the video he had given Sam and pushed it into the video machine. He then sat back down on the sofa next to her.

'This isn't another of those snuff movies, is it, Stan? I couldn't stand to see another one of those.'

Sharman shook his head. 'Just watch.'

Sam concentrated as the video flashed on. She was genuinely shocked as the pictures of Sophie Clarke suddenly emerged. She was even more dumbfounded when she saw the shots of her making love to Ward. 'Where did you get this?'

'Rogers' place. It was hidden under the television.'

'What did he say when you found it?'

'He was a bit nervous, but nothing really. I think he had something wrong with his throat.'

'So you'll be paying him another visit?'

Sharman smiled and nodded. 'First thing in the morning. There's as much on him now as there is on Ward.'

'That should put the cat amongst the pigeons, then.'

Before Sharman could say more there was a loud rap on the front door. She was surprised and glanced at her watch. It had just gone midnight. Who the hell could that be? Standing up, she made her way to the door and opened it. Much to her surprise, standing in front of her were Adams, Meadows and at least half a dozen uniformed officers. Adams spoke first. 'Good evening, Dr Ryan. Is Stan Sharman here?'

Before Sam realized, Sharman was by her side. 'I'm here, what's the problem?'

Adams looked him straight in the face. 'Stanley Sharman, I am arresting you for the murder of Michael John Rogers. You do not have to say anything . . .'

Sam looked first at Sharman then back at Adams in shock. This was ridiculous – there had to be some kind of mistake. But there wasn't. Adams stepped into the hall and took hold of Sharman's arm. Sharman pulled away and the police officers outside moved quickly towards him. Sam held on gently to his other arm.

'It's OK, Stan, we'll sort it out.'

Sharman looked at her and in that moment all the anger seemed to leave him. He put out his hands and Meadows, not wishing to take chances, handcuffed him quickly before leading him out to the awaiting van. As they left Adams turned to her. 'I'll want a word with you later.'

Sam wanted to come back at him, but this didn't seem

the time or the place and she was unnerved by the turn of events so she let it go. Wandering back into the sitting room, her mind racing with thoughts of what had just happened, she saw the present Sharman had brought her still sitting on the table unopened. She picked it up and carefully unwrapped it. It was the Lancer she had admired on his shelf.

CHAPTER SEVEN

Sam knew there was nothing further she could do that evening, so after tidying up she decided to go to bed. It was a mistake and sleep was impossible. Sharman's arrest and the events surrounding it just kept playing itself over in her mind. Finally, tired of looking at the ceiling of her own bedroom through the light of the moon which had risen high above her cottage, she dragged herself out of bed. As she passed through the sitting room on her way to the kitchen she glanced at the wall clock. It was three thirty, almost too late to go back to bed. She made herself a coffee and let a surprised Shaw back into the cottage early. Slowly making her way back into the sitting room she slumped herself down on to the settee and tried to relax. It was impossible. Finally running out of ideas she dressed and made her way into the greenhouse to pot up some late plants. She knew it was the only thing that was guaranteed to make the time pass quickly and relax her at the same time.

Sam arrived at the Park early, but still not early enough to beat Fred there. He was sitting in his small room at the back of the mortuary, sipping from a mug of tea and listening to the radio. Sam knocked.

'Morning, Fred. There isn't another one in the pot, is there?'

Surprised by her voice, Fred jumped up, spilling the tea

across his lap. Brushing it off quickly before he scalded himself he looked up at Sam.

'Dr Ryan, didn't expect to see you here this early.'

Sam grabbed a cloth from the kitchen sink and wiped his trousers down quickly. 'Sorry, Fred, that was stupid. Are you OK?'

Fred nodded unconvincingly, 'I'll be OK, Dr Ryan, please don't worry.'

Sam pushed Fred back on to his seat. 'I'll make the tea, you sit down.'

Sam poured two more mugs. It was a bit stewed but she'd drunk worse and she knew Fred liked his tea strong. She passed Fred's over to him. 'Send me the cleaning bill.'

Fred shook his head. 'Not necessary, Dr Ryan, they're only my old work ones. They've already got a few dodgy stains on them.'

Sam looked at the work board. 'Much on today?'

Fred nodded enthusiastically.

'That murder in Grantchester, it was the same place as Sophie Clarke was killed. They've got Stan Sharman in for it. Who'd have believed it?'

Sam winced. 'I know, he was at my house having dinner when they came to get him.'

This time Fred winced, 'Sorry, Dr Ryan, I had no idea. Explains one thing though—'

Sam cut in. 'What's that?'

'Why Dr Stuart is doing the PM.'

Although Sam felt she ought to be, she wasn't surprised. 'Did he go out to the scene?'

'Special request of Superintendent Adams.'

There's a surprise, Sam thought sarcastically. 'Don't suppose he's done his initial report yet, has he, Fred?'

Fred got up and began to walk across the mortuary towards the office. 'I'll look, stay here, Doctor, no point both of us getting nicked for theft.'

Sam did as she was told and waited. Sipping at the hardly drinkable mug of tea she wondered what the implications of the last forty-eight hours were going to be.

Although it seemed to take Fred longer than she had anticipated, he was soon back in the office with Trevor Stuart's report in his hand. 'Here you go, Dr Ryan.'

She snatched it from his hand and opened it without a word of thanks, keen to examine its contents. 'I'll be as quick as I can, Fred.'

Fred crossed the room and took a large mouthful of his tea. 'Take your time, Doctor, I photostatted it all.'

Sam looked across at him, smiling broadly. She should have known.

The report was pretty standard. Mrs Waddam, who seemed to be making a career of it, discovered his body at ten past seven when she came to lock the house up for the evening. John Clarke being away in London. Her husband informed the police who arrived at blah, blah, blah. The report followed the usual formula. Cause of death was massive injuries to the head caused by an unknown blunt instrument. Stuart continued with a bit of speculation. From the oval and blunt shape of the injuries he surmised it might possibly be a baseball bat, or similar. Well, that's Stan out, Sam thought. If he'd done it he wouldn't have used a bat, he'd have used his fists. He was proud that way. She continued to read the report. There were also further defensive and superficial injuries to his hands, back, neck and legs. Stuart, rather arrogantly, Sam thought, put the time of death at approximately 3 p.m. Sure it wasn't three minutes past? Sam sarcastically wondered. The rest of the report was fairly standard. Room temperature, Colin Flannery's initial report, including a blood-splatter chart, report on the scene, photographs of the scene and body, which had come out surprisingly well on the copier. Even in black and white he was still a bit of a mess. Sam looked back at Fred. 'What time's the PM?'

'Ten.'

'Are you assisting?'

Fred nodded. 'By special request, and yes I will call you

and tell you everything there is to know when the PM's over.'

As usual Fred was way ahead of her. 'Thanks, Fred. It's just that Stan Sharman's a friend and I know he didn't bloody well do it.'

Fred put his mug down and sat next to Sam. 'Even if you weren't so sure, I'd have still given you the report.'

After Fred had brewed a second and more manageable mug of tea, Sam made her way up to Trevor Stuart's office to see if he had arrived at work yet. She was in luck. He, like Sam, had come in early to prepare for the day's work. Sam knew it had been some time since Trevor had conducted a full forensic post-mortem and she wasn't convinced that he was the best person for the job. She knocked and entered his office. Stuart was sitting at his desk poring over his notes from the previous day.

'Morning, Trevor.'

Stuart looked up, removing his glasses. 'Morning, Sam. I'm glad you're here.'

Sam crossed the room towards him. 'Saves you sending for me, Trevor. You're beginning to sound more like a headmaster than a pathologist.'

Stuart stood and walked across to the coffee maker at the far side of the office. 'And whose fault is that. Coffee?'

Sam perched herself on his rather smart settee. 'Yes, thank you. I take it you are referring to last night?'

Stuart began to pour the coffee. 'Amongst other things.' He brought the coffee across to Sam and sat beside her at the far side of the settee. 'So where do I start?'

Sam raised an eyebrow and prepared herself. 'Sorry to sound like a cliché but what about the beginning?'

'OK. What the hell was a murder suspect doing at your cottage last night?'

Annoyed by the question, Sam decided to keep her composure. 'He wasn't when he arrived, only when he left.'

Stuart wasn't keen on her attitude but let it go for the moment. 'I told you Sharman was a bad lot, I told you to keep away from him.'

'Who I do and don't associate with is hardly your concern, Trevor. You're my boss not my father.'

'And as your boss I have a duty to point out that your public persona makes your actions a matter of public interest. We have already had one incident with the papers, we don't want any more, do we?'

Sam could feel herself becoming increasingly agitated by Stuart's attitude.

'I was not responsible for the paper's smutty pictures, other than answering my own door in my own cottage. Stan Sharman has been convicted of nothing and I doubt very much he will be.'

'That's not Superintendent Adams' opinion,' Stuart cut in.

'And as we know, with the likelihood of him being the next deputy chief constable he can't possibly be wrong.'

Stuart stood and began to pace, which was always a bad sign.

'He is the senior investigating officer, his voice does have some weight.'

'Doesn't mean he's right, though, does it?'

'Doesn't mean he's wrong either.'

Sam felt the conversation was going around in circles and tried to change the subject. 'Have you managed to do the second PM on the girl yet?'

Stuart began to shuffle his feet. 'Yes.'

Sam could see by his attitude there was a problem. 'And?'

'I'm afraid I don't agree with your finding.'

She could feel herself beginning to lose it. 'What, that she was a girl or that she was murdered?'

'That she was murdered.'

Sam stood suddenly, her face reddening. 'And what do you think made the mark on her rib?'

'Rats. I don't see the difference between the mark you place so much store by and the other marks and indentations I found on the body.'

Sam picked up her bag and for a moment Stuart thought she was going to hit him with it.

'Is that your opinion, Trevor, or that of your new friend Tom Adams? You really have sold out, haven't you?'

'That was uncalled for. Look, you're supposed to be on leave. Why don't you finish it and come back next week? We can talk it through in a much calmer way.'

Sam glared at him angrily before marching towards his door. 'You don't have to worry about me coming back, Trevor, because I resign.'

With that she pulled open the door and stormed out, leaving Stuart bemused and confused.

Mr Morris Quick was known to be the best solicitor in Cambridgeshire, that's why the police used him when they were in trouble. Sam didn't need to be told that he was the first person Stan Sharman would have contacted on his arrest. Stan had a serious contempt for solicitors but had a stronger sense of self-preservation. Quick was at least responsive to Sam's request to come with him to see Sharman. Stan had already given him some information about their relationship and Sam filled in the holes. When they arrived they were shown into interview room number four, where a dishevelled Sharman stood to greet them. He looked both surprised and pleased to see Sam there.

'Sam, nice surprise.'

Sam stepped over to him and shook his hand. She wanted to give him a hug and tell him everything was going to be OK but it seemed inappropriate.

Quick looked at the formidable-looking constable standing in the corner of the room. 'I'd like some time with my client on my own.'

The constable hesitated, unsure about the request. Quick responded without hesitation.

'Don't make me ask you again, Constable, I'll be seriously upset if I have to.'

This more positive approach seemed to do the trick and

the burly young officer left them alone immediately. Quick looked across at his client.

'So, Stan, this has got a bit out of hand. What's going on?'

Sharman shrugged. 'Adams barking up the wrong tree again.'

'He doesn't think so or you wouldn't be here.'

Sharman bit his lip. He didn't like what Quick was saying but knew it was true.

Quick continued, 'Did you visit Rogers shortly before he was killed?'

'I visited him on the day, I don't know if it was shortly before.'

Quick examined his briefing sheet. 'According to Dr Stuart he was killed at approximately 3 p.m. When did you see him?'

Sharman considered the question. Although he hadn't looked at his watch at the time he was sure it was about two. 'Some time around two.'

'And how long were you with him for?'

Sharman thought seriously again. 'Half an hour max.'

'Why did you go to see him?'

Sharman looked at Sam for support. She shrugged.

'I was investigating the Clarke murder.'

Quick looked confused. 'I thought you'd been thrown off that?'

Sharman wasn't sure how much to confide in Quick. He wasn't the kind of man that anyone confided in easily. 'I was doing a bit of after hours.'

'Bit stupid. I take it this has got more to do with your feud with Adams than any particular search for justice.'

Sharman was impressed and embarrassed by his knowledge. 'Bit of both.'

'How does that work, then?'

'I get a result, he's embarrassed.'

Quick leaned back. 'Now he's got a result and you're embarrassed.'

Sharman put his hands on his head. Quick had a
horrible habit of being right.

After an hour, Quick had asked Sharman every con-
ceivable question he could think of, plus a few Sharman
couldn't. He had even persuaded Sharman to admit
beating Rogers, something Sharman thought he would
never do no matter who was asking. In fact Sharman was
so impressed by the way Quick had put him through the
wringer that he wondered how good a copper Quick
would have made. But then Quick was earning three
times his income, and didn't have to get his hands dirty to
get it. So it was clear which of them had made the best
decisions in life.

As he packed his papers away he looked across at Sam.
'Would you two like a few minutes to plan your strategy?'

Sam and Sharman nodded together as Quick clicked his
briefcase shut.

'I can only get you a couple of minutes so be quick.'

As soon as Quick had left the room Sharman began.
'Look, you're on your own now, Sam, so be bloody careful.
There are some very rough people involved in this. I'd like
to tell you to stop the investigation but as you are now my
only hope that would be difficult.'

'What do you want me to do?'

'Go and see DS Bill Flemming in King's Lynn. See what
you can find out about Spade. Try and discover where he
is. He is definitely the key to the murder of the girl.'

Sam was more concerned about Sharman's current
situation. 'What about the situation now?'

'It'll resolve itself. Beside the fact I was there shortly
before he died, they've got nothing. No forensics, no eye-
witness and they certainly aren't going to get a cough.'

Sam thought about what he'd had said for a moment.

'Then how the hell did they know you were there, and
more to the point where to find you?'

'Anonymous tip-off, apparently.'

Sam gave a false laugh. 'Another one. They must have

some serious curtain-twitchers in Grantchester, because nothing much gets past them.'

Sharman sat up and looked across at her. 'I think it's a bit more serious than curtain-twitching. Whoever it is wanted to get rid of two problems in one go. Rogers is dead and I'm in the nick. Nice work if you can get it.'

Sam nodded, exasperated with the situation. 'Are you sure you'll be all right?'

Sharman nodded. 'Yeah, I'll be fine. I just hope Adams decides to interview me. At least I'll have the satisfaction of tying him in knots. Just get yourself across to King's Lynn and find Spade.'

'Not a problem.'

The door opened and the large police officer who had previously been shown the door by Quick entered and began to escort Sharman back to his cell. As he left and made his way down the corridor he turned quickly. 'Sam, find Kate and tell her what's happened. Look after her. As soon as the pimps know I'm in here they'll go after her.'

'Leave it with me, Stan, I'll sort her out.'

Sharman gave her a grateful look before finally being pushed bodily into his cell. As Sam turned to leave she found Adams standing in front of her.

'Can I have a word, Dr Ryan?'

Although Quick offered to come with her, Sam felt more than capable of handling Adams, so she declined the offer. She followed him along the maze of corridors that made up force headquarters to his office. On reaching the office he turned to Sam.

'Coffee?'

She shook her head. 'No, thanks, I won't be staying.'

Adams didn't try to hide his contempt. 'OK. What was Sharman doing at your cottage last night?'

Sam resented the question. 'Me, if you must know.'

It wasn't true, of course, but she felt she wanted to hit back after he had hit her with the news that Rebecca was pregnant.

Adams didn't try and disguise his anger. 'You stupid bitch, well I hope he wore something because if he's not doing you then he's doing some whore.'

She was pleased, she'd clearly got through. 'I've been made to feel like a tart for years, so why not be used like one?'

Adams suddenly stepped forward and for a minute Sam thought he was going to hit her and she stepped back, putting her hands up in front of her face to protect herself. The sight of Sam cowering slowed him down and he regained his composure.

'What time did he get to your cottage?'

Sam put her arms down and glared into Adams' face. After that exhibition all she wanted to do was turn around and storm out of the room, but she decided to stay. She realized she would have to answer his questions eventually and decided now would be as good a time as any.

'What time did Sharman reach your cottage last night?'

'Some time after nine.'

'Did he seem all right?'

'He seemed fine. He didn't confess, he wasn't covered in blood, and he wasn't carrying a bag with the word swag on.'

Despite Sam's sarcasm Adams pressed on. 'Did he say anything to you at all about the day's events?'

Sam shook her head. 'Nothing.'

'So what did you talk about?'

Sam thought about the question for a minute.

'The Seventeenth Lancers and their role in the Charge of the Light Brigade.'

Adams looked at her, exasperated. 'For an intelligent woman you really can be a idiot when you want to be.'

Sam stared arrogantly at him, despising his presence in the same room. 'If you want any more information, talk to Mr Quick. I'm sure he'll be glad to help.'

'I'll need a statement.'

'You can have one. Just let me know when.'

With that Sam turned and marched out of the room without looking back despite Adams calling to her several times.

Once outside, she made her way to her car, which was parked in a small side street just behind the police station. As she approached it she was surprised to find Kate leaning against the bonnet waiting for her.

Although Sam knew she was a prostitute she could also see what Sharman saw in her. She really was very beautiful. Long natural black hair surrounded a light brown oval face and her eyes were the darkest brown Sam could ever remember seeing. With so many striking features Sam considered it gave her a real Spanish look. She was also dressed immaculately with a three-quarter-length light pink dress, wonderful Italian high-heel shoes and thick silver jewellery. The look was both expensive and classic and not at all what she expected from Kate. She also wondered how Kate recognized her car or knew where she was.

'Kate. What are you doing here?'

Kate stood, dwarfing Sam. She was very tall, and seemed to tower over her.

'Come to try and help Stan out if I can.'

Sam smiled at her, wondering how she had found out so quickly. Not even the papers had picked it up yet. 'What had you got in mind?'

Kate shrugged. 'Don't know, thought you might have a few ideas.'

'Not yet. If you contact Mr Quick he might be able to get you in to see him.'

'I don't want to go in to see him. I've seen enough of those bloody cells to last me a lifetime. I want him back out here to see me.'

Sam decided she liked Kate. 'I'm on the case right now. I don't think he'll be in there long. How did you recognize my car, by the way?'

'It was outside Stan's flat the other day.'

'So were dozens of others.'

'Yours was the only one I didn't recognize, and it was a bit posh for round there. If you know what I mean?'

'How did you know where to find me?'

Kate put a finger to her nose. 'Now that would be telling, wouldn't it?'

Sharman clearly wasn't the only policeman Kate knew. She opened the car door. 'Can I offer you a lift anywhere?'

Kate nodded. 'A decent class hotel.'

'Meeting a gentleman?'

'I hope not. With Stan inside the pimps are starting to move in. Thought I'd make myself scarce for a while. Until Stan gets out anyway.'

'And if he doesn't?'

Kate shrugged. 'New town, new life. Wait for him. I've got enough put by to survive for a while. Open a flower shop, perhaps.'

The expression 'wait for him' surprised Sam. She had thought their relationship was just based on sex and completely one-sided. She'd been wrong. She wondered if Sharman knew how Kate felt about him. If he did then he'd never said.

'Where to then?'

'Garden House Hotel, please.'

Sam nodded and after grabbing her case, which was hidden behind the car, they set off.

Kate and her relationship with Sharman fascinated Sam. She even found herself being quite jealous of her. 'How long have you and Stan been together?'

'Two years, off and on. If you know what I mean.'

'Where did you meet?'

Kate laughed. 'He nicked me when he was on Vice. We got on after that. Going out with a copper, who'd have thought it?'

Sam found herself warming to Kate. If she was honest, and she knew it was a terrible thing to think, she could never imagine liking a prostitute, but she liked Kate.

'Kate, I was wondering – just while Stan's locked up – whether you would like to come and stay with me. It will be safer than any hotel, including the Garden House, and Stan will be able to get hold of you easily.'

Kate looked surprised and pleased. She put on a refined accent. 'If you're sure, that would be lovely.'

In truth Sam was lonely and considered having Kate around for a while might be quite pleasant.

'No working from home, though.'

Kate looked annoyed by the comment but seeing the broad grin on Sam's face began to laugh.

After Sam had dropped Kate at the cottage and introduced her to Shaw, she left her to settle in while she travelled back into Cambridge to see Dr Andy Herman. Herman had based himself in offices just behind the Round Church and Cambridge Union Society building. It was a handy spot, close to the colleges with a large car park opposite. The offices were modern and plush with a clear attempt by studied use of pictures and colours to give the place a calm, soothing effect. The only thing it lacked, Sam considered, was some of that awful lift music. Entering the office, Sam was met by a pretty young woman in her mid-twenties. She looked at Sam through her clear blue eyes, smiling with such charm that Sam could see at once why Andy had employed her.

'Can I help you?'

Sam noticed a hint of an accent. Swedish, she thought. Andy really was acting out his fantasies. 'I've come to see Dr Herman. It's Dr Ryan from the Park.'

'Ah yes, he is expecting you.'

She put her finger down on a small intercom and leaning down spoke through it. As she did Sam was able to see down the front of her white lab coat. She wasn't wearing a bra. Sam wondered what else she wasn't wearing. Andy's voice came back at once. 'Send her in, please.'

The girl indicated to the door. 'Please go through.'

Sam did as she was bid and after knocking lightly on the door, entered. Herman was already on his feet making coffee. Herman liked his coffee. He would never use instant but liked to buy it off a man on the market who specialized in coffee and tea and had a wonderful international selection.

'I've got a new Cuban blend I'd rather like you to try. Grab a seat.'

Sam sat down in a comfortable armchair while Herman finished pouring the two coffees.

'Your new receptionist seems very nice. Different to Betty.'

Herman laughed. 'Just a bit. Betty was wonderful in her way, but for a private practice you need to be a little sexier, if you follow what I mean.'

Sam did. Like most men his age, he was having a mid-life crisis.

'She's Dutch.' Sam had been close. 'Picked her up from one of the language schools about a month ago. She's very good.'

'Picked up' and 'very good' seemed appropriate phrases, Sam thought.

He brought the coffees across and placed them on the table. 'So, Sam, is this a social or professional visit?'

Sam sipped at the coffee. It was very good.

'Neither. I want some information on one of your cases.'

Herman looked concerned. 'You should know better than that, Sam. Can't possibly.'

Sam shook her head. 'Don't get the wrong idea. I don't want anything too detailed, just a feel, if you know what I mean?'

Herman wasn't sure he did. 'Which patient?'

Sam braced herself. 'Sophie Clarke.'

Herman put his mug down. 'I can only tell you what I told the police. The files are confidential and I'm under an obligation not to reveal their contents. You know that, Sam.'

After another mouthful, it really was good, Sam put her mug down next to his.

'I'm not the police, Andy, and I don't want to look inside her file. Just want to ask you some basic questions to get a feel for the woman.'

Herman thought about it for a moment. 'You always did like to discover more about a person than just what their dead body told you, didn't you, Sam?'

She smiled sweetly. She knew he'd always fancied her and now was the time to take advantage of that situation.

'OK, ask away, but I can't guarantee to answer them all and it must be done in the strictest confidence.'

'How long was Sophie Clark seeing you for?'

'About a year.'

'Why?'

Herman thought about that question. He wanted to answer it but didn't want to give away too much detail.

'Depression, mostly.'

'What had she got to be depressed about? She'd got everything, hadn't she? Famous well-connected husband. Rich jet-setting lifestyle. What more could she want?'

Herman shrugged. 'I don't know, but she wasn't happy.'

Money isn't everything, Sam pondered. 'Was it her husband? He is older?'

Herman shook his head deliberately. 'No, I don't think so, she seemed happy enough with him. Age isn't everything, you know, Sam.'

There speaks a man having a crisis, Sam considered.

'Clarke was rich, successful and powerful, they can be very attractive qualities.'

Sam knew he was right, but she still wondered if he was speaking professionally or from personal experience. 'So what was it?'

'I was never really sure. She wasn't one to let go easily. She'd hold things back, almost frightened to speak about them.'

Sam jumped on the important word. 'Frightened?'

Herman nodded. 'Yes, there was certainly a bit of that. Something or someone was certainly upsetting her.'

Sam was intrigued. 'Any idea who?'

'No, none. I did ask, even tried to get a hint, but she would never say.' He thought about his last comment for a moment. 'Well, I say never. We were due to have a meeting the day after she was killed when she told me she wanted to tell me something important. So maybe she had made up her mind to say something.'

'So we'll never know?' She couldn't help feeling disappointed.

Herman agreed. 'Unfortunately, no.'

Sam picked up her coffee and sipped at it for a moment before putting it down again. 'Did she ever say something about having an affair?'

'No, why, was she?'

'With Ward.'

'The man they arrested for her murder?'

Sam nodded.

'She never said a word. But then, like I said, the biggest problem I had with her was getting her to tell me anything about her personal life.'

'Did you ever talk to her about sex?'

'Occasionally.'

'Was she into anything out of the ordinary?'

Herman felt confused. 'Like?'

'I don't know. Bondage, leather, handcuffs. Mickey Mouse mask. You know what I mean.'

Herman shook his head again. 'No, nothing like that. She clearly liked sex but I got the impression that it was all very straightforward stuff. Nothing out of the ordinary.'

Sam had run out of questions and coffee so she stood to leave. 'Thank you, Andy.'

He stood up opposite her. 'Well, I'm not sure how much help I've been, but if it was any good I'm glad.'

'You have, so thanks again.' Sam thought for a moment then asked one last question. 'Did you find Sophie Clarke attractive?'

Herman thought before replying, trying to establish in his mind whether or not it was a loaded question.

'Yes, I did, because she was. That's as far as it went,

though, Sam. I hope you understand that?'

Sam smiled sweetly again. 'Of course I do. I just wanted to establish how other men saw her, that was all.'

It wasn't she wanted to know if Herman had ever tried it on or was perhaps having an affair with her. Despite their code of ethics, doctors often did have affairs with their patients.

Herman asked, 'I take it from this conversation that you don't think Ward was the killer?'

Sam shook her head. 'I know he wasn't.'

Herman smiled. He knew that if that was what Sam thought she was probably right. 'When you do find the killer, let me know, would you, I'd love to have a word with him.'

It was a bizarre request but Sam understood.

Sam knew her next journey would have to be to see DS Flemming, to try and find out all she could about Spade and his activities. She made her way back to her cottage to change and pack an overnight case. She didn't envisage being there for more than a couple of days, but you never knew. Besides, she thought, if she was there any longer she could always shop. Letting herself in through the back door she called out to Kate, who she hoped had settled in by now.

'Kate!'

Kate's voice came back immediately, 'In here, Dr Ryan!'

Sam made her way into the sitting room to find Kate lying naked on the settee, with Hudd, who was sitting in the armchair opposite her, sketchpad in hand, drawing her. Hudd turned to greet her.

'Sam, good to see you. Wondered how long you were going to be.'

The sight of Kate naked on the settee took the wind out of Sam's sails and for a minute she wasn't sure what to do. Finally, not wanting to make too much of a fuss, she crossed the room and stood behind Hudd, observing what he did. The drawing was beautiful. She looked at Kate and then back to Hudd's sketchpad. Kate really was very beautiful and she could see why Sharman was so excited by her.

Kate called across to her, 'What do I look like? He won't let me see it until he's finished.'

Sam was amused by her concern. 'It's a very good likeness.'

Kate wasn't convinced. 'Is that good or bad?'

'Good. You're very beautiful.'

Kate smiled, pleased and flattered by the compliment.

Sam returned her attention to Hudd. 'Besides sketching Kate, what are you doing here?'

Hudd continued to draw Kate while he spoke. 'I heard that that policeman you brought to my rooms had been arrested for murder. Thought I'd find out what was going on.'

Sam shook her head. 'Nothing. They've got the wrong man, that's all.'

Hudd was clearly not convinced by Sam's reassurance. 'Do you think it might have been him that destroyed the bust?'

'No.'

Kate suddenly jumped off the settee and stormed across to Hudd. 'Stan Sharman wouldn't hurt a fly!' She thought about the statement for a moment. 'Well he wouldn't kill one anyway. If you've nothing good to say about him then why don't you just keep your gob shut?'

Hudd looked both surprised and concerned by Kate's sudden outburst.

Sam explained, 'Kate is Stan's girlfriend.'

Hudd looked up at her still red face. 'Sorry, I didn't mean to be—'

Kate cut him off, 'Didn't mean to be what? Fucking rude!'

Hudd looked back at his drawing, put a couple of finishing lines to it, and handed it to Kate. It was a bad moment. Without looking at it she ripped it in half, threw it back at him, grabbed her clothes and ran upstairs.

Hudd followed Sam into the kitchen.

'Coffee? No, sorry, you don't drink poison, do you. Water?'

Hudd nodded. 'Please.'

Sam picked up a glass. 'I've only got tap.'

Hudd nodded his acceptance. 'That will be fine. I didn't mean to be rude.'

Sam poured his drink and handed it to him. 'You weren't, really, she's just a bit sensitive at the moment.'

Hudd took the glass and began to drink from it. 'She seems a little young for your friend?'

Sam shrugged. 'What's age got to do with it? It's all down to feelings.'

Hudd wasn't convinced. 'There must be twenty years between them.'

Sam poured her coffee. 'Never had you down as a bigot.'

Hudd became defensive. 'I'm not, just realistic. They can't have that much in common?'

Sam sipped the hot liquid from her mug. 'Probably, but they still love and care for each other and that's worth more than most things.'

Hudd nodded. 'Maybe. Sure he's not just having a mid-life crisis?'

Sam shook her head. 'I thought he might be at first, but after talking to Kate I think there is far more to it than that.'

Hudd nodded in a lazy, vaguely interested way. Then, bored with the topic, he moved on. 'So what's new with the unknown mystery girl?'

'I might have some information for you later.'

'How much later?'

Sam thought about it for a moment. 'Couple of days. I've got to go and see a detective in King's Lynn. He might have some information on her.'

Hudd suddenly lost his bored lethargy and began to spark, the thought of finally discovering who the girl was exciting him. 'Can I come?'

Sam shook her head. 'No. This is a murder investigation.'

Hudd gave a shallow laugh. 'An unofficial one, with no money. I'm not sure that counts.'

Sam put her mug down. 'You don't have the background or experience for something like this.'

Hudd put his half-finished glass of water down on to the kitchen table. 'Funny, that's not what you said when you asked me to do the bust for free.'

Sam thought about what he said for a moment. 'That was different.'

Hudd shrugged. 'Thought it might be. Look, I'm either in or I'm out. If I'm out I leave now and that will be it.'

Sam pondered his threat. She knew that if nothing came of the King's Lynn trip, then the only chance she stood of ever identifying the girl was Hudd and she knew she mustn't alienate him at this stage.

'OK, you can come. But keep out of the way, keep your mouth shut, and do as you're told.'

Hudd smiled broadly. 'Thanks, thanks a lot, brilliant.'

Sam hadn't finished. 'One more thing?'

Hudd looked contrite. 'Anything.'

'I'm not posing in the nude.'

He laughed. 'Deal.'

A voice from the far side of the kitchen suddenly cut through their conversation.

'If he's going, I'm going too. Stan needs friends looking after his interests. Not wet-behind-the ears students.'

Sam looked across at Kate, who had dressed and was now standing with a determined look on her face by the kitchen door.

'Besides,' Kate continued, 'I'm not keen to be left here on my own. Bit isolated, if you know what I mean.'

Sam shook her head. After inviting Hudd she could hardly not invite Kate. What a team she thought, a pathologist, an art student and a prostitute. If Adams ever found out, she'd have to leave the country, never mind the county.

'OK, Kate, you can come too.'

Kate smiled, holding up the drawing she had just

ripped in half. 'Anyone got any sticky tape? This is rather good.'

Everyone burst out laughing.

The road from Cambridge to King's Lynn, although not long, certainly wasn't straight. Sam seemed to find herself behind every slow lorry, tractor and caravan on the road. It wasn't the easiest place in the world to pass other vehicles either. So she had to be content to sit behind these slow-moving vehicles for hours. Finally, they reached the old square known locally as Tuesday Market Place and parked. Sam was lucky, and The George, the hotel she had booked herself into, had two spare rooms so she was able to get her two companions in with her – although neither offered to pay, she noticed. Once Sam was settled in her room she rang Detective Sergeant Flemming and arranged to meet him the following day.

After dinner Sam went for a wander on her own while Kate and Hudd went to try and find a club. As Sam walked along the waterfront, past the old warehouses and custom buildings, the events of the last few weeks spun around her head. It seemed remarkable that over the course of a few days Sharman had been arrested for murder, she had resigned, and there were still three unsolved murders. She looked out over the Wash watching the reflection from the moon shimmer across the murky waters that lapped along the shore. She tried to make sense of it all, but couldn't. It was like a giant jigsaw with several of the pieces missing. As she looked around herself she suddenly realized she was alone. King's Lynn had to be one of the quietest places she had ever visited. Even now, at ten thirty in the evening, the avenues and streets were practically empty and although it was still summer, as the nights drew on and the breeze across the Wash stiffened, it began to get cold. A shiver ran through her. Pulling her jacket tightly around her shoulders, she began to make her way back to the hotel.

Suddenly she began to have the feeling of being

followed. In such a quiet spot anything out of the ordinary became startlingly obvious. Sam wasn't sure what she noticed at first – the footsteps, that feeling of an unknown and unwanted presence? Whatever it was, she knew she was being followed. She quickened her step, and as expected, so did the steps behind her. All this situation needed, Sam thought, was a thick fog floating from the sea. As she reached the far side of the harbour the person behind her who she had managed to keep at a reasonable distance called out, 'Dr Ryan!'

Sam stopped and then turned, surprised to hear her own name. The man who approached her wasn't anything like she imagined. He was about fifty and about as menacing as a carrot. She waited while, coughing and wheezing, he eventually caught up. While she watched, the man who had been following her grabbed a lamppost to steady himself. He looked across at her.

'Bloody hell, lady, you can shift.'

Sam watched him for a moment. 'Who the hell are you?'

The man was now doubled over, trying desperately to regain his breath. 'Stan, Stan Sharman sent me.'

Sam was surprised. 'Stan, why?'

The man was slowly recovering. 'He said you were looking for a man called Spade.'

'Yes, but what's that got to do with you?'

He put his hand out. 'David Cross. Stan and I were policemen together a few years back.'

Sam hoped he was fitter then.

'Mr Quick gave me a call on Stan's behalf. Said you needed help.'

Sam put her hand under his arm to help steady him. 'Why you?'

'I'm a private detective now. Owed Stan a few favours.'

Sam was never surprised how many people owed Stan a favour.

'So how can you help?'

'I know where he is.'

'Spade?'

He nodded. 'Yes.'

Sam could feel herself becoming excited. 'Do the police know?'

He shook his head. 'I wouldn't tell those prats.'

She was surprised at his attitude. 'Weren't you one?'

'I was a real one. Different age, different job.'

Sam didn't really want to know his opinion of the modern police force, just where Spade was. 'So where is he?'

'A field just outside Diss.' It was accurate but not accurate enough.

'Diss is a big place. Where exactly?'

The man put his hand in his pocket and handed Sam a crude map. 'That will show you where. Be careful, he's a nasty bastard. You know he's wanted for murder, don't you?'

'Yes.' She took a quick glance at the map. 'Thanks for this.'

'Tell Stan we're even now.'

With that he turned and walked away towards the Market Place.

Crossing the Tuesday Market Place Sam noticed Kate climbing into an unknown car on the far side of the square. She searched through the darkness of the car's interior to try and catch a glimpse of the driver. She'd often wondered what men who used woman in this way looked like. It's like being cut up in your car and staring at the person who did it. Just trying to establish what a dick looked like. Sam thought about calling out to her, but then changed her mind. It was her life, after all. As she reached the George, Hudd suddenly appeared behind her.

'Fancy a drink, Sam?'

Sam looked at him, surprised. 'I thought you didn't drink?'

He shrugged. 'I'll have a fruit juice. What about you?'

'Brandy, large one.'

The two of them made their way into the bar, where they were just calling last orders.

'Orange juice and a large brandy please.'

The barman nodded, looking at his watch. 'Only just in time.'

Hudd took the drinks across to Sam. 'Here we go. That should help you sleep.'

Sam took it, raised her glass, and took a large mouthful, swallowing hard. Putting her glass down she looked across at Hudd and smiled. She wasn't sure whether to tell him about her clandestine meeting with Sharman's friend down by the quay. However, as he was almost certainly going to accompany her to Spade's lair she felt obliged to.

'I know where Spade is.'

Hudd looked startled. 'What, where?'

She took another large mouthful, this time almost emptying her glass. 'A field just outside Diss.' She handed him the rough sketch map. 'This should show us exactly where.'

Hudd examined the map intensely. He was so close now to finding what he had been searching for, he could almost feel it. 'When are we going?'

'Tomorrow afternoon, after we've seen DS Flemming.'

'Good. Sooner the better as far as I'm concerned.'

That established, Sam changed the subject. 'Seen anything of Kate?' She knew where Kate was but wanted to hear what Hudd had to say about it. Judging his honesty, she supposed. 'No. Couldn't find a decent club so she headed off to see some old friends. Said she would be late.'

I bet she did, Sam pondered.

The following morning Sam woke early, and after a short walk by the quay went into breakfast. She'd had a restless night. The face of the unknown girl floated in and out of her dreams, her features almost visible before drifting back to the dark recesses of her mind. Sam knew she was so close to identifying the girl, yet she still, somehow, seemed to be beyond reach. She had only been at the table for a few minutes when Kate appeared and sat opposite her. She examined her face looking for signs of the hard night she imagined she must have had, but there wasn't a trace. She was as beautiful as ever. Smooth features, wide bright eyes and hair like silken yarn. After ordering her food she dipped into her bag and handed Sam a wad of notes.

'There's about a hundred pounds there. Hope it's enough to cover the hotel and your petrol.'

Sam pushed her hand away. 'No thanks. Not sure I liked the way you earned it.'

Kate looked surprised, shocked and upset. 'What do you mean by that?'

Sam bit into a small slice of dry toast. 'I saw you last night, getting into that car.'

Kate glared at her. 'Oh you did, did you? Put two and two together and made six.'

Sam leaned back in her seat, certain of her facts.

'And Stan told me you were intelligent. For your information, that man was a friend of Stan's. He said he'd seen you already. He gave me some money from Stan to help out with your expenses.'

Kate stood up sharply, glaring at Sam. 'Next time get your facts right before you start pointing the finger. And I thought you were a friend. How wrong can you get.' She threw the money across the table and into Sam's face before storming out of the breakfast room.

Sam was pleased and surprised when she found Kate, along with Hudd, waiting by the car when she re-emerged from the hotel. The short journey from the Market Place to the police station was made in silence. Hudd made several attempts to start a conversation but his efforts were met with a stony silence. Sam wanted to apologize but certainly didn't want to do it in front of Hudd. She'd been wrong and had assumed rather too much. She of all people should know never to assume anything; it was almost a watchword for the profession. Yet she had done it to Kate and now she felt terribly guilty. She parked her car at the back of the police station and a young and nervous looking PC showed them up to Bill Flemming's office.

As she entered he stood and put out his hand. 'Dr Ryan, I presume?'

Sam was amused by the greeting and shook his hand firmly before turning to introduce her two companions. Although looking a little confused, he shook both their hands and was genial enough to both of them, without asking the awkward questions she'd been dreading. As the three of them sat down on prepared chairs Flemming came straight to the point and began the conversation. 'Stan Sharman tells me you are looking for Spade?'

'We are.'

'You know he's wanted for murder, don't you?'

Sam nodded. 'Yes, we heard.'

'And that he's a very dangerous man?'

Sam nodded again. 'I think we assumed that, given what he's wanted for.'

Flemming paused for a moment, looking at Sam, trying to read her thoughts. 'So what can I do to help? If you want to know where Spade is I haven't a clue. If I did I wouldn't be sitting here now.'

'We realize that, we just wanted to know if you had any background information on him.'

Flemming sighed. 'Very little. His real name is Alex Johnson. He's been in trouble all his life; approved school, Borstal, and prison. Convictions for just about everything you can think of. Other than that, nothing. He's a traveller, hard to pin down, if you know what I mean?'

'What about travelling companions?'

Hudd leaned forward on hearing the question.

'He's always been nicked on his own. Doesn't have a partner that we know of.'

Sam could feel herself becoming frustrated. 'Any criminal intelligence on him that might give a clue to associates?'

Flemming shook his head again. 'Next to none outside what I've already told you. Like I said, he's a traveller, a loner.'

Sam wasn't quite sure what else to say. Flemming either didn't know very much about Spade or wasn't willing to divulge what he knew to three people representing a suspected murderer, friend or no friend.

Flemming interrupted her thoughts with his own inquiry. 'I'm sorry to have to ask you this, but from the note I got from Stan I formed the impression that you might already know where he is?'

Sam wasn't sure what to say. Saying too much would give away Spade's location, then they might never get to talk to him properly. Withholding information was a criminal offence and might leave her in more trouble than she was already in. As if spotting Sam's dilemma Flemming gave her a workable solution.

'Why don't we do this? You go and see Spade, wherever he is, and get the information Stan and you need. Once you have, call me, tell me where he is, and we'll go and pick him up. That way, you get what you want and I get to nick a killer. Sound fair?'

Flemming sat back and waited for Sam's response. She quickly scanned the faces of her two companions, looking for inspiration, but there was nothing. She looked back at Flemming. 'OK, you've got a deal. But no tricks. This has been too long a road and Stan's freedom might well depend on what we are going to find when we see Spade.'

Flemming put his hand over his heart. 'You have my word. I like Stan, he's helped me out more than once. I wouldn't do anything to jeopardize his freedom. Trust me.'

Sam smiled, feeling more confident. Stan's friends were, if nothing else, loyal.

As soon as they had finished talking to DS Flemming, they headed off in the direction of Diss. Sam still hadn't had a chance to speak to Kate about their conversation at breakfast but was hoping to later. The trip to Diss was quicker than she'd had imagined. She'd been lucky and for some reason the great long queues of slow-moving traffic she had experienced on her way to King's Lynn just weren't about. As they entered the small market town Sam handed Kate, who was sitting next to her, the rough map Cross had given her. As she did Sam gave Kate's hand a squeeze, as a sort of apology for what had happened earlier. Kate looked at her and smiled. Sam was relieved. She knew she didn't deserve it.

'Can you see if you can follow that to Spade's caravan?'

Kate nodded and began to read the map earnestly. As Sam reached the centre of the town Kate told her to take a right. Sam followed her instructions. After about half a mile Kate directed her off the main road and on to a narrow dirt track that was signposted to 'Blood Farm' – very appropriate, Sam thought. A few hundred yards along the track Sam reached a small clearing backed by a deciduous wood, where Kate told her to stop. She looked across at Sam. 'Well, if Stan's mate's map is right we're here.'

Sam looked around but there was no sign of life, or a caravan for that matter. Kate began to open the car door.

'The caravan should be at the far side of the wood. Can't see it from here. We'll have to walk.'

Sam and Hudd followed Kate's lead. They climbed out of the car and began to follow her through the woods. As they began to emerge from the far side of the wood Sam suddenly spotted the caravan with a large silver Volvo estate parked next to it. The small party made their way towards it.

Reaching the caravan, Sam knocked on the door and waited. There was no reply. She knocked again, this time shouting Spade's real name.

'Mr Johnson, are you there? Mr Johnson?'

There was no reply. Sam turned to her two companions, wondering what to do next. Kate was the first with a suggestion. 'Give the door a push.'

Sam pondered the idea for a moment, considering

whether actually entering the caravan without permission was a step too far. She quickly made her mind up, however. She'd come this far and everything she'd done along the way had been pretty unorthodox, so why stop now? She pushed down the handle and pulled at the door, it wasn't locked and opened easily. The three friends looked at each other for support, for what was quite obviously the next step. Kate, as usual, was the first to make up her mind and, pushing gently past Sam and Hudd, pulled herself into the caravan.

Kate's screams were the next thing Sam remembered. That and the brutal voice of a man shouting at her, 'Who the fuck are you? Who the fuck are you?'

Sam looked up to see Kate standing with her back to a scruffy dishevelled man who had one arm around her waist while the other held an evil-looking lino knife to her throat. After a few moments Sam had regained enough of her composure to react.

'Calm down, we just want some information.'

The man, whom Sam presumed was Spade, glared down at her. He had the most evil and angry face she had ever seen.

'Who are you, the fucking police?'

Sam noticed that the point of the knife had already pierced Kate's skin, and a thin trickle of blood was running down her neck on to her dress. She knew she would have to explain quickly.

'I'm a doctor, we found a girl's body and thought she might be a friend of yours.'

Spade was still highly agitated and disbelieving. 'What girl, what's her name?'

Sam shook her head desperately. 'We don't know, that's why we are here.'

Spade stepped out of the caravan, pushing Kate in front of him, the knife still firmly at her throat. Once outside he began to look around, searching for any unseen foes. Sam tried to be reassuring.

'We're on our own, honestly. Do we look like the police?'

Spade stopped his search and looked at Hudd and then Sam, then making his mind up pushed Kate roughly to the floor and stepped towards Sam and with the same evil look put the edge of the knife hard against her throat.

'Well, you seem to be the leader. Cross me, and before anyone can save you, I'll have cut your throat, do you understand?'

Sam swallowed hard and nodded. She understood only too well.

As Hudd helped Kate to her feet, giving her a handkerchief to hold to the small wound on her throat, Spade guided the three of them into his caravan, closing and locking the door behind him. Sam sat with her friends on the settee at the far side of the caravan while Spade sat opposite them, the knife still held hard in his hand.

'So, what girl and where?'

Although still nervous, Sam managed to compose herself enough to reply without stuttering. 'Her body was discovered about a month ago under a railway bridge. She'd been there for a while and I'm afraid it was in a bit of a state. There was nothing to identify her with but we do know she was murdered.'

Spade glared at Sam again, hitting his knife down hard on the tabletop. 'And you think I killed her?'

Sam shook her head vigorously and reassuringly. 'No, we don't!' That wasn't entirely true but seemed the sensible thing to say given the circumstances. 'But we do think you knew her and might be able to help identify her.'

Spade's face began to relax. Sam put her hand inside her bag. As she did so Spade leant forward, knife in hand and pointed at her. 'Don't try anything stupid.'

Sam shook her head. 'I'm not going to, I just wanted to show you this. We found it on her body.'

Sam carefully pulled the watch from her bag and

handed it to Spade, who reached out with his free hand
and took it. He stared at it for a moment running it around
in his hand and staring at the erased engraving at the back
of the watch. He finally looked up at Sam. 'Her name was
Claire Armstrong. She was my girlfriend. I gave her the
watch for her birthday.'

Sam wasn't going to get into the issue of where it came
from. 'When did you last see her?'

'About a month ago. She had some deal going down in
Cambridge, wouldn't say what it was, only that it was
likely to make us some money.'

Hudd interrupted. 'Have you got any photographs of
her?'

Spade eyed him for a moment, 'Yeah, somewhere.' He
looked across the caravan. 'Look in that drawer, I think
there's some in there.'

Hudd began to search through the drawer.

'Are you sure you have no idea what Claire was doing
in Cambridge?'

'Only like I said she'd got some sort of deal going
down.'

Sam continued, 'What about her background?'

Spade shrugged. 'She never talked about it. I think she
ran away because of problems with her parents. Can't be
sure, through.'

'What about her date of birth, National Insurance
number?'

Spade looked across at Hudd. 'Her social security card
and stuff should be in there too. Take it if you want.'

Hudd suddenly shouted out, alarming everyone in the
caravan, 'She was just how I pictured her. I was right, I
was bloody well right.'

Spade glared at him, annoyed at being startled. Hudd
handed the photograph to Sam, a triumphant smile all
over his face. Once Sam had taken it he continued to
search for more information. Sam looked at the photograph with increasing emotion. Before her was the picture
of an attractive, vibrant young woman, a far cry from the

dried-out and decomposing remains she had been working on only a short time before.

Sam turned her attention back to Spade. Considering that they had just told him his girlfriend had been murdered, she was surprised that there was no sign of any emotion. Looking at Spade she wondered whether, short of anger, this man had an emotional bone in his body. She considered that his lack of response might make him a suspect, but then suspects usually made a show of emotion to cover their tracks. This certainly wasn't the case with Spade, he just couldn't care less. Spade looked across at Sam. 'Look, I'm giving you all this information. I mean, you know, how much?'

Sam decided on a tactic. 'For what? A few photographs and Claire's social security card? I'll give you ten pounds.'

Spade gave a sarcastic laugh. 'That wouldn't fill my petrol tank.'

Sam shrugged. 'I'll give you more if you've got more to tell me.'

Spade stared hard into Sam's eyes, trying to intimidate her. 'I could just take it.'

Sam smiled. She was frightened but she wasn't going to show it. 'What makes you think I've got it on me?'

'I could search.'

Sam picked up her handbag and put it on the table. It had over three hundred pounds in cash in plus all her credit cards. It was the biggest bluff she had ever tried to pull off. Spade looked at the bag and then at Sam.

'So how are you going to pay me, then, if I do tell you something else?'

Sam put her handbag back on the floor. 'Cashpoint. You take me to the bank, I take out the money, you give me the information, and we go our separate ways.'

Spade thought about it for a moment. 'How much?'

'Depends on what you've got.'

Sam knew it was a risk. The moment she got the money out he could just force her to hand it over. The only thing in her favour was the fact it was a public place and he might not be so keen to try something with so many people about.

'I can tell you who she was meeting.'

Sam started to get excited, but remained outwardly calm. 'How do you know that?

Spade gave her an evil smile. 'Thought she was clever, did Claire, but she wasn't as clever as she thought and I found out what she was up to.'

Sam cut in. 'And what was she up to?'

Spade laughed. 'Money first. How much?'

Sam thought about it for a moment. 'Five hundred pounds?'

Spade looked contemptuous. 'Thousand.'

Sam tried to looked surprised and shocked but she wasn't. It was just what she had expected him to say. If she gave in too easily, however, he might ask for more.

'How much? You must be joking!'

Spade, annoyed at her attitude, became stubborn. 'Take it or leave it.'

Sam looked at Kate and Hudd, who both shrugged, before turning her attention back to Spade and trying to look as defeated as possible. She gave a loud sigh.

'OK, you win, you can have your money.'

Spade leaned across the table, pushing his face into Sam's. 'I always fucking do. You might as well get used to that fact.'

Sam wanted to slap his face but knew that would be insane.

Spade began to climb out of his seat. 'Right, you can all help me hook up my caravan.'

Sam was confused by the request. 'Why?'

Spade hated people questioning him. Especially people in their position. 'If you think I'm hanging about here so you can tell the filth where I am, then you've got another think coming.'

Sam shrugged. 'Whatever makes you feel comfortable.'

Spade moved his attention to Kate. 'And you're staying with me until I've got the money!'

Sam looked at Kate and then Spade. 'Is that really necessary?'

Kate put her hand on Sam's arm. 'It's OK, Dr Ryan, I'll go with him. I'm used to getting into strange cars with odd people, remember?'

Sam was impressed by Kate's bravery, while at the same time feeling like a complete bitch. She nodded, she could do little else. Just had to hope that it didn't all go horribly wrong.

As Sam and Kate got to their feet Spade walked across to a cupboard. He opened the door, took out the bottom drawer and removed a pistol and a small package from a secret alcove situated underneath the drawer. Spade showed them the gun, waving it around deliberately. 'Insurance. Piss me about and I'll fucking kill all of you, street or no street. Understand?'

Sam nodded. It was an unexpected development and one that might well ruin all her plans. Spade was now in a position to take the money and still tell her nothing. Pushing the gun inside his belt he ushered them all outside. Sam, Kate and Hudd climbed down the single step that led from the caravan and waited for further instructions. Spade followed them out.

'Wait here, I'll get the car.' With that he began to walk towards his Volvo, parked at the far side of the clearing.

'Get down, get down, armed police!'

The loud and commanding voice seemed to come from nowhere. Sam was slow to react and felt herself suddenly being dragged to the ground by Kate, who fell across her body. As Sam looked up the entire scene seemed to have gone into slow motion. Spade turned to face the unseen voices, an angry almost insane look on his face. As he did he drew his gun. Sam knew he was screaming something, but the words were muffled and drawn. With a brilliant flash, followed by a deep explosion, his gun went off again and again. Then, as Sam watched, his chest seemed to explode and he was thrown backwards on to the ground. Sam knew he was dead before his body finally collapsed into a disorganized mess on the grass. As her mind and senses went back to real time, men and feet seemed to be everywhere. People were shouting and screaming out their orders, but Sam couldn't understand a word they were saying. Finally recovering a little from the past few seconds she called to Kate.

'It's OK, Kate, you can get off now, I think it's over.'

Kate didn't move and it was only then that Sam noticed the blood dripping past her head and on to the dirt by the side of her face. Sam could feel the panic begin to rise up within her. She pushed Kate gently off her before turning to see how badly she had been hurt. The bullet had entered Kate's right eye and exited at the back of her skull taking a large portion of her head with it. Sam screamed, cradling the dead girl's head in her lap, 'Kate, Kate, oh no, oh for God's sake no!'

CHAPTER EIGHT

Sam's next few hours passed in a muddled haze. She knew there were people around her, but she didn't know or care who. They spoke to her in low, slow, sentences, their voices calm and reassuring, before they disappeared again into the fog of her consciousness.

Sam lived surrounded by death; it was her work, her passion. She saw and dealt with it every day. Up to this point she had thought she understood it. Cold, undemocratic, unfeeling. Yet death for Sam was always at a distance. She saw what was left after death had taken the rest. Bodies were nothing, just a memory of what once was. Yet this was so close. Life and death in a heart beat. Her only serious experience of death at a personal level had been the demise of her mother, and although she had been devastated by her loss, there had been a certain expectation and inevitability about it.

There was none of that with Kate. She was young and vibrant with everything to live for. Sam might not have approved of her lifestyle, but then who was she to judge? Despite her misgivings, she really had liked Kate. The fact that she had died trying to protect her was an added wound, and one Sam knew she would have to live with for the rest of her life.

Sam couldn't remember who finally moved her; she thought it was probably the ambulance drivers. All she could really remember was being placed gently in a seat and wheeled across the field into a waiting ambulance. She thought Hudd might have been by her side but wasn't sure. What she did remember vividly, however, was seeing Kate's body still lying out in the field as a murder tent was slowly erected over and around her.

She wasn't sure how long the trip to the hospital took but then it didn't really matter, time seemed to have stopped the moment she realized that Kate had been killed. In the casualty unit Sam was examined by both a casualty doctor and a nurse who found little, save the odd bruise and shock, wrong with her. They wanted her to stay in hospital overnight for observation but despite her depression Sam refused, choosing instead to return with Hudd to her hotel for the evening. As they travelled back towards the Tuesday Market Place, one thought kept rolling over and over in her mind: how the hell was she going to tell Sharman? Kate was her responsibility and she'd let him down terribly.

As soon as they arrived back at the hotel, Hudd helped Sam up to her room, settling her in before leaving her to sleep. He desperately wanted to talk to her, reassure her about the day's events as well as reassuring himself about what had happened. But above all he wanted to get back to the safety of Cambridge and the cloistered calm of his own college. He had never expected this. The project was meant to have been an unusual route into his art. He had wanted to be famous, but now all he wanted to do was go home and forget the last twenty-four hours. Yet he knew he couldn't, he still had work to do, enquiries to make, and he knew that more than ever before Sam would need him.

After Hudd left, Sam slowly stripped off her clothes, dumping them in the white linen bag provided by the hotel. Her coat, trousers and shoes were covered with Kate's blood. Sam felt a little like Jackie O and began to realize how she must have felt as she crawled out of the back of the official car covered in her husband's blood. She didn't want the clothes back. She wouldn't put them out for a clean but would take them home and burn them.

Stepping into the shower, she let the warm water run slowly over her body and through her hair. She stood, arms by her side, as her tears, which up to then she had managed to suppress, mingled with the water from the shower as the droplets trickled down her cheek. Finally she started to scrub herself vigorously, desperately trying to wash away the memory of Kate's blood soaking through her clothes. When she eventually stepped out of the shower, she dried herself quickly before collapsing into bed and falling into a dreamless sleep.

Despite her exhaustion Sam didn't sleep late, waking at six and staring up at the ceiling for half an hour before pulling herself out of bed and dressing. Once wrapped up warm she went for a walk along the front, enjoying the cooling breeze. Wrapping the thick wool coat tightly around her body she perched herself on a bench over-looking the mud flats and reconstructed the previous day and her part in it. She suddenly began to realize how arrogant she had been. If she hadn't involved herself in the investigation in the first place, Kate would still be alive, Sharman probably wouldn't be in prison, she wouldn't have resigned and the mess that she felt she had personally created would never have happened. It was all her fault and she knew it. After this, she vowed, she would stick to her job, just do what she needed to do and not involve herself in anything that wasn't strictly her business. It still didn't solve the problem of how she was going to tell Sharman, however.

   As she stood to return to the hotel she was surprised by a voice behind her.

   'Hudd told me I might find you here.'

   She turned to see Sharman looming over her. In an instant her legs felt weak and she could feel herself falling loosely through the air.

When she came round, she found herself sitting back on the bench. Her head had been pushed firmly down between her legs. After a few moments she pushed against Sharman's hand. 'It's OK, Stan, I'm with it again. Sorry.'

Sharman eased his hold as Sam sat up, still breathing deeply. When she had finally recovered, she looked across at her friend. 'I take it you know?'

Sharman nodded. 'Adams told me.'

'I bet he enjoyed that,' Sam said wearily.

Sharman shook his head. 'No, to be fair, I don't think he did. That's why I'm here. It was on his orders they let me go.'

Sam wasn't in a forgiving mood. 'Seen the light, has he?'

Sharman nodded, reaching into his pocket for cigarettes and sparking one up quickly. 'Was it quick?' He didn't look at Sam, just kept staring out over the Wash.

'Yes, very. She wouldn't have known anything.'

Sharman remained silent, waiting for more.

'She saved my life. Threw me on to the floor and covered me with her body. Otherwise it would have been me not her laid out in the mortuary.'

Sharman gave a sort of half-smile but without the pleasure. 'Sounds like her, stupid cow. There was so much more to her. Oddest prostitute I ever met.'

'She was very special, Stan. I'm so sorry.'

Sharman turned to her. 'It wasn't your fault, so don't even think that.'

Sam could feel her eyes begin to fill with tears. 'I just think that if I hadn't . . .'

Sharman shook his head. 'Kate was a big girl, she knew what she was doing. It was just one of those things. Fate, if you like.'

Sam reached out and took Sharman's hand. 'I really am sorry, Stan, I know how much she meant to you.'

Sharman squeezed Sam's hand before putting it back on her lap. 'Thank you. I'll get used to it.'

Sam wasn't sure what the rejection of her hand meant but wasn't in the mood to analyse it. 'What do we do now?'

Sharman took one last slow draw from his cigarette. 'We catch the killers.'

He stood, and taking Sam by the arm pulled her to her feet. 'Come on, let's get on with it.'

Detective Sergeant Bill Flemming was waiting for them when they arrived back at the hotel. He was the last person Sam wanted to see. He stood as the two companions arrived. He put his hand out in Sam's direction but she pointedly refused to take it.

'Why the hell didn't you stick to the bloody plan? You said you wouldn't move in until we'd got the information we wanted.'

Flemming shrugged. 'Operational decision made above my head.'

Sam wasn't satisfied. 'But you had some say in it?'

'Some.'

'Then why the hell didn't you stick to the original plan? Kate might still be alive.'

Flemming sucked his teeth for a moment, clearly pondering what Sam had said before answering. 'We were frightened of losing him, or letting him get to an area where it would be difficult to pick him up.'

'Then why didn't you let us in on your little scam, then perhaps we would have stood a chance?'

'The decision wasn't made until after you'd left and we couldn't get hold of you.'

Sharman cut in. 'Or their nervousness might have given the game away?'

Flemming knew there was no point in lying to Sharman, he'd been around too long. 'There was an element of that. He was a dangerous man. We couldn't afford to lose him.'

'Why were you armed? Did you know he would have a bloody gun?'

Flemming considered his reply again. 'We had some intelligence that he might be armed.'

'But you chose not to say?'

'As I said, it was only intelligence. It's not always accurate.'

Sharman cut in again. 'You thought it was accurate enough to call out an armed special operation unit, though.'

'No point taking chances.'

Sam felt like hitting him. 'Except with other people's lives. You set us up, you bastard.' Suddenly the anger within her reached boiling point and she finally and unexpectedly lashed out with her fist, striking Flemming on the side of the face and knocking him back down into the chair. 'Don't you bloody well care? A girl is dead because of you, you piece of shit!'

As Sam moved towards Bill Flemming, her fist raised again, Sharman grabbed her around the waist and picked her up.

'That's enough. That's enough.' He pulled her behind him before turning his attention back to Flemming. 'I think you'd better leave.'

Flemming stood and nodded to Sharman. 'Thank you.'

Sharman glared at him. 'Don't thank me. If I see your face for much longer I'll alter it. Am I making myself clear?'

Flemming ignored him. 'We'll need a statement.'

Sharman nodded. 'You'll get your statement. Just leave.'

Flemming looked at Sam and Sharman one last time. 'I really am sorry. This was never meant to—'

Sharman cut in, sickened by his attempt at an apology. 'Keep it. Just piss off, OK.'

Flemming finally took the hint and left. Sharman turned to Sam. 'Come on, I'll get you a brandy.'

Sam looked up at him. 'Bit early, isn't it?'

Sharman shrugged. 'It's six o'clock somewhere in the world.'

Sam smiled and followed him into the bar.

'Where did you learn to punch like that?'

'An old boyfriend used to box for Cambridge. He taught me a trick or two.'

Sharman smiled. 'He certainly did.'

She was just finishing a very large brandy when Hudd entered the bar. He was surprised to see Sharman. 'Thought you were in prison?'

Sam shook her head. 'As diplomatic as ever.'

Hudd looked embarrassed for the first time since Sam had known him. 'Sorry, I didn't mean – I mean I'm glad you're out of . . . of . . . It's good to see you.'

Sharman put his hand out, stopping him struggling any further. 'It's good to see you too.'

Hudd smiled, appreciating the help. 'For what it's worth I'm really sorry about Kate. She was one cool chick. Didn't know her long but I really liked her.'

Sharman nodded. 'Thanks.'

'I've got some drawings of her, if you'd like them?'

Sharman nodded again. 'I'd like that a lot.'

'They're in my room. I'll get them for you. Would you like to come?'

Sharman shook his head, 'No, it's OK, you can bring them down.'

Sam leaned across to Sharman. 'It might be a better idea to see them in his room.'

Sharman looked confused. 'Why?'

'She's in the nude.'

Sharman stared at Sam for a moment then back to Hudd. 'In the what?'

Hudd gulped deeply as he noticed the look on Sharman's face. 'It was just art, Stan, nothing happened.'

Sharman was still clearly upset so Hudd changed the subject quickly as an act of self-preservation. 'I've got something else in my room I'd like you both to see.'

Sam studied his face suspiciously. 'What?'

'I'd rather show you upstairs, it's rather private.'

Sam looked across at Sharman, who nodded. 'OK, lead on, I just hope it's worth it.'

Hudd nodded. 'Oh, I think you'll find it's worth it.'

*

Hudd's room was at the back of the hotel. Sam was surprised to discover it was bigger and much more spacious than her own.

The surprise must have shown. 'I like my space.'

Sam looked around. 'Must have cost a pretty penny?'

Hudd shrugged. 'There's money in the family.'

Sam smiled sarcastically. 'Of course there is. Now what is it you want to show us, besides the pictures, that is?'

Hudd smiled broadly, amused at Sam's disapproval of his old-money values. Wandering over to his cupboard, he removed several shirts before pulling out an oblong parcel wrapped tightly in brown paper. Sam had a feeling she had seen the parcel before but for the moment just couldn't remember where. He smiled at Sam before holding it up in front of her. 'Remember this?'

As Hudd said it Sam did. It was the parcel Spade had removed from the cupboard in the caravan just before he was shot. Sam reached out to try and grab it but Hudd was too quick and he pulled it away from her.

'No, no, I found it, I'll open it.' As he crossed towards the table at the far side of the room to open the tightly sealed packet Sam began her questioning.

'Where the hell did you get that from?'

Hudd dropped the parcel on the table and pulled a clasp knife from his pocket. He pulled it open and looked at Sharman. 'I use it to cut clay, that's all.'

Sharman didn't really care what he used it for but nodded his understanding in an official way.

Sam persisted, 'Are you going to tell us where you got it from or not?'

Hudd began to cut the string free. 'From his body. Well, close to it anyway.'

Sam was amazed and surprised. 'And the police didn't stop you?'

Hudd gave a short sarcastic laugh. 'They didn't see me. I pretended I was trying to help him and slipped the parcel inside my shirt during the confusion.'

Sam shook her head. 'If you'd been caught—'

Hudd cut in. 'Well, I wasn't, so shall we see what we've got?'

Sam looked across at Sharman, who was smiling broadly. Yes, she thought, you would approve of that.

Hudd continued to open the packet until its contents lay exposed on the table. Sam stepped forward and began to run the various items through her hands. There was a bank book, a VHS video, and two small rings. Sam opened the bank book and began to examine it. The book was in Claire's name. The deposit account had been opened several months previously and had regular payments transferred into it. As Sam began to flick through the pages she was surprised to see how much money had been paid into it. She turned to Sharman. 'Look at this!' Sharman leaned over the book as Sam showed him the entries. 'Look, a thousand pounds a month for three months, two thousand for two months and the last entry for three thousand. Who the hell was paying her that kind of money?'

Hudd cut in. 'Prostitution?'

Sharman shook his head. 'No, far too much, even for a young one. She was blackmailing someone. Look at the last entry, for three thousand pounds. Paid in about a month before we think she died. Looks like she was becoming too demanding, getting greedy. Whoever it was decided enough was enough and got sick of paying her.'

Hudd cut in again. 'You can't be sure of that?'

Sharman shook his head. 'Just look at the entries. They're too controlled. One thousand, two thousand, then three, then nothing. I'm certain, seen it too many times before.'

Sam picked up the book and began to flick through it again, hoping to see something she hadn't noticed before, but there was nothing. 'But who?'

Sharman shrugged. 'Whoever it was had money and was clearly worth blackmailing.'

'They were also bloody dangerous.'

'She might not have known that.'

'So someone rich and not obviously dangerous. Cast of thousands.'

Sharman smiled. 'Everyone's capable of murder, given the right circumstances.'

Sharman picked up the two rings, turning them around his fingers. They were two of the most distinctive rings he had ever seen. White gold with an odd but not unattractive twist at their centre with three rubies along the length of one and three diamonds along the length of the other. They were both expensive and unique.

'Who do you think these belong to?'

Sam shrugged. 'Who knows?'

Hudd's hand suddenly darted forward and he picked up the video. '*Star Trek*, my favourite, hope it's the episode with the Furbys, I loved that one.'

Sharman reached over and snatched the video from Hudd's hand, irritated by his interruption. He looked at Sam. 'Can we get a video in here?'

Sam nodded. 'We'll see.'

Walking across to the phone Sam called down to reception and was pleasantly surprised to find that they were able to supply a machine almost at once. As they waited Hudd went through the objects yet again, hoping to discover something his two expert friends had missed. While he searched, Sharman brooded quietly by the window. Sam joined him. 'Are you OK?'

Sharman glanced at her for a moment before looking back through the window. 'Memories are a difficult thing sometimes.'

'I know. I am so sorry about Kate,' she said quietly.

'I know you are, you don't have to keep repeating yourself.' He looked back down at her. 'I know it wasn't your fault either. So shall we just leave it at that. I don't need your guilt on top of mine.'

A loud knock on the bedroom door broke the moment. Hudd answered it, allowing room service into the room with a state-of-the-art video player. The video was quickly attached to the television and the tape slipped into the machine. As expected, an episode of *Star Trek* began. Sharman picked up the remote control and, much to Hudd's disgust, scanned through the tape quickly, until shortly after the episode finished he came to the section he was looking for. As the pictures slowly revealed themselves both Sam and Sharman became increasingly astonished. Instead of the pictures they had expected to see of some seedy room and a poor Eastern European girl being attacked and murdered, they were presented with the interior of John Clarke's bedroom and his wife Sophie tied to the bed, clearly scared and waiting for the inevitable. As they continued to watch half in shock and half in amazement, Michael Rogers appeared and began to abuse the helpless Sophie Clarke. Sam noticed that throughout the attack Rogers was careful about wearing a condom. She found it difficult to watch but realized she had to. As the camera moved from scene to scene, from close up to wide shot, long shot to big close up, the attack continued in graphic detail. Although the attack, rape and torture were terrible, the tape ended with Sophie Clarke still alive. Hudd had been stunned into total silence. As the video continued to play Sam suddenly shouted out, 'Stop, stop the video there.'

Sharman reacted at once but not quite quickly enough. Sam could feel herself becoming very agitated. 'Back, go back to the hands.' Sharman jogged the video back slowly until he reached Sophie Clarke's hands. They were tied tightly together around the metal bedpost.

'There, stop there.'

Sharman froze the picture. He looked at her slightly confused. 'What am I supposed to be seeing?'

Sam stood and pressed her finger hard against the screen. 'There on her hands, the rings.'

Sharman and Hudd studied the picture hard as Sam dashed back to the table and picked up the rings they had found inside Spade's packet. Racing back to the screen she held the rings up to the picture of Sophie Clarke's hands. 'Look, they're the same.'

Sharman looked at the rings and then the picture. He knew at once Sam was right, they were the same rings. Hudd examined the frozen frame before looking across at Sam.

'Were any other rings found on her body?'

Sam re-examined the picture. There were rings on most of Sophie's fingers. She shook her head. 'No, they must have been stolen from her body. I wonder where they are now?'

Sharman stared at the picture for a moment and then at Sam. 'I think I know.'

After one final night at the hotel the small group began to make their way back to Cambridge. They had all retired early, desperate for sleep and some respite from their thoughts of the previous day's encounters. Not that any of them slept much. Their minds were still so full of the events and the tragedies of the previous few days. Sharman travelled back to Cambridge on his own. He said he had an appointment with a postman, which Sam didn't really understand but decided to leave for the present. For Sam and Hudd the journey back was both long and slow, and they drove in almost total silence. There was such a strong sense that somebody was missing. Three of them had set out, full of excitement and interest, and now only two were coming home. It reinforced Sam's sense of loss and guilt. All Kate's luggage was in the back. Sam had folded it all neatly before putting it inside the case. The one thing she'd kept back was a photograph of Sharman and Kate taken at a dinner party. They both looked so happy. She had decided to give it to Sharman the next time they met, which, if Stan was right about the rings, wouldn't be long.

Arriving at the Backs behind Trinity College, Sam parked and turned to Hudd. 'I'm sorry about involving you in all this.'

Hudd shook his head. 'I'm not. I'm sorry about Kate, of course I am, but my God it has been exciting. I've finally got my picture of Claire as well, so perhaps now I can do her mask justice, it'll only take me a couple of days to bring her back.'

Sam looked at him for a moment considering what he had just said. 'It was you, wasn't it?'

Hudd feigned confusion. 'What?'

'You smashed your own bust, didn't you? Why?'

Hudd shrugged and smiled. 'It wasn't her. She just wasn't there and I knew it. I couldn't bring her back if I didn't believe in what I was doing. She became special to me. I fell in love with her, I guess.'

Sam shook her head in disbelief at Hudd's bizarre statement. 'But she was dead.'

He looked away across the Backs towards the river and the back of the Wren Library. 'The spirit is never dead, just the body. If I couldn't capture that, I didn't want to portray her at all.'

'And if we hadn't found the picture of her?'

'Then I wouldn't have done it. She would have stayed smashed on my floor.'

'Just like her memory.'

Hudd's smile broadened. 'Just like her memory.'

They looked at each other for a moment before Hudd opened the passenger door and stepped out. As he closed the door he looked back through the window. 'I'll call you when I've finished, then perhaps you can see what she looked like in the flesh, so to speak.'

Sam smiled at him. 'I look forward to it.'

Pushing the car into first gear Sam pulled away from the Backs and headed for home.

Adams was waiting for her when she arrived. She noticed that he was on his own this time and she was grateful for that. As he stood waiting patiently by the door, she brushed past him, put her key firmly in the lock and pushed the door open. She glanced back at him. 'You can come in as long as you're not going to give me a lecture.'

Adams shook his head. 'No lectures.'

Sam nodded and they both entered the house. Walking through to the kitchen she put the kettle on. 'Tea or coffee?'

'Tea, thank you.'

Sam turned to Adams. 'So what can I do for you, other than make you tea?'

Adams hesitated for a moment, compiling his words. 'I just came to say how sorry I was and to see if you're OK?'

Despite his kind words Sam couldn't help distrusting him. 'Thanks for that. Thank you for releasing Stan as well, especially right now.'

'No need to keep him, he clearly hadn't done anything. If I'm honest I probably locked him up because I was pissed off with him, I never really thought he'd done anything. Stan can be a pain in the arse but he's a good cop and no killer.'

'Well, I'm glad you've realized that at last.'

Sam poured the tea and handed a mug to Adams. 'So now you've told me why you're here, is there anything else?'

Adams sipped at his tea before putting it down and looking across at Sam. 'You've resigned?'

Sam nodded. 'Thought you would be pleased. Got rid of the old witch at last.'

Adams shook his head. 'That was never the idea. Sam, you're the best pathologist I have ever known and I – the force – can't afford to lose you.'

'Even though I'm unconventional and interfere?'

'And that interference led to the death of a young girl. Even then, Sam. If it hadn't been for your unconventional habits I wouldn't be a detective superintendent and there would be a good few murderers still on the loose. It's one of the things that attracted me to you in the first place.'

Sam hadn't touched her tea, she was too nervous but she didn't know why. 'If that's how you felt then why have you been on my case?'

'Because despite your unorthodox approach you have to appreciate that at the end of the day it's police business.

If you'd kept me informed of your progress then perhaps Kate would still be alive and this case would have been solved a darn sight quicker.'

'And if you'd believed she had been murdered when I proved she had been, instead of putting your economic imperatives before good police work, perhaps Kate wouldn't have been dead either.'

Adams was silent for a moment pondering what Sam had just said and considering whether it was the right time to bring up the real reason for his visit. 'OK, you were right about the girl, sorry. With her killer dead I don't see what else I can do.'

Sam stared at him in disbelief. 'What do you mean, with her killer dead?'

'Spade, I think it's quite clear he followed her to Cambridge and killed her.'

Sam shook her head. 'How handy for you. From refusing to admit you even had a murder on your hands, you've now got a detected murder and it hasn't cost you a penny. Bet that will help your promotion chances. You'll have to head up a new department, Murders on the Cheap. Well, you're wrong, Spade didn't do it.'

Adams stood and said angrily, 'Then who did?'

Sam smiled. 'I'll let you know when I've finally sorted it out.'

'I've told you before, Sam, it's an offence to withhold information.'

She felt like throwing her mug at him. 'Oh, don't worry, Superintendent, you'll be the first to know when I finally discover who really did it.'

Adams glared at her for a moment before turning and making his way back towards the front door. Sam waited for him to open the door before shouting out her final insult, 'And for what it's worth her murder is linked with Sophie Clarke's.'

Adams stopped for a moment but didn't turn. Sam knew she'd got through to him and it made her feel good.

*

The following morning Sam showered and changed quickly. She had slept surprisingly well. She thought it might have been the effect of Adams' visit. It was the first positive thing she felt she'd done for a couple of days. She'd enjoyed putting him in his place. She was due to meet Sharman outside his flat at eleven thirty. She had hoped to see him earlier but he'd put her off saying he had a couple of important things to do first. She glanced at her watch, it was just before eleven. Putting Shaw out into the back garden she secured her house and jumped into her car. As Sam turned on to the dirt track that led from her cottage to the main road, she noticed a dark blue Ford Escort parked amongst the trees at the bottom of the track. She wouldn't have noticed it at all but the driver hadn't pulled the car off the road fully and the bonnet jutted out on to the verge by a good few feet. Instinct told her that it was an unmarked police car, and that Adams had put it there to keep an eye on her. She'd rattled him more than she realized. Perhaps playing games with Adams wasn't such a good idea. He was after all head of a very powerful police department and an extremely ambitious man. As much as she knew and thought she understood Adams for the first time for a long time she found herself slightly frightened of him. She hadn't driven far enough along the track to have been spotted by Adams' men, so pushing the car into reverse she pulled back on to her drive. Securing her vehicle she made her way back into the cottage switching on the TV set to give the impression she was at home, before setting off across the fields at the back of the house for the half-mile walk into the next village. On arrival she made her way to a public call box and phoned for a taxi. She had thought about calling from home, or calling on her mobile, but she wasn't sure how serious Adams was taking her comments and who might be listening in.

Stan Sharman was waiting for Sam outside the Waddams' house by the time she arrived. Although he eyed the taxi he didn't seem surprised. Sam paid the driver and stepped across to Sharman.

'Adams' lads waiting for you, were they?'

'Yes, how did you know?'

Sharman smiled. 'I had to lose a couple of flat feet too.'

Sam felt concerned. 'They don't know where we are, do they?'

'Do you honestly think I'd let Adams steal my thunder now?'

Sam took the point. Sharman stared into her face. 'Are you ready?'

Sam nodded. 'As I'll ever be.'

Sharman felt in his pocket to make sure the tightly packed roll of coins was handy before opening the gate and following Sam up the drive.

Bill Waddam answered the door. He seemed surprised to see them. 'Mr Sharman, what can I do for you?'

Sharman gave him a sickly sweet smile. 'Is Mrs Waddam in?'

Bill Waddam nodded. 'She's in the sitting room.'

'Can I have a quick word with her?'

Waddam hesitated for a moment, but finally made his mind up and nodded. 'Certainly, come in.'

He showed them through to the sitting room, where Betty Waddam was sitting on the settee knitting while watching some mind-numbing daytime soap on the TV. Sharman immediately crossed the room and sat down next to her before she had time to react. Taking her hand, he examined the rings. Betty looked surprised.

'Not only did you murder her, you had to take her rings as well, didn't you?'

Mrs Waddam paled visibly as Sharman kept hold of her hand. She looked across at her husband, who stood transfixed to the spot. Recovering a little she tried to stand, but Sharman kept hold of her hand, forcing her to remain seated. Swinging her arm sideways she tried to hit him across the face, but Sharman was too quick for her and parried the blow, causing a reaction from Mr Waddam.

'For God's sake, Betty, stop, it's over. You and those

bloody rings, I told you to bloody well leave them. You stupid bitch.'

Mrs Waddam suddenly rounded on her husband. 'Shut up, you stupid bastard, they've got nothing, they can't prove a thing.'

Sam watched as Sharman's eyes narrowed. 'Oh, I'm afraid we can. You see we have a copy of the video you took when you murdered Sophie Clarke. She was wearing the rings then. Now, only a few weeks later, you are. What do you think a jury is going to make of that?'

Mr Waddam shook his head as he looked across at his wife. 'You've finished us, you greedy bitch, you've finished us.' He moved his attention from his wife to Sharman. 'We did kill her. It wasn't done on purpose, it was an accident.'

Sharman shook his head. 'Accident! Don't tell me, you didn't know it was loaded.'

Betty Waddam suddenly exploded with rage. Such was the anger that this time she managed to pulled free of Sharman and rushed across the room towards her husband, a raised knitting needle in her hand. Sharman caught up with her quickly and grabbing her by the hair forced her to the ground still screaming and threatening her husband. Sharman pulled his handcuffs from his back pocket and secured Betty Waddam's hands behind her back. Once she was secure Sharman turned his attention to Bill Waddam. 'So do you want to tell us what happened, or do you want to join your wife on the floor?'

He shook his head. 'There's no need for that. I'll tell you what you want to know.'

Betty Waddam looked up at her husband, screaming, 'Keep your mouth shut, keep your fucking mouth shut. He'll kill you for this, just like he did Rogers.'

Sam noticed the fear in William Waddam's face. Fortunately so did Sharman. Picking Betty Waddam up by her secured hands he took her into the hall locking her into the downstairs toilet. She continued to scream but at least it was now difficult to hear what she was saying.

Returning to the sitting room, Sharman took hold of William Waddam by the lapels and pushed him into a chair. 'Right, we're all ears.'

William Waddam gulped deeply before commencing. 'It was Rogers that got us involved. He knew I was struggling to make ends meet. Van driver's money doesn't go that far even with a porter's pension. He offered us this job picking videos up from Europe, and bringing them into the country.'

Sharman sat on the arm of the chair trying not to appear less menacing. 'Did you know what was on the videos?'

Waddam nodded. 'I knew it was porn but didn't know what kind. Well, not at first anyway.'

Sam could see Sharman's mind ticking over. 'These trips, who went on them?'

'Rogers, me and a bloke we picked up at the port called Spade. Nasty piece of work he was. Violent.'

'Rogers knew Spade, then?'

Waddam nodded. 'They'd been in the Royal Marines together.'

The links were beginning to drop into place, and for the first time in a while Sharman was beginning to feel confident about the case. 'How long have you been making these trips?'

Waddam thought for a moment. 'About a year.'

'And your main pick-up points?'

'Amsterdam and Paris. Used to quite enjoy the trips.'

Sam noticed that Waddam was becoming increasingly agitated and had actually begun to look ill as Sharman continued to ask his questions. She wondered whether to intervene but decided to leave it for a little while longer and give him a chance to finish.

'When did you realize what kind of material you were bringing in?'

'Couple of months ago. When Rogers showed me, I was disgusted.'

Sharman gave a sarcastic laugh. 'Not disgusted enough to stop dealing with it, though?'

Sam noticed that Waddam's breathing was becoming more laboured.

'I was in too deep. These weren't men you said no to. And Betty was enjoying the money.'

'Whose idea was it to kill Sophie Clarke?'

Waddam undid the top button on his shirt and loosened his tie. Sam decided it was time to intervene.

'Stan I think it might be time to—'

Sharman put his hand up cutting her short. 'Leave it, Sam, not now.'

Although unsure whether she should, Sam remained silent, deciding to give Sharman a little more time.

'We never meant to kill her.'

Sharman was clearly unconvinced. 'So what happened?'

'Rogers was blackmailing her. He knew about the affair she was having with Ward. Told her that if she didn't do what he wanted he would tell her husband. He had a video of the two of them having sex. Took it through the bedroom window so she could hardly deny it.'

'So what did she have to do?'

'Rogers said that we should make our own films, cut out the travelling costs.'

'So you knew it was a snuff movie?'

He shook his head. 'No, no, it wasn't going to be like that. It was only going to be simulated.'

Sharman cut in. 'Just pretend to kill her?'

'Yes. I know it sounds stupid but that's what we decided.'

'And she agreed to that?'

'She agreed to do it once, and then Rogers was going to give her the video back and keep his mouth shut.'

Sharman gave a sarcastic laugh as Sam cut in, 'She believed that?'

Waddam shrugged. 'She was desperate, I suppose you'll believe anything.'

Sharman cut back in. 'So who strangled her?'

Sam noticed that Waddam was in considerable distress. 'Stan, you're going to have to stop.'

Even Sharman was beginning to notice he was suffering but if he was honest he didn't really care. 'Couple more questions. So who was it?'

'Rogers raped her and then began to burn her. She began to scream, she hadn't agreed to that, you see. She started to say she was going to tell her husband and call the police.'

'So what happened?'

'Betty came across and gagged her while Rogers kept burning her. You see, Betty really hated her because she'd betrayed John.'

'So Betty was the cameraman?'

Waddam nodded. 'She was very good, she's done a course in media studies.'

'So when he'd finished burning her he strangled her?'

'No, he just pretended to strangle her. She was still alive when we left the room.'

Sharman was confused. 'Who's we?'

'Me and Rogers. We went and had a drink, when we got back, she was dead.'

'Who was in the room when you left?'

Waddam was struggling but it was already obvious so Sharman helped him out. 'It was Betty, wasn't it? She finished the job for you, so you got your snuff movie after all.'

Waddam nodded. 'Yes. She wanted her dead all along, planned it the moment she knew about her affair with Ward. She wanted Sophie dead and Ward doing life. Almost worked.'

Sharman had one final question. 'Betty said "he" will kill you. Who was he?'

Now Waddam looked very frightened. 'I'd rather not – not say . . .' Suddenly he went a deathly shade of pale, clawed at his shirt and slumped forward. Sam was at his side in an instant. Checking his pulse she looked up at Sharman. 'He's had a heart attack, you'd better call an ambulance quickly.'

Despite Sam's best efforts William Waddam was dead, and with him the only and best witness they had. He was probably dead before he hit the ground. Sam had done her best but it wasn't enough. They'd waited for both the ambulance and the local police to turn up. After Sharman had explained the situation, they made their excuses and left quickly to finish what they had started, before Adams turned up and had them both locked up.

Sharman drove them to a terraced house just outside the city centre and parked. He looked across at Sam. 'Come on.'

She followed without question. As Sharman opened the door and they entered, Sam's curiosity finally got the better of her. 'Where the hell are we?'

Sharman pushed open the hall door and they entered the a small smartly furnished sitting room.

'It's Kate's old house. She's left it to her mum. I'm sorting things out for her. Might buy it myself. Had a few good times in here.'

Sam was still confused. 'But why are we here?'

'Because within the hour Adams will have sent his lads to your house and my flat to pick us up. He must be wondering what the hell is going on. Wish I could be there to see his face. He doesn't know about this place so it's going to give us a bit of time to sort a few things out before he finally catches up with us.'

'What about your car?'

Sharman smiled. 'In case you hadn't noticed, that's not my car. I hired it yesterday. Parked it a bit away from the house. Thought Adams might try something. Although I didn't know he had it in him to do it.'

Sam pulled off her coat and slumped down on the settee. 'So what now?'

Sharman searched through the inside pocket of his jacket and handed Sam an envelope addressed to Mr John Clarke MP.

'Where the hell did you get this from?'

'Mark Anderson.'

'Who the hell is he?'

'Clarke's postman. I nicked him for theft a few years back, which he forgot to declare to the Post Office when he got the job.'

'You blackmailed him?'

Sharman lit a cigarette. 'Bet your bloody life I did, and he's not off the hook yet either.'

'I'm sorry, but I still don't get it.'

Sharman took a long drag on his cigarette. 'Look inside the envelope.'

Sam did as she was bid. Inside the envelope were several bank statements covering John Clarke's account for the past twelve months.

'This has to be against the law.'

Sharman shrugged. 'What he's up to isn't exactly honest, is it?' He fumbled in his pocket again, this time producing the bank book that Hudd had retrieved from Spade's body. 'Check the dates and the amounts of the deposit entries in Claire's bank book against the withdrawals on Clarke's statements.'

Sam did. They all matched within a day or two, and the amounts were exactly the same. She looked across at Sharman. 'But how did you get them?'

'Clarke's away until tomorrow. Broke in . . .'

Sharman was so nonchalant it took a moment for his words to sink in.

'You broke in?'

Sharman smiled and nodded. 'Bloody right. Well, there was no one there to stop me, was there? Used Mr Anderson as lookout.'

Sam was still amazed at Sharman's cheek. 'What if he says something? Goes to Adams?'

'Not a chance. He's more frightened of me than Adams.'

'And the alarms?'

'I set them off and then waited for the plods to arrive. There was no sign of a break-in at that point so they marked it off as a false alarm and because his system is so complicated they had to ring the alarm company to re-set it. That gave me about an hour, which was more than I needed.'

They say there's a very thin line between being a good policeman and being a good criminal. Sam wondered sometimes how close Sharman got to crossing it.

'Anyway once I'd got in I ordered a bank statement and then got my friendly postman to hold it back and give it to me.'

'It's not that easy to get a bank statement. Is it?'

Sharman smiled ruefully. 'It is if you know how.'

Sam still wasn't convinced. 'What about passwords, mother's maiden name, things like that?'

'His mother's maiden name was Russell—'

'How do you know that?' Sam cut in.

Sharman shrugged. 'It's my job to know that sort of thing.'

Sam hadn't finished her cross-examination. 'And his password?'

'He leaves his password stuck to the side of his computer. Noticed it there last time I was in. Lots of people do it. Defeats the object, really, don't you think?'

Sam thought nothing, still too aghast by Sharman's actions to say or do anything.

'You know the poor old postman will probably lose his job?'

Sharman lit his second cigarette. 'I doubt it. I'll square it off for him. He isn't the only postal worker I've got something on.'

Sam would liked to have been shocked by the way Sharman did business but she wasn't. In fact if she was honest she rather liked it. Sharman continued, 'There was a bit of a bonus too. If you check his account month on month you'll see that there are very large deposits paid in on or about the fifteenth.'

Sam shook her head. 'So?'

Sharman smiled mischievously. 'After I came out of Clarke's house I thought I might as well have a look around Roger's flat. All the alarms were off by now so I thought I might as well take advantage of the situation and broke in there too.'

Sam could feel herself becoming irritated. 'And the point is?'

Sharman shook his head. 'There was no real point, just wanted to sniff around a bit. But then I found these.'

He handed a pile of petrol receipts over to Sam. 'The receipts come from all over Europe and correspond with the trips Waddam and his friends made to Europe. Which correspond precisely with the large amounts of cash paid into Clarke's account.'

Sam was surprised and shocked at how large the amounts were. She had had no idea how much money there was in porn.

'But Clarke's already a rich man. Why would he do this?'

Sharman laughed. 'What do they say? You can never be too rich or too thin.'

Sam and Sharman spent the rest of the day and night at the house, Sam sleeping on the settee while Stan slept in Kate's bed. Sharman did offer her the bed, but Sam didn't have the heart to take it. The only surprise of the evening was the lack of news about the Waddams. Adams had clearly acted quickly to suppress any information until he'd had time to pick them up, and find out what was going on. It was an odd feeling, 'being on the run'. A wanted woman, who would have thought it? Sam mused grimly. What odd games life plays.

They both got up late. There seemed no point in rushing. Sam had had yet another restless night. This time it wasn't the dreams but the state of the settee she had decided to spend the night on. After a large mug of coffee and a quick shower the two companions were ready to leave.

As Sam pulled herself into the passenger seat Sharman glanced across at her. 'We'll take the scenic route, no point looking for a problem.'

Sam nodded. She'd forgotten they were still on the run.

Sharman seemed to use every back road and side-street in Cambridge, stopping every now and then to make sure they weren't being followed. After what seemed an age, they finally arrived at Clarke's home in Grantchester. Sam half expected an army of police officers to be waiting there to meet them, and was relieved when there wasn't.

They parked on the drive and marched up to the door. Sharman rang the bell long and hard. A few moments later Clarke appeared at the door. He seemed calm and unruffled. 'Dr Ryan, DS Sharman, to what do I owe this honour?'

Sharman was having none of it. 'I thought you ought to know that your cleaner Betty Waddam has been arrested for the murder of your wife and I'm afraid Bill Waddam is dead.'

Clarke tried to look shocked, but Sam could see it was somehow false.

'So it wasn't Ward at all. I never thought it was. But Mrs Waddam, that is shocking news. Are you sure?'

Sharman smiled. 'Positive. What's more interesting, however, is that Mr Waddam implicated you in the murders before he died.'

Clarke shook his head and gave a false laugh. 'He gave you a statement to that effect, did he?'

Sharman shook his head. 'He didn't get the chance. He told Dr Ryan here and myself before he died, though.'

Clarke shrugged. 'He was lying. Think you might be struggling with that one in court. Don't you?'

Sharman could feel himself becoming annoyed. 'Mrs Waddam's still alive. She might become helpful when she knows how long she is about to spend at Her Majesty's pleasure.'

Clarke was as confident as ever. 'I doubt it. Have you got the poor woman in custody? I must arrange for some decent legal representation for her. You've probably made another mistake. You lot seem good at that. Must ask a question in the House about it.'

Sharman changed tack. 'Did you know a girl named Claire?'

Clarke thought for a moment then shook his head. 'I know a lot of women, none named Claire, though.'

Sharman persisted. 'She was a man called Spade's girlfriend, but I don't suppose you've ever heard of him either?'

Clarke shook his head. 'No, never. Unusual name, though, sure I would have remembered that one.'

'He was a friend of your handyman, Rogers.'

Clarke shrugged again. 'The late Mr Rogers had a lot of friends. Not the kind I was likely to associate myself with, though. Good man, Rogers, but a bit of a rough diamond.'

'Do you like to watch porn, well to be more exact snuff movies? Films where young girls are raped and then murdered, Mr Clarke?' Sharman asked bluntly. Sam noticed that Clarke's face reddened slightly. Sharman had hit a nerve.

'No, certainly not. Now look here, I've had enough of this. I think I'll ring your boss, Superintendent Adams, isn't it? I'm sure he'll be able to sort out any problems you might have with me, Mr Sharman. Besides, didn't I hear that you had been suspended? I'm not sure you should even be here. So please leave.'

Sam watched as Sharman's eyes began to narrow. She knew it was a bad sign. She knew all Sharman wanted to do was hit Clarke right between the eyes. 'Come on, Stan, there are other things we can be doing.'

Sam pulled him away gently towards the car as Clarke closed the door firmly behind them.

As they pulled out of the drive Sam looked across at Sharman. 'What now?'

He shrugged. 'God knows. Unless Mrs Waddam decides to make a full confession, which with Clarke's legal adviser on the way seems unlikely.'

Sam thought for a moment. 'What about the bank statements and receipts. That's pretty conclusive?'

Sharman shrugged. 'Not really, remember how I got them. We now know he's involved but they'd never let us use them in evidence. I'm not sure I'd even dare admit I've got them. Not to mention how I got them. I can see it'll be me that gets banged up on this one.'

Sam looked out of the side window as Sharman drove back through Grantchester. Suddenly her mobile phone burst into life. She checked the number before answering – it was Hudd. In that moment the answer to all their problems flashed through her head. Sam wasn't sure why she hadn't thought of it before. She looked across at Sharman. 'Stan, get us to Trinity quickly and by the most direct route you know.'

It was a risk but one Sam considered worth taking.

John Clarke was sitting by his pool when she appeared. He didn't notice her at first, too busy considering the implications of Sharman's visit. He wasn't too worried about Betty Waddam, he'd already called his solicitor and he was travelling down. If nothing else he would make sure she kept her mouth shut. Not that that worried him. It would take more than the local CID to make someone like Betty talk, but there was no point in taking chances. Suddenly he became aware that someone was watching him. He turned slowly to see a girl waving.

'Hello, John, remember me? I'm Claire.'

Clarke couldn't stop staring at her. Staring into her dead face, because if there was one thing he did know for sure it was that she was dead. He knew that because he had killed her. His mind began to race. 'You're dead.'

Claire began to walk towards him slowly, her hands outstretched. Clarke could feel his legs begin to shake and his stomach knot.

'Keep away from me, you bitch, keep away.'

Claire continued to walk towards him, a smile

broadening on her face as she did. Clarke began to step backwards.

'I killed you once, I can do it again!' Too shocked and frightened to talk at the apparition, Clarke looked wildly around him before turning and running into the house.

Sharman, Sam and Hudd, who had been concealed behind a low hedge, suddenly appeared. Hudd was by his girlfriend's side in a trice, while Sam and Sharman pursued Clarke into the house. As they approached the french windows that opened up on to the poolside Clarke suddenly re-emerged, an over-and-under shotgun pressed hard into his shoulder. He seemed surprised to see Sam and Sharman standing in front of him. 'What the hell are you doing here?'

Sharman looked him straight in the eye. 'I've come to arrest you for the murder of Claire Armstrong, the murder of Michael Rogers and conspiracy to murder your own wife, Sophie Clarke.'

Sam could see Clarke was becoming increasingly agitated. 'How can you accuse me of murdering Claire, she's there, look behind you, she's there!'

As he spoke Hudd peeled the silicone mask from his girlfriend's face. Clarke just stared in total disbelief. 'You tricked me. This will never stand up in court.'

Sam glared at him. 'You told us you'd never met Claire, yet you seemed to recognize her quickly enough, and admitted that you killed her.'

Clarke kept the gun hard against his shoulder. 'Your word against mine, you've still got nothing.'

Sam turned to Hudd and nodded. Hudd held up a video camera. Sam returned her attention to Clarke. 'You see, we can prove everything. A full confession.'

Clarke was swinging the gun from Sam to Sharman and then back again, clearly uncertain what to do, while Hudd continued filming events. 'They deserved to die. She was sleeping with my political agent, a fucking nobody, a nobody, when she had me. She deserved to die.'

Sharman's nerve was holding. 'Did you kill her?'

'Me, soil my hands on that bitch? No, got Betty to sort that out and a bloody good job she did too.'

'What about Claire and Rogers?'

'Blackmailers. Well, they tangled with the wrong man. Rogers actually tried to frighten me. You should have seen the look on his face when his life ended.'

Sharman continued. 'Did you kill them?'

'Yes, I killed them, they had it coming.' He pointed the gun at Sam. 'And if it hadn't been for that bitch I'd have got away with it.'

As he continued to train the gun at Sam, Sharman pushed her behind his body.

'So what now? You going to open fire or not? You won't get us all, you know, maybe two, but Hudd will get away and then you're finished. Life in prison, disgrace, humiliation. People will spit on your memory.'

Sam was alarmed at Sharman's comments. The last thing they needed to do was upset him further. Sharman put out his hand and began to walk towards him. 'Why don't you just give me the gun and I'll see what I can do for you. You've got good solicitors, I'm sure they'll sort it out for you. Come on, give me the gun.'

'Sort it out? I'm finished. Finished by a cheap music hall trick. Who would have thought it?' Clarke's shoulders slumped.

Sensing victory Sharman moved forward, but he wasn't quick enough. Without another word, Clarke pushed the gun under his chin and pulled the trigger. His head exploded into a mess of blood and brains, before his body finally toppled into the swimming pool, turning the water a crimson red. Sam ran up to Sharman, who was covered in Clarke's blood.

'You knew he was going to do that, didn't you?'

Sharman nodded. 'Thought he might. Can't say I'm sorry.'

Sam wanted to ask what made him judge, jury, and executioner but despite the grim satisfaction behind his words, his eyes were full of pain and he looked defeated.

Considering what he'd lost, Sam's heart contracted with sympathy and tears filled her eyes. Besides, she couldn't help agreeing with him. It was the best thing that could have happened.